T0149639

Life in
Cythera

Life in

Cythera

2 Tales 2 Tickle

CHARLES CODDINGTON

LIFE IN CYTHERA
2 TALES 2 TICKLE

This is a work of fiction. All of the characters, names, incidents, organizations, and dialogue in this novel are either the products of the author's imagination or are used fictitiously.

iUniverse books may be ordered through booksellers or by contacting:

iUniverse
1663 Liberty Drive
Bloomington, IN 47403
www.iuniverse.com
1-800-Authors (1-800-288-4677)

ISBN: 978-1-5320-3158-8 (sc)
ISBN: 978-1-5320-3159-5 (e)

Print information available on the last page.

iUniverse rev. date: 09/01/2017

Tale the First:
"You Call a Cab?"

The Author wishes to inform
the Reader that
all of the events in this narrative
actually happened
(well, most of them anyway –
oh, all right! half of them!),
so help him Vonnegut.

1

Monday
(an arbitrary choice)
07:59:40 am
(also arbitrary)

Ring-ring! says the telephone cheerfully. *Ring-ring!*

The dispatcher looks at the telephone with one bleary eye (which one matters not). His other eye is half-closed, and it is too much of an effort to open it fully.

Ring-ring! says the telephone happily. *Ring-ring!*

"Honk you!" says the dispatcher unenthusiastically.

The dispatcher, a grizzled, unkempt, and overweight fellow whose clothes appear to be older (and dirtier) than he is, takes a short pull from a pint of Jack Daniels and a short drag from a Marlboro, belches, farts, and scratches his privates (not necessarily in that order).

Ring-ring! says the telephone joyfully. *Ring-ring!*

As soon as the amenities are taken care of, the dispatcher reaches for the telephone.

Ring –

"Cythera Cab Company," the dispatcher says unenthusiastically. "Service with a smile."

Even though the caller cannot see him, the dispatcher exposes a mouthful of yellowed teeth in a grotesque facsimile of a smile.

"I need a cab going to the train depot," the caller says forcefully.

"Where you at?"

"460 Garfield Avenue."

"OK. Be about ten minutes." *Give or take an hour.*

"Thank you."

Click.

"Honk you, poo-head!"

The dispatcher takes another short pull from the pint of Jack Daniels and another short drag from the Marlboro, belches, farts, and scratches his privates (not necessarily in that order). As soon as the amenities are taken care of, he reaches for the two-way radio.

"Dispatch to 65," he says unenthusiastically.

"65 here. Go ahead, dispatch."

"You still at the casino?"

"Yeah. It's dead around here. Even the whores have packed it in."

"Got one at 460 Garfield – goin' to the depot."

"10-4, Uncle Gordy."

The dispatcher, who hates to be called "Uncle Gordy," flips the bird, even though the driver of taxi #65 of the Cythera Cab Company cannot see him. Then he takes another short pull from the pint of Jack Daniels and another short drag from the Marlboro, belches, farts, and scratches his privates (not necessarily in that order). As soon as the amenities are taken care of, he nods off.

8:01 am
(more or less)

Deliberately, taxi #65 of the Cythera Cab Company pulled up in front of the building located at 460 Garfield Avenue. Taxi #65 of the Cythera Cab Company did not, of course, pull up in front of the building located at 460 Garfield Avenue by itself. It had a driver who did the actual pulling up. The driver also applied the brake and stopped; otherwise, taxi #65 would not have stopped (even by itself) and most likely would have proceeded into the lobby of the building located at 460 Garfield Avenue, produced an uproar amongst the staff and patrons in the building, caused considerable injuries to said staff and patrons and damage to the building, taxi, and its driver, moderately to severely, and forced the management to register a polite complaint.

The driver of taxi #65 of the Cythera Cab Company – call him "Fred," because that was his name – gazed upon the building before him while not-so-fond memories dragged themselves out of his subconscious. He thought briefly – perhaps a second or two – how improved the building might be if he had crashed into it. He smiled at the brief thought and said to himself "Someday, maybe." ("Someday, maybe" was Fred's favorite expression, and he used it at least twice a day.)

The building, located at 460 Garfield Avenue, which provoked not-so-fond memories in the conscious mind of Fred, the driver of taxi #65 of the Cythera Cab Company, was a five-story, yellow brick-and-ceramic structure hunkering at the bottom of a decline leading from the street. The property on which it hunkered – plus the land behind it – had been donated to the City of Cythera by a wealthy local manufacturer (whose factory was not far away from 460 Garfield Avenue) with no strings

3

attached to the usage of the property. What the City Fathers did not know – or kept to themselves – was that the donated property had once been a wetland in the days when Cythera was not yet a twinkle in the eyes of the first white settlers in the area.

Nevertheless, the City Fathers were pleased to receive this property, because they wished to build a new YMCA to replace the old one which had become too small for its purposes. The new YMCA was duly constructed (and the old one torn down) and opened for business. The main floor housed the administrative offices, a small but homey restaurant at the east end, a large banquet room at the west end, a lounge in the center for the members and residents to relax in, and a children's play area between the lounge and the banquet area. The recreational facilities were all in the lower level – all state-of-the-art for its day. The second floor was given over to conference rooms, rented out to various community organizations for their own purposes. The upper three floors functioned as a dormitory for transient young men who were newly arrived in Cythera and needed a place to stay while they sought employment and eventually their own lodgings. (Some residents, however, enjoyed the ambience of the YMCA so much that they became permanent residents.)

Fred, the driver of taxi #65 of the Cythera Cab Company, had been one of those transients, and he had looked to be as temporary a one as he could. He had not enjoyed the building, its ambience, or anything else about the organization, and their combination had constantly provoked not-so-fond memories in his conscious mind whenever he chanced to pass through the neighborhood (which was more often than he cared to) or to hear someone mention the name "YMCA" (which was more often than he cared to). As it happened, he had spent a year and four months there, all the while collecting not-so-fond memories and saving up his earnings as a dedicated driver for the Cythera Cab Company so that he could "move the honk out" of the place.

Now, Fred sat in taxi #65 in front of the building located at 460 Garfield Avenue, a.k.a. the YMCA, and nursed his not-so-fond memories while waiting for his fare to exit the building and enter his cab.

Said fare exited the building five minutes later and entered his cab. He immediately ceased nursing his not-so-fond memories and put on his best smile. Fred had several different smiles for all occasions, and he had used all of them at one time or another over the course of his career as a taxi driver. On this occasion, he took his best smile out of his tote bag, put it on, and adjusted it for maximum effect.

The reason that he took his best smile out of his tote bag, put it on, and adjusted it for maximum effect was that the fare which had exited the building and entered his cab took the form of two striking young women. One of the striking young women was a striking redhead wearing a maroon knit dress which both complimented her hair and emphasized certain physical features. The other one of the striking young women was a striking strawberry blonde wearing a yellow T-shirt which complimented her hair and tight jeans which emphasized certain physical features. Fred, being a long-time, self-avowed connoisseur of the female form, took instant notice and therefore took his best smile out of his tote bag, put it on, and adjusted it for maximum effect. *[Author's note: the Reader may wonder why two striking young women were in a YMCA in the first place. In order to dispel any prurient thinking on the part of the Reader, the Author hastens to point out that the two striking young women had availed themselves of the Olympic-sized swimming pool on the lower level and had swum several dozen laps as their daily exercise regimen. That's the Author's story, and he is sticking to it.]*

"Good morning, ladies," Fred greeted the two striking young women lecherously.

"Morning," one of the striking young women mumbled (it matters not which one).

"We want to go to the depot," the other one of the striking young women mumbled.

"Oakie-doakie," Fred said lecherously.

Taxi #65 of the Cythera Cab Company pulled away from the YMCA and moved down Garfield Avenue. Taxi #65 of the Cythera Cab Company did not, of course, pull away from the YMCA and move down Garfield Avenue by itself. It had a driver (identified as one Fred) who did the actual pulling away and moving down. The driver released the taxi's brake and applied a foot (the right one, as it happened) to the taxi's accelerator. Otherwise, taxi #65 would not have gone anywhere (even by itself) and most likely would have remained in front of the YMCA for all of Eternity (more or less).

Fred would have lost a fare – plus a spectacular view.

"Do you mind if we smoke?" one of the striking young women asked (it matters not which one).

"Sorry, ma'am." Fred (a non-smoker) replied less lecherously. "I have an asthmatic condition. Smoking would cause me severe distress."

"Well, *honk!*" the other one of the striking young women muttered.

[Author's note: it was a blatant lie on Fred's part that he had an asthmatic condition. His normal response to that specific question was a five-minute lecture on the dangers of smoking. Claiming an asthmatic condition was his way of sparing the feelings of certain fares.]

The fact that he had two striking young women in his cab notwithstanding, Fred did not care for the fare in general. The depot was only a five-minute drive from the YMCA (seven minutes if the traffic was heavy), and he did not stand to make very much money on this trip. *[Author's note: there were other types of fares from which he did not make very much money, and they will be mentioned later in this narrative.]* Suffice it to say that Fred had to settle for a spectacular view to compensate for a meager fare.

The train depot in Cythera squatted on a chunk of land just south of the business district and adjacent to the east bank of the river which divided the City in two. It was a non-descript, functional, red-brick building fronting on a street which was actually part of a state highway. It was Cythera's second depot, the first one having been located a block east of the same state highway north of the business district; the first one had to be torn down when the tracks were elevated in 1921. The new depot was, of course considerably larger to accommodate the increased traffic, both in trains and in people using them. It was a matter of pride (more or less) that the City Fathers called their town a major transportation hub.

Behind the depot lay three boarding platforms (such was the aforementioned traffic that three were justified). One reached the boarding platforms in one's choice of two methods: (1) the rear door of the depot from which one walked across the tracks to whichever boarding platform one desired; and (2) the tunnel in the lower level of the depot down which one passed under the tracks and emerged via a stairway to whichever boarding platform one desired. During inclement weather, (2) was the preferred choice.

South of the depot and the boarding platforms, other tracks ran off the three main lines. In point of fact, the depot possessed a freight-train switching yard, a railway express office, and a place for minor repairs to the locomotives/cars. The railroad company which owned and operated the facilities had a reputation for reliable service to maintain, and nothing was left to chance in maintaining said reputation. And such was the service (and reputation) that the City Fathers took pride (more or less) in calling their town a major transportation hub.

Forcefully, taxi #65 of the Cythera Cab Company pulled up before this major transportation. Taxi #65 of the Cythera Cab Company did not, of course, pull up before this major transportation hub by itself. It had a driver (identified as one Fred) who did the actual pulling up. The driver also applied the brake and stopped; otherwise, taxi #65 would not have stopped (even by itself) and most likely would have proceeded into the depot, alarmed employees and passengers, caused considerable injury to said employees and passengers and damage to the depot, taxi, and its driver, moderately to severely, and moved the railroad to complain vigorously.

"Here you are, ladies," Fred announced lecherously. "That'll be, um" – he peered at the taxi's meter -- $8.20, please."

One of the two striking young women (it matters not which one) fished in her handbag, produced a ten-dollar bill, and handed it to Fred.

"Keep the change, buster," she said gratuitously. "You'll need it for asthma medication."

Both of the striking young women giggled incessantly as they exited the taxi and sashayed into the depot. Fred eyed them every step of the way. When they had disappeared from view, he sighed deeply and deposited the ten-dollar bill in his money pouch.

"65 to dispatch."

"Dispatch here. Go ahead, 65."

"I'm clear at the depot, Uncle Gordy."

"Goody. Head for Plum Street. I'll give you the street number when you're there."

"10-4."

Uncle Gordy, who hated to be called "Uncle Gordy," flipped the bird even though the cab driver could not see him. Then he took a short pull from the pint of Jack Daniels and a short drag from the Marlboro, belched, farted, and scratched his privates (not necessarily in that order). As soon as the amenities had been taken care of, he nodded off.

0811 UT
(and counting)

One of Cythera's local writers, an individual well-known for his flammatory style of writing and controversial subject matter – which usually garnered an equal amount of respect and disrespect – had on occasion dug into his own life experiences to make a point. He did this only sparingly because, as he once remarked, his life experiences were none of anybody's business but his own. The casual observer might have concluded that, because the said life experiences were so sparingly dug into, they were probably fictional, that the writer had nothing else upon which to excuse his flammatory style of writing and controversial subject matter, and that therefore one could easily ignore his arguments and/or write them off as delusions. The casual observer might have been greatly surprised to learn that the ignoring of his arguments or the writing them off as delusions only *encouraged* the said writer in his flammatory style of writing and controversial subject matter.

One life experience of the said writer provoked in him fond memories each and every time he dug it up. He had spent his teen years in an old neighborhood on Cythera's northwest side in which an industrial park was surrounded by residential structures. All except one of the industries dealt with light or heavy manufacturing. The one exception was, of all things, a bakery. Why the owner of the bakery had seen fit to locate it there might have made for an interesting story; but no one – not even the aforementioned local writer with a flammatory style of writing and controversial subject matter – had ever bothered to research the motive behind the siting of the bakery.

Be that as it may, the bakery, as it happened, was the one positive element in this northwest neighborhood of the City of Cythera. For, when the wind was just right – and it was just right at least three mornings a week – the nearby residents woke up to the aroma of freshly-baked bread. This was a life experience which no amount of prose or poetry could adequately describe. One had to experience it him/herself in order to appreciate the full flavor of it. The said writer had remarked on a number of occasions that filling one's lungs with the delicious aroma of freshly-baked bread was the next best thing to being in Heaven (or words to that effect).

The said neighborhood which was the recipient of the delicious aroma of freshly-baked bread was pure Middle America – upper-lower-class and lower-middle-class in equal proportions – which was the backbone of any community, and Cythera was no exception. The houses were mostly two-story, wooden A-frames with an occasional brickwork here and there, with a garage (attached or unattached) and a neatly trimmed lawn of varying sizes. All yards had trees, and some also had shrubbery and flowers. It was a matter of civic responsibility (and pride) to keep one's property free of garbage and debris; if any such appeared anywhere in the neighborhood, it was attributed to the nasty dispositions of "outsiders."

"Outsiders" were welcome in this neighborhood only if they knew someone who lived there. Otherwise, they were looked upon with suspicion; "state your business or move on" was the unofficial motto. Even though the neighborhood was ethnically diverse, no one who lived there was considered an "outsider." No muggings or burglaries or rapes occurred there – unless "outsiders" were responsible – and all was peace and tranquility (which was saying a lot for a city like Cythera, where, if anything could go wrong, it would). That was how it was in the youth of the said writer of flammatory style of writing and controversial subject matter.

At the time of the present narrative, the neighborhood had changed considerably. The industrial part now contained only light manufacturing. New social-service organizations replaced several factories. And, alas! the bakery with its delicious aroma of freshly-baked bread was also gone, to be replaced by a discount furniture outlet. The surrounding residential structures were older and their occupants still more ethnically diverse. But the residents lacked neighborliness; they took no responsibility for, or pride in, the appearance of the neighborhood. The lawns were shabby-looking, the trees chopped down, and the shrubbery and flowers uprooted. Garbage and debris were strewn everywhere.

And no one could blame this sea change on "outsiders." What had been done had been done by "insiders." No one greeted each other as members of a larger family but looked at each other with suspicion. Muggings and burglaries and rapes were commonplace; if they weren't perpetrated by "insiders," then they were perpetrated by "outsiders" who associated with "insiders." In short, this neighborhood was full of vermin, scum, riff-raff, and animals which infected the streets of Cythera; and the Chief of Police had sworn to harass, arrest, detain, or otherwise crimp the activities of as many as he could get his hands on.

Three-quarters of a block from the former bakery stood a typical two-story, wooden A-frame with an unattached garage and a small yard with one tree and some shrubbery. It was one of many houses in the neighborhood with an enclosed front porch (*screen-enclosed*, if you please). Said enclosed porch had been an excellent place to relax and watch the neighborhood go through its daily routine – and to fill one's lungs with the delicious aroma of freshly-baked bread. This house – at 543 Plum Street -- was where the aforementioned writer had misspent his youth dreaming of the day when he could engage in a flammatory writing style and controversial subject matter. *[Author's note: the aforementioned writer with the flammatory writing style and controversial subject matter no longer lives there. His present whereabouts is a closely guarded secret for obvious reasons.]*

This typical two-story, wooden A-frame with an unattached garage and a small yard with one tree and some shrubbery at 543 Plum Street was the destination of Fred, the driver of taxi #65 of the Cythera Cab Company. Fred had no problem in finding it as he'd been here any number of times, both professionally and socially. Nevertheless, he had to notify his dispatcher where he was.

"65 to dispatch."

"Dispatch here. Go ahead, 65."

"I'm on Plum Street, Uncle Gordy."

"Goody. The number is 543. Goin' to City Hall."

"10-4."

Honk you, poohead!

Stealthily, taxi #65 of the Cythera Cab Company pulled up in front of 543 Plum Street. Taxi #65 of the Cythera Cab Company did not, of course, pull up by itself; it had a driver (identified as one Fred) who did the actual pulling up. The driver also applied the brake and stopped; otherwise, taxi #65 of the Cythera Cab Company would not have stopped (even by itself) and most likely would have proceeded into the house at 543 Plum Street, provoked outrage in its occupants, caused considerable injury to said occupants and damage to their house, the taxi, and its driver, moderately to severely, and invoked a torrent of obscenities.

No sooner had Fred stopped than the front door opened (but not by itself) and two individuals (who did the actual opening) emerged. One individual was a European-American male with a ruddy complexion, brown eyes, reddish-brown hair, and a hawk-like projection for a nose. The other individual was an African-American female, petite, slender, and exceedingly buxom. *[Author's note: the Reader will excuse the use of politically correct ethnic designations; he has received any number of anonymous letters and phone calls pointing out the error of his ways and wishes to mollify everyone regardless of race, creed, national origin, age, gender, or sexual orientation.]*

The two individuals took a moment or two to embrace and to engage in a long, lingering kiss and some moderate petting. Then the male scrambled down the front steps and walked briskly to the waiting taxi. The female watched him every step of the way and did not re-enter the house until taxi #65 of the Cythera Cab Company had departed. The male jumped into the taxi, recognized the driver, and slapped him on the shoulder.

"Hiya, Fred!" he greeted Fred boisterously. "How's it hangin'?"

"Hiya, Tommy!" Fred greeted Tommy boisterously. "Same ol,' same ol.' I see you and Amber are still together."

"Yeah. She's the best thing that ever happened to me. Got me straightened out. We're getting married."

"No poo?"

"No poo, man. Donny's goin' to be my best man. You're invited."

"Wouldn't miss it for the world. But, say, how come you're getting all – all –"

"Sentimental? Well, Fred old buddy, I got to start bein' *respectable*. I'm runnin' for mayor in the upcomin' election, and I got to present a new image."

"Holy poo! Russell the Rat – *respectable?* Man, you've come a long way since the Commandos. Time was you'd've been sent to jail for some the stunts you pulled."

"Yep. Those were the days all right. But no more. You're lookin' at the new Thomas Albert Russell."

"I'm afraid to."

"You'll get over it. Now, take me to City Hall. I got to register my candidacy."

"Right on, bro."

Taxi #65 of the Cythera Cab Company pulled away from the curb and moved down Plum Street toward downtown. Taxi #65 did not, of course, pull away and move down by itself; it had a driver (identified as one Fred) who did the actual pulling away and moving down. The driver also released the brake and applied a foot (the right one, as it happened) to the accelerator. Otherwise, taxi #65 would not have gone anywhere (even by itself) and most likely would have remained in front of the house at 543 Plum Street for all of Eternity (more or less).

Fred the driver would have lost a fare – and a friend.

8:31:33 am
(depending on which clock you are looking at)

Ring-ring! says the telephone cheerfully. *Ring-ring!*

The dispatcher looks at the telephone with one bleary eye (it matters not which one). His other eye is half-closed, and it is too much effort to open it fully.

Ring-ring! says the telephone happily. *Ring-ring!*

"Honk you!" says the dispatcher unenthusiastically.

He takes a short pull from the pint of Jack Daniels and a short drag from the Marlboro, belches, farts, and scratches his privates (not necessarily in that order). As soon as the amenities are taken care of, he reaches for the telephone.

Ring-

"Cythera Cab Company," says the dispatcher unenthusiastically. "Service with a smile."

Even though the caller cannot see him, the dispatcher exposes a mouthful of yellow teeth in a grotesque facsimile of a smile.

"I'm at the casino," says the caller slurredly. "I wanna go to Duncan Grove."

"OK. Be about ten minutes." *Give or take an hour.*

"Thanks."

Click.

"Honk you, poohead!"

The dispatcher takes a short pull from the pint of Jack Daniels and a short drag from the Marlboro, belches, farts, and scratches his privates (not necessarily in that order). As soon as the amenities are taken care of, he reaches for the two-way radio.

"Dispatch to 65."

"65 here. Go ahead, dispatch."

"Where you at?"

"I don't rightly know, Uncle Gordy. Is the sky supposed to be green?"

"You been smokin' pot again, Fred?"

"Nah. I haven't had a joint since breakfast."

"Get serious, willya?"

"I'm back at the depot, waiting for the Chattanooga choo-choo (track #9)."

Even though the cab driver cannot see him, the dispatcher flips the bird.

"Got a goody fer ya, despite my reservations. Casino, goin' to Duncan Grove."

"Meter or flat rate?"

"Meter, unless he asks fer the flat rate. Then it's $40."

"Money in the bank. You're a sweetheart, Uncle Gordy. 10-4."

Uncle Gordy, who hates to be called "Uncle Gordy," flips the bird again. Then he takes another short pull from the pint of Jack Daniels and a short drag from the Marlboro, belches, farts, and scratches his privates (not necessarily in that order). As soon as the amenities are taken care of, he nods off.

(The big hand is two-thirds of the way to the twelve, while the little hand is three-fourths of the way to the nine.)

The aforementioned local writer, an individual well-known for his flammatory style of writing and controversial subject matter – which usually garners an equal measure of respect and disrespect – has called it (as often as he can) "Pilsner's Folly" in "honor" of a former mayor of Cythera who was instrumental in having a casino constructed in downtown Cythera, straddling one of the bridges which crossed the river which divided the City.

Former Mayor Pilsner believed in his heart of hearts that his town had been ripe for Cythera to have a casino to rival all casinos in the northeastern part of the state. He believed in his heart of hearts that having a casino in downtown Cythera would generate needed revenue into the City's coffers, needed jobs for the city's unemployed, and needed tourists for the City's businesses. He believed in his heart of hearts that the casino would restore Cythera to its former heyday as a major economic player in the Midwest. And so, he raised funds by any means available (within the law, of course) to construct the thing – tax dollars, individual and corporate donations, bond issues, public and private grants, and bake sales.

No expense had been spared in the construction. Former Mayor Pilsner wanted *his* casino to equal in splendor anything Las Vegas had to offer. He hired the best architects, the best contractors, and the best interior designers. He purchased the best furnishings, the best gaming equipment, and the best amenities. And he hired the best management team and the best work force. When all was said and done, the Cythera Classic Casino looked like a royal palace, fit for anyone who had a lot of extra cash lying about and was willing to throw it around in order to have a really good time.

There was one glitch, however, and the aforementioned local writer, an individual well-known for his flammatory style of writing and controversial subject matter – which garnered an equal measure of respect and disrespect – was quick to point out as often as he possibly could. The Cythera Classic Casino was situated adjacent to a war memorial located in the middle of the bridge and was deemed to be an insult to the City's war dead. For this and other reasons did he dub the casino "Pilsner's Folly."

One of the local businesses which hailed the construction of the Cythera Classic Casino as a boon to the city was the Cythera Cab Company. The owner believed in his heart of hearts that his cab company would find plenty of customers and make the company lots of money transporting casino goers hither and yon. *[Author's note: the use of the expression "hither and yon" has been deemed by the Author's many critics as obsolete and therefore ought to be replaced by an expression more reflective of the modern era. The Author has duly noted the criticism and assures the Reader that he will employ said expression more suitable to the modern era as soon as he finds one and that the Reader should hold his/her breath until he does find one.]* Alas! for owner and cab drivers alike, this did not turn out to be the case. Local casino goers usually arrived in private automobiles and availed themselves of the casino's parking garage; out-of-town casino goers were generally senior citizens looking to spend their Social Security checks in the hopes to realizing a huge retirement nest egg, and they usually arrived by charter buses. It was mostly slim pickings as far as the cab drivers were concerned, and rarely did they get a large fare.

At the time of the present narrative, a driver lucked out.

Fretfully, taxi #65 of the Cythera Cab Company pulled up in front of the Cythera Classic Casino. Taxi #65 of the Cythera Cab Company did not, of course, pull up by itself; it had a driver (identified as one Fred) who did the actual pulling up. The driver also applied the brake and stopped; otherwise, taxi #65 of the Cythera Cab Company would not have stopped (even by itself) and most likely would have proceeded into the lobby of the Cythera Classic Casino, inconvenienced the staff and patrons, caused considerable injury to said staff and patrons and damage to the casino, the taxi, and its driver, moderately to severely, and motivated several large security guards to remonstrate.

Presently (that is to say, half an hour, give or take ten minutes or so), the fare half-reeled/half-staggered out of the casino, because he was – as they say – "three sheets to the wind." He blinked his eyes rapidly in the bright sunlight in an attempt to focus them and half-reeled/ half-staggered even more. Presently (that is to say, ten minutes, give or take thirty seconds or so), the fare reached taxi #65 of the Cythera Cab Company, fumbled for the door handle, lost his grip, cursed a while (that is to say, a minute, give or take five seconds), fumbled for the door handle again, pulled on it hard, yanked the door open, fell in, and collapsed on the seat. He wheezed a bit (that is to say, two minutes, give or take fifteen seconds), peered at Fred with bloodshot eyes, realized vaguely where he was and why he was there, smiled crookedly, and chortled in embarrassment (which sounded like a series of short grunts).

"Good morning, sir," Fred greeted him cheerfully.

"Mornin'," the fare responded slurredly. "What the honk time is it?"

"It is" – Fred checked his watch – "exactly 8:45, sir."

"Oh, man. I got to get home. Gonna sleep all honkin' day."

"Yes, sir, that's a good idea. Did you have a good night at the casino?"

The fare chortled in glee (which sounded like series of short grunts).

"You honkin' betcha, buddy-boy. I made a honkin' *killing*!"

"Congratulations, sir. So, it's off to Duncan Grove?"

"Honkin' A! How much this trip gonna cost me?"

"Forty dollars, sir."

The fare reached into his coat pocket, pulled out a wad of bills, peered at the wad of bills with bloodshot eyes, peeled off four bills, and handed them to Fred. Fred took the bills, peered at them with clear eyes, and goggled.

"Sir? These are not ten-dollar bills. They're one-hundred-dollar bills."

"Huh? The honk you say!"

"I do say, sir."

"Well, what the honk? You keep 'em. I made a honkin' *killing* tonight!"

"Are you sure, sir?"

"Honkin' A! An' jus' for bein' honest about it, here's another one."

The fare peered at the wad of bills with bloodshot eyes, peeled off one, and handed to Fred. Fred took it with a poo-eating grin on his face – he had really lucked out! – and reached for the two-way radio.

"65 to dispatch."

"Dispatch here. Go ahead, 65."

"I'm on my way to Duncan Grove, Uncle Gordy."

"Goody. 10-4." *AMH.*

[Author's note: "AMH" is an obscene way to say 'good-bye.' It stands for 'adios, m----- - h-----.' Whoever coined it was apparently having a bad-hair day. Needless to say, it is not to be used in polite company – unless one is hard pressed to say something polite.]

Uncle Gordy then took a short pull from the pint of Jack Daniels and a short drag from the Marlboro, belched, farted, and scratched his privates (not necessarily in that order). As soon as the amenities were taken care of, he nodded off.

INTERLUDE THE FIRST

The Visitor halts in front of the sign at the edge of the city and studies it carefully.

The Visitor is on foot, having walked from the nearby woods to his present location. He had walked because he had parked his vehicle in the said woods. He had parked the said vehicle in the said woods because the sight of the said vehicle might have tended to alarm the local population. The Visitor does not wish to alarm the said local population; rather, he wishes to observe the said local population unobtrusively. And so, he has walked from the said woods to the said sign at the edge of the said city, hoping to be as unobtrusive as he can.

The Visitor's walk from the said woods to the said sign at the edge of the said city has, unfortunately, not been as unobtrusive as he would have liked. He does not understand why. He has walked along the yellow line running down the middle of the highway which passes the said woods and heads for the said city as he has done countless times in the place of his origin and has never thought anything of it.

Yet, members of the said local population operating their own vehicles have signaled to him in two different fashions. One, some of the members of the said local population have switched on a mechanical noise-making device within their vehicles and created a long series of beeps. Two, some of the members of the said local population have deployed a specific hand gesture. He assumes they are greeting him in welcome. Because he has parked his own vehicle in the said woods, he cannot return the mechanical first greeting; but, he can and does return the hand-gesture greeting in an effort to be courteous. Part of his training has been to assimilate into the local culture as quickly as possible.

Once more, the Visitor studies the said sign at the edge of the said city carefully and remembers his language lessons. The sign is yet another form of greeting to visitors (more or less). It reads:

WELCOME TO CYTHERA
CITY OF LIGHTS
POP. 101,010

The Visitor is pleased with his first use of his translating skills and is about to move on toward the said city. But wait! He has spied an anomaly on the said sign that he had not noticed before, because the said anomaly was not written in the same style as the other wording.

This anomaly, a single character of the local language, has been prefixed to the word "lights" in a crude, hand-written fashion. The said single character of the said local language is a "B," and its addition to the original word creates a new word – "blights" –which, if the Visitor is not sadly mistaken, signifies a state of ruination. Some member of the said local population has obviously attempted to make a sociological observation but has also obviously employed a very non-scientific manner of expressing himself.

In any event, the Visitor now must pay close attention to the physical structure of the said city in order to determine (if possible) the derivation of the said sociological observation inscribed upon the said sign. It seems to him that his task has just been made more complex. He slaps his forehead in resignation and walks into Cythera, the city of blights.

THE INTERVIEW
PART I

[*Author's note: venerable taxi driver and dispatcher for the Cythera Cab Company, "Uncle Gordy" (who hated to be called "Uncle Gordy"), whose real name has never been divulged by any of the employees of the Cythera Cab Company for reasons known only to themselves, deigned to give an interview to one Harriet Methune Beiderbeck, star reporter (in her humble estimation) for the Cythera* Clarion-News, *who had won several awards for her reporting which (in her humble estimation) she had deserved and who was generally referred to (though not to her face) as "Harry the Hatchet," thanks to her reputation for sniffing out and pursuing a story until (1) it became old news or (2) some other story needed to be sniffed out and pursued.*

[*The reason Harriet Methune Beiderbeck, star reporter (in her humble estimation) for the Cythera* Clarion-News, *had been assigned a bland assignment like an interview with an old cab driver and dispatcher for the Cythera Cab Company was because she was, as they used to say, "in a family way," and her publisher, the redoubtable Michael John McNamara, wanted to spare her the rigors of star reporting, much to her everlasting disgust. What follows is the first of several excerpts from said interview.*]

I been drivin' a cab [Uncle Gordy began] fer forty honkin' years, and I seen plenty o' poo what would curl yer hair, Blondie. They's a lot o' reasons *not* to be cab driver – the long honkin' hours, the meager honkin' pay, the ingratitude of too many honkin' passengers – and on'y one to be one. Truth is, I *like* to drive. I don't like sittin' around on my honkin' butt – like I'm doin' now. I got to be movin' around, and I can do that when I'm drivin'.

I been up and down and back and forth in this honkin' town, and I know it like the back o' my hand. Got a honkin' map up here. [He taps his forehead.] They's places I been in I don't honkin' care to be in

23

more'n I have to – places with honkin' pooheads runnin' all over the honkin' streets – but I go there 'cause a fare is a fare. Can't make no honkin' money of they ain't no honkin' fares, and that's the honkin' truth, Blondie.

…I mentioned some o' the reasons *not* to be a taxi driver. I saved the biggest reason fer last, 'cause I can go on and on about it and never repeat my honkin' self. It's them *other* drivers out there, them honkers with their big honkin' expensive automobiles who think they honkin' own the honkin' streets. I call 'em "Crackerjacks," 'cause they must've got their honkin' driver's license from a box o' Crackerjacks. Pooheads, ever' honkin' one o' them! They don't know poo! I like to get rid o' them and leave the streets safe fer people who know what the honk they're doin'.

I'll give ya an example, Blondie.

"Beepers." You get in their honkin' way, and *beep-beep!* Beepers must own automobiles what ain't got no honkin' brakes. That's why they beep – to warn other folks to get out o' their honkin' way 'cause they don't want to honkin' slow down or stop when they're barrelin' down the honkin' streets. They must have some real honkin' important business to attend to, doncha know? Beep-beep! Get out o' my way! Man, I hope they all go honkin' deaf!

Give ya another example.

"Gaters." Honkin' younger brothers to the beepers. Gaters look like they're in yer honkin' back seat, lookin' over yer honkin' shoulder, and checkin' out yer honkin' speedometer to see why you ain't movin' any faster. They's one way to cure a honkin' gater: make a sudden stop. If he crashes into ya, you can sue his butt off for damages. Heh-heh-heh.

One more example, Blondie.

"Weavers." They're also in a honkin' hurry, doncha know. They ain't no space in traffic too honkin' small fer weavers to enter so's they can honkin' move ahead of ever'body else. They got more honkin' moves than some honkin' NFL running back, jumpin' from lane to lane, always lookin' fer the least honkin' advantage. What they do is called the "Los Angeles Shuffle," 'cause that's where it honkin' started. Real honkin' pooheads they are!

9:30 am
(or as close as anyone can tell)

"65 to dispatch."

"Dispatch here. Go ahead, 65."

"I'm back in town, Uncle Gordy."

"Goody. Head over to Provisional Medical Center, pick up a package, and deliver it to Dunlap Hospital."

"Money in the bank. 10-4."

Honk you, poohead!

[Author's note: at this particular time, the dispatcher at the Cythera Cab Company who hated to be called "Uncle Gordy," would have uttered the words "honk you, poohead" aloud as was his habit. He then would have taken a short pull from the pint of Jack Daniels and a short drag from the Marlboro, belched, farted, and scratched his privates (not necessarily in that order). Finally, as soon as the amenities had been taken care of, he would have nodded off.

[At this particular moment, however, he could not utter the words "honk you, poohead," take care of the amenities, and nod off as was his habit. At this particular time, he was just beginning to be interviewed by one Harriet Methune Beiderbeck, star reporter (in her humble estimation) for the Cythera Clarion-News, *who had won several awards for her reporting which (in her humble estimation) she had deserved and who was generally referred to (though not to her face) as "Harry the Hatchet," thanks to her reputation for sniffing out a story and pursuing it until (1) it became old news or (2) some other story needed to be sniffed out and pursued. She had been given a choice by her publisher, the aforementioned redoubtable Michael John McNamara, either to cover the monthly meeting*

of a local garden club or to interview a long-time resident of Cythera. She had chosen Uncle Gordy, dispatcher for the Cythera Cab Company, just to spite the said publisher.

{The narrative continues as regularly scheduled.}

Fred, driver of taxi #65 of the Cythera Cab Company drove though the business district of Cythera on his way to his next fare. Ordinarily, he would have avoided the business district of Cythera like the plague because (1) the streets were too narrow to drive through safely, (2) the automobile traffic was too congested to drive through safely, and (3) the human traffic was too disdainful of the traffic laws to drive though safely. The only reason Fred chose to drive through the business district of Cythera was that it was the shortest route toward his next fare. Taxi Driver Rule #1: *always* take the shortest route to a fare, even if it means driving through alleyways or over someone's front lawn, all the while avoiding as many traffic signals and stop signs as humanly possible. Taxi Driver Rule #2: forget Taxi Driver Rule #1 *after* the fare is in the cab. Fred was not as diligent as he should have been, but he applied himself as best he could.

While on route through the business district of Cythera, he spotted a familiar sight parked on Downer Street: the "lemon car." Some enterprising citizen of Cythera either had bought the vehicle in question as is or had had it re-painted (no one knew which, and no one cared). Whoever had dubbed it the "lemon car" was unknown (no one knew, and no one cared), but the vehicle had the exact same color as a lemon. Moreover, since the vehicle in question was a Volkswagen, it also had the exact same shape as a lemon and was so comical as to be comical in the extreme. All who saw it pointed at it and laughed uproariously.

Fred saw it, pointed at it, and laughed uproariously – and nearly ran over a pedestrian who shook his fist in righteous wrath and cursed a bright blue streak. *[Author's note: the color of the streak has generated some controversy. Some witnesses say it was more navy-blue, while others say it was robin's-egg blue. Fred kept his own observation to himself.]* Fred ignored the shaking of the fist in righteous wrath and the cursing of a blue streak. Taxi Driver Rule #3: ignore the petty concerns of other drivers and pedestrians as your business is more important than theirs.

Fred was exceptionally diligent in this regard, and he continued on his merry way.

As Fred continued on his merry way, he spotted a fixture in Cythera. The fixture was not of the mechanical, inanimate sort (as fixtures go) that one can see anywhere in twenty-first-century America. The reason Cytherans called it a "fixture" was that it had been around for a very long time and seemed like a permanent part of the environment.

This fixture was none other than Albert Weldon (whose family had donated the land for Weldon Park to the City), reputedly the oldest living citizen in Cythera. No one knew how old the gentleman was, and no one cared; most estimates put him at the century mark, although he didn't look a day over ninety-nine, while some estimates put him as high as one-hundred-and-twenty, although he didn't behave a day over one-hundred-and-nineteen (as many females of the City will attest!). Whatever the truth of his age, Albert Weldon was referred to as "Uncle Bert" by most residents because he was full of tall tales and never missed an opportunity to tell two or three or more tall tales at the drop of a hat (or any other article of clothing). Some few called him "Batty Bert" for the exact same reason, but they were mostly sourpusses who did not appreciate a good tall tale when they heard one.

"Uncle Bert" (as he will be dubbed in this narrative) was out and about on his daily morning walk as was his wont. *[Author's note: use of the archaic word "wont" in this context is more appropriate than the modern word "habit," because Uncle Bert was also archaic.]* He was wearing his usual bright red shirt, blue trousers, and trademark rainbow suspenders without which he never went anywhere, but no overcoat and multi-colored matching stocking cap and scarf. Only in inclement weather did he wear over his usual bright red shirt, blue trousers, and trademark rainbow suspenders without which he never went anywhere his overcoat and multi-colored matching stocking cap and scarf, at which time one could not view his bright red shirt, blue trousers, and trademark rainbow suspenders without which he never went anywhere.

Uncle Bert walked everywhere, and one could see him in any part of Cythera on any given day. He did not own an automobile; whether he had ever owned an automobile no one knew and no one cared. He simply walked and walked and walked for no other reason than he liked to walk. And everyone respected him for it, and that was another reason he was called "Uncle Bert" – or "Batty Bert" by the sourpusses who did not appreciate a good walk when they saw one.

When Fred, the driver of taxi #65 of the Cythera Cab Company, spotted Uncle Bert, he tooted his taxi's horn. Everyone in Cythera who drove past Uncle Bert tooted their automobile's horn out of respect for him, and so Fred tooted. In response, Uncle Bert shook his fist at the tooters because he didn't like tooting horns. This did not prevent anyone from tooting their automobile's horns; everyone knew that Uncle Bert had his little eccentricities, and shaking his fist at drivers who tooted their automobile's horn was one of them. And that was yet another reason he was called "Uncle Bert" – or "Batty Bert" by the sourpusses who did not appreciate a good eccentricity when they saw one.

Fred laughed uproariously at Uncle Bert's shaking fist and continued on his merry way.

The Provisional Medical Center was a tall structure, spread out over five acres of former farm land on the northern edge of Cythera, constructed of white concrete. Its architecture was functional in nature; no added color, abutments, or spires adorned any part of it. It had not been designed to capture any awards for architectural sophistication but was simply a plain old, dull hospital where people went to be healed or to die trying.

Zestfully, taxi #65 of the Cythera Cab Company pulled up in front of the Provisional Medical Center located on the northern edge of Cythera. Taxi #65 of the Cythera Cab company did not, of course, pull up by itself; it had a driver (identified as one Fred) who did the actual pulling up. The driver also applied the brake and stopped; otherwise, taxi #65 would not have stopped (even by itself) and most likely would have proceeded into the lobby of the Provisional Medical Center, frightened the hospital staff and patients, caused considerable injury to the said hospital staff and patients and damage to the hospital, taxi, and taxi driver, moderately to severely (providing the hospital more people to be healed or to die trying), and initiated some running about in circles.

Fred exited his cab, went inside, identified himself to the receptionist (who gave him a "Visitor" badge and a dirty look), signed the guest register, asked for directions to the package pick-up office (a mere formality since he had been there many times before), and marched at a brisk pace to said office.

At the package pick-up office, he was greeted by a pretty little blonde technician with dimpled cheeks, sparkling blue eyes, an hour-glass figure, and an infectious smile. He was instantly smitten and wished he weren't otherwise occupied. Reluctantly, he identified himself, stated his business, and waited patiently while the pretty little blonde technician with dimpled cheeks, sparkling blue eyes, an hour-glass figure, and an infectious smile retrieved the desired package. She returned in a trice with the desired package and handed Fred a transfer form for him to sign. *[Author's note: the trice in this instance was the avoirdupois trice which is observed in the United States of America and not the metric trice which is observed in other parts of the world.]* Fred signed the form, accepted the package and gave the pretty little blonde technician with dimpled cheeks, sparkling blue eyes, an hour-glass figure, and an infectious smile a smile of his own designed to send provocative signals and to raise certain hopes.

With the desired package in hand, he marched at a brisk pace back to the receptionist's desk, returned the "Visitor" badge (and the dirty look), exited the hospital, and continued on his merry way.

THE INTERVIEW
PART II

So, ya wanna know [Uncle Gordy continued] what my best and worst drivin' experiences were, eh, Blondie?

Well, I'll tell ya, in this honkin' business, they's good days and bad days – mostly pee-poor days, if ya wanna know the honkin' truth. In my forty years of drivin,' it's been a real struggle to take home enough dough to make honkin' ends meet.

But, yeah, they's a few times what stand out at both ends of the honkin' stick. Lessee now, the *best* day I ever had – oh, yeah, that was one honkin' *super* day, I wanna tell ya, Blondie. I get the call at 5:30 in the a.m. to pick up a fare at the casino. We get them honkers all o' the time – three sheets to the honkin' wind and moanin' about their honkin' bad luck. Can't shut 'em the honk up. They go on and on and on. Honkin' pooheads!

Anyways, this honker jumps in the cab with the biggest poo-eatin' grin on his face I ever seen. And he don't look too buzzed neither. So, I sez, where to, and he sez, Elmont. I sez, do ya want the meter or the flat rate, and he sez, what's the flat rate. I sez, forty bucks, and he sez, OK, the flat rate.

I'll let ya in on a little secret, Blondie. Us cabbies prefer the meter on these long-distance fares, 'cause mebbe we can squeeze an extra couple o' bucks out of 'em. Honkin company offers flat rates in order to get the business, but they don't do the cabbies no favor. Still, we gotta offer the fare his choice.

Anyways, we're off to Elmont. Wouldn't ya know, the honker falls asleep right away, so the honkin' trip is a quiet one. At 5:30 in the a.m., I'm still half asleep my honkin' self. When we get to Elmont, I wake the fare up in order to get his street info – took a couple o' shakes before he opened his honkin' eyes. He looks around for a couple o' minutes before he recognizes where he is. Then he gives me the street info, and I take 'im there. When we pull into his driveway, he hands over a couple o' twenties. *Then*, he whips out a plain white envelope and hands *it* over. I sez, what's this, and he sez, that's yer tip for excellent service. And he jumps out o' the honkin' cab.

I wanna tell ya, Blondie, we hardly get much honkin' praise in this honkin' business. Most of our fares think we overcharge 'em or we take the 'scenic route' in order to jack up the fare. So, when we get a word of praise, we consider it a good day.

But, that wasn't the honkin' half of it that day. I looked at that honkin' envelope for the longest time, wonderin' what the honk's in it. Sometimes we get advertisin' flyers or religious leaflets or poo. Anyways, I finally get the nerve to open that honkin' envelope. I like to have a honkin' heart attack, Blondie! Inside was *ten honkin' one-hundred-dollar bills. A thousand honkin' dollars!* Made my day, I wanna tell ya. Natcherly, I kept quiet about it. Ain't never told nobody until now. Heh-heh-heh.

Now the worst experience? Yeah, I remember that honkin' day like it was honkin' yesterday. Ya gotta unnerstand, Blondie, us cabbies are like honkin' postmen. We got to go out in all sorts o' weather and do our job. 'Neither rain or snow or sleet' and all that poo.

So, I'm a half hour from the end o' my shift, and I'm anxious to get home 'cause it's honkin' winter, and the sky looks ready to drop a honkin' load. Matter o' fact, it was flakin' at the time. Anyways, the honkin' dispatcher (the honker's dead now, and good riddance too) gets on the honkin' horn and sends me over to West Indian Trail fer a final fare. He didn't say where the honk the fare was goin.' That shoulda been my first honkin' clue.

So, I pull into the fare's driveway, and now the snow is really comin' down. The fare comes out with his old lady and two kids and a bunch o' suitcases. Red flag time, Blondie! I sez to my honkin' self, oh, poo, a honkin' *airport* run. Sure enough, that's what it was.

So, I get on the interstate. It's honkin' 'rush hour,' and the honkin' traffic is backed up from Cythera to the airport turn-off. It's a honkin' snail-crawl all the way, and the honkin' snow is cuttin' vision down to, mebbe, ten yards. The fare in the back seat is makin' little honkin' whiney noises and wonderin' if he'll catch his plane. Me, I'm cursin' the honkin' dispatcher for sendin' me out on this trip.

Anyways, we get to the honkin' airport, and I help the fare unload his suitcases. He pays me off – exact amount – no honkin' tip for services rendered above and beyond, doncha know? Like it was my honkin' fault it was snowin' and the honkin' traffic was backed up. Believe me, Blondie, they ain't no honkin' justice in this honkin' world.

So, now I got to make the long trip back to Cythera. I'm runnin' out o' gas, the honkin' windshield is iced over, and my honkin' bladder is sendin' me an urgent message. It was a good thing they's a rest stop with full services not far from the airport, or there'da been a honkin' 'accident,' if ya know what I mean. First thing I do is take care of the bladder. Then I knock off all the ice on the windshield. Then I gas up.

The trip back wasn't as bad as the trip in. It was still snowin,' but the traffic was light. Even so, I don't get back until honkin' 7:30 in the p.m. I'd put in a honkin' fifteen-and-a-half-hour day, and I wasn't home yet. I like to strangle the honkin' dispatcher! Know what I mean, Blondie?

So. There ya are, the best and the worst. Next question?

[Author's note: if truth be told, at this juncture, one supposes that Uncle Gordy would desperately like to take a long pull from the pint of Jack Daniels and a long drag from the Marlboro, belch, fart, and scratch his privates (not necessarily in that order), then nod off. Alas! he cannot on pain of looking foolish in the presence of the press, represented in this case by one Harriet Methune Beiderbeck, star reporter (in her humble estimation) for the Cythera Clarion-News, who had won several awards for her reporting which (in her humble estimation) she had deserved for sniffing out and pursuing stories until (1) they became old news or (2) some other stories needed to be sniffed out and pursued. So he endures – but none too graciously.]

INTERLUDE THE SECOND

The Visitor has been strolling along the main thoroughfare of the city for the better part of forty-five minutes (local reckoning). He has taken his time about reaching the city's core because he does not wish to miss a single aspect of the local culture. There is, he has realized, much to see; and, if he should overlook anything, his understanding of the local customs would be incomplete. And, therefore, his report to his superiors would likewise be incomplete to the detriment not only to their understanding but also to his chances for promotion to a higher status. Remaining in his current grade for longer than necessary would be rather unpleasant, to say the least.

So far in his observations of the fringe of the city, he has noted an interesting complex of structures. The sign in front of the complex states that it is a replica of an agricultural station commonly found in the area two centuries ago (local reckoning). Judging by the number of units who are walking about and examining every single part of the complex, the designers must have intended to make a museum out of it. The Visitor would surely like to examine the complex himself; but his prime goal is to examine the city's core as thoroughly as possible. Perhaps, later, when he has a few moments (local reckoning) to spare, he might avail himself of the opportunity to absorb some of the local history.

Another interesting complex is what seems to be a bio-engineering station. He had been led to believe, during his period of indoctrination, that this culture had not yet achieved the scientific sophistication to perform such experiments. He is secretly pleased to learn that his indoctrination was in error; now he will be able to correct the error and enhance his chances of promotion to a higher status. It is unfortunate, however, that he cannot examine this complex in more detail as the knowledge would make for a very interesting report. Perhaps, later, if he has a few spare *moments (local reckoning), he might avail himself of the opportunity to absorb some of the local science.*

The Visitor has been strolling along this major thoroughfare, all the while greeting passersby in their vehicles with the accepted hand gesture. That they return the hand gesture assures him that he is not out of place here; for, if he were seen as being out of place here, his mission might be compromised and his person might suffer harm. Then there would be no chance at all for a promotion to a higher status. He is also adding to his basic lexicon some of the local idiomatic expressions because, when some of the passersby in their vehicles greet him with the accepted hand gesture, they also call out to him. The words are, of course, unfamiliar to him; but, in the context of the setting, he believes they constitute both an acknowledgement of his presence and a form of introduction. Words like "sunuvab-----," "a---hole," "s----head," and "m------f------," repeatedly so many times by so many units cannot be construed otherwise, even if he is unfamiliar with their derivation. [Author's note: ever mindful of the Reader's sensibilities, the Author has abbreviated the above terminology and begs his/her indulgence.]

VII

9:45 am
(give or take two seconds)

As he went on his merry way, Fred, the driver of taxi #65 of the Cythera Cab Company, passed by another familiar sight: the "Pepto-Bismol" car. Now, the Reader might be led to believe that the said vehicle was a company-owned vehicle and displayed the company logo on both sides of the vehicle. The Reader would have been misled if (s)he believed such a thing. The fact of the matter was that the said vehicle was *not* a company car nor did it display the company logo on both sides. Rather, the said vehicle was privately-owned car owned by persons unknown (said unknown persons being totally irrelevant to this narrative). The "Pepto-Bismol" car had been so-named because its color matched exactly the color of that esteemed product. It had been so-named by some local wag (said local wag being totally irrelevant to this narrative) who believed (s)he was quite clever.

As soon as Fred, the driver of taxi #65 of the Cythera Cab Company, spotted the "Pepto-Bismol" car, he put one of his fingers (it matters not which one) in his mouth and made a gagging motion. Fred believed he was being quite clever too. How the driver of the "Pepto-Bismol" car responded to this bit of cleverness – if (s)he responded at all – was unknown and may or may not be totally irrelevant to this narrative. Be that as it may, Fred continued on his merry way. *[Author's note: continual use of the word "merry" may be an exaggeration on the Author's part. The fact of the matter is that Dunlap Hospital was located in another community north of Cythera, and so Fred would have had to battle traffic both ways and burn up costly gasoline, neither action of which can be considered "merry."]*

Morosely, battling traffic and burning up costly gasoline, taxi #65 of the Cythera Cab Company pulled up in front of Dunlap Hospital located in another community north of Cythera. Taxi #65 of the Cythera Cab Company did not, of course, battle traffic, burn up costly gasoline, and pull up in front of Dunlap Hospital by itself; it had a driver (identified as one Fred) who did the actual battling, burning up, and pulling up. The driver also applied the brake and stopped; otherwise, taxi #65 would not have stopped (even by itself) and most likely would have proceeded into the lobby of Dunlap Hospital, surprised hospital staff and patients, caused considerable injury to said hospital staff and patients and damage to hospital, taxi, and driver, moderately to severely, and had the administration wailing and gnashing their teeth.

Fred exited his cab, went inside, identified himself to the receptionist (who gave him a "Visitor" badge and a dirty look), signed the guest register, asked for directions to the package drop-off office (a mere formality since he had been there many times), and marched at a brisk pace to said office.

At the package drop-off office, he was greeted by a gorgeous little red-haired technician with dimpled cheeks, sparkling green eyes, an hour-glass figure, and a come-hither smile. He was instantly smitten and wished he weren't otherwise occupied. Reluctantly, he identified himself, stated his business, and waited patiently while the gorgeous little red-haired technician with dimpled cheeks, sparkling green eyes, an hour-glass figure, and a come-hither smile accepted the package and wrote out a receipt. Fred accepted the receipt and gave the gorgeous little red-haired technician with dimpled cheeks, sparkling green eyes, an hour-glass figure, and a come-hither smile a smile of his own designed to send provocative signals and to raise certain hopes.

With the receipt in hand, he marched at a brisk pace back to the receptionist, returned the "Visitor" badge (and the dirty look), exited the hospital, jumped into his cab, and went on his merry way. As soon as he returned to Cythera, he reached for the two-way radio.

"65 to dispatch."

"Dispatch here. Go ahead, 65."

"I'm back in town, Uncle Gordy."

"Whoopy-doo. Got a laundry run fer ya."

Yuck, Fred thought.

"Yuck," Fred said vigorously.

"Sorry, 65. All the other drivers are busy. Head for Smith and Ohio."

"10-4, Uncle Gordy."

Honk you, poohead!

[Author's note: Uncle Gordy still did not utter the words "honk you, poohead!" out loud, as he was still constrained at this time by the fact that he was still being interviewed by one Harriet Methune Beiderbeck, star reporter (in her humble estimation) for the Cythera Clarion-News, and saying "honk you, poohead" in the presence of "Harry the Hatchet," who had the reputation, when disturbed, of fixing said disturber with such a menacing glare that an army of rats would flee for their very lives and of holding that glare until such time as the said disturber vacated the premises (presumably fleeing for his very life), was not a wise thing to say, even for an old curmudgeon like Uncle Gordy.]

# VIII

16:17:18 pm
(GMT)

Fred, the driver of taxi #65 of the Cythera Cab Company, hated laundry runs. Laundry runs were the second worst fares he could think of. *[Author's note: Fred's worst fare will be explained later in this narrative. The Reader need not worry over missing some valuable information.]* In the first place, laundry runs tended to be only three- or four-dollar fares. Drivers hardly made any money on them, unless those were the only fares they made every day of their lives; but, before then they would have gone stark raving mad and driven their taxis off the High Street bridge, thus damaging their taxis and themselves beyond all recognition (not that most people recognized taxis and taxi drivers *before* they drove off the High Street bridge).

In the second place, laundry runs meant having to get out the taxi, open up the trunk, help the fare put three or four baskets/bags of dirty, smelly clothes into the trunk, close the trunk, and get back into the taxi. And once the driver arrived at the laundromat, he had to get out of the taxi, open up the trunk, help the fare remove three or four baskets/bags of dirty, smelly clothes from the trunk, close the trunk, and get back into the taxi. And sometimes the fare did not opt to use the trunk but instead put three or four baskets/bags of dirty, smelly clothes in the back seat and place herself in the front seat next to the driver.

And, in the third place, the fare was apt to load up her dirty, smelly children in the back seat instead of in the trunk where they belonged.

But, since the taxi driver is not allowed to refuse a fare (except under extraordinary circumstances), Fred was obliged to make laundry runs. So, off he went on his unmerry way, mumbling to himself all the while. *[Author's note: what Fred mumbled to himself all the while on his unmerry way is not relevant to this narrative. Neither is it printable. The Author has his scruples (such as they are), and the Reader is obliged to use his/her imagination as to what Fred mumbled to himself all the while on his unmerry way.]*

When he had neared the intersection of Smith and Ohio in the southeast quadrant of Cythera, Fred duly reported his position to Uncle Gordy [who was still being interviewed by one Harriet Methune Beiderbeck, star reporter (in her humble estimation) for the Cythera *Clarion-News*, who was now regretting her choice of interviewee]. Uncle Gordy gave him the address of the fare which was quite unnecessary because Fred already knew where the fare was, having been sent there more times than he cared to think about during the course of his career. But, since a taxi driver was not allowed to refuse a fare, Fred was obliged to go to that address and pick up that fare and her dirty, smelly clothes/children.

The address to which Fred was driving to pick up the fare and her dirty, smelly clothes/children was a large brick building and was in fact an apartment complex for low-income families. Few residents in the said apartment complex could afford an automobile to transport their dirty, smelly clothes/children, and so they were limited to the use of a taxi which was the reason for frequent laundry runs at an average of two a day.

Cautiously, taxi #65 of the Cythera Cab Company pulled into the parking lot of the said apartment complex. Taxi #65 of the Cythera Cab Company did not, of course, pull into the parking lot of the said apartment complex by itself; it had a driver (identified as one Fred) who did the actual pulling in. The driver also applied the brake and stopped; otherwise, taxi #65 would not have stopped (even by itself) and most likely would have proceeded into a grove of trees located at the south end of the said parking lot, caused considerable damage the trees, itself and its driver, moderately to severely, and left much wildlife fleeing for their very lives.

Fred did not have to wait long for the fare and her dirty, smelly clothes/children, because the fare and her dirty, smelly clothes/children were all waiting for him at the entrance to the said apartment complex.

The fare carried a large plastic basket overloaded with dirty, smelly clothes; she was followed by two dirty, smelly boys who each carried an overloaded bag of dirty, smelly clothes. (Actually, the said boys *dragged* their bags of dirty, smelly clothes because the bags were as large as they were.)

Fred heaved a sigh of resignation (it matters not in which direction or how far he heaved the sigh of resignation), got out of the taxi, opened the trunk, helped the fare load the plastic basket and the two bags with dirty, smelly clothes into the trunk, closed the trunk, and got back into the taxi. The fare threw the two dirty, smelly boys into the back seat and jumped in herself. Fred drove off toward a laundromat six blocks away from the said apartment complex, eager to collect his three- or four-dollar fare and be off to some more lucrative destination.

10:27/28

[depending on whether you were looking at Fred's watch
or the time/temperature sign on the bank across
the street from the laundromat
(it matters not which is which)]

"65 to dispatch."

"Dispatch here. Go ahead, 65."

"I am clear at the laundromat."

"Whoopee-doo. Go back to Provisional Medical Center. Got another package pick-up, goin' to Dunlap Hospital."

"Money in the bank. 10-4, Uncle Gordy."

Honk you, poohead!

Fred, the driver of taxi #65 of the Cythera Cab Company, departed with glee the said laundromat – which, curiously, was named for a marsupial creature indigenous to Australia but for some unfathomable reason was colored blue instead of the normal brown – and proceeded north on Farnsworth Avenue. He proceeded north on Farnsworth Avenue very slowly at this point as it was a major north-south thoroughfare on the east side of Cythera and therefore heavily congested with vehicular traffic, both private and commercial (although more commercial than private). The aforementioned writer well-known for his flammatory style of writing and controversial subject matter – which usually garnered an equal measure of respect and disrespect – has often declared that, no matter what time of the day or night, there is always heavy traffic on Farnsworth Avenue and proceeding up it is always slow and that crossing it is next to impossible. Traffic at this particular hour included a

43

city bus which delighted in stopping every fifty feet to pick up or drop off passengers. Fred had the misfortune to be behind it and unable to turn into a passing lane due to the large number of persons hurrying hither and yon to be somewhere. *[Author's note: "hither and yon" is a more accurate description than most people have been led to believe. Originally, it meant traveling to unknown places at a great distance; nowadays, it means traveling to known places at a short distance. The number of people who hither-and-yon is irrelevant.]* Fred duly proceeded slowly.

Eventually, the city bus turned off of Farnsworth Avenue, but Fred was not in the clear just yet. He now found himself behind a semi-trailer (whose cargo is not relevant to this narrative), and he was treated to a barrage of diesel-fuel fumes. He quickly rolled up the window of the taxi and sent the driver of the said semi-trailer a few well-chosen thoughts concerning his parentage and sexual habits. Eventually, the said semi-trailer turned off of Farnsworth Avenue, but Fred was still not in the clear. He now found himself behind a gravel truck whose driver had neglected to throw a tarpaulin over the load of gravel, and he was treated to a barrage of flying gravel which pelted the taxi's hood and windshield with regularity. Fred also sent the driver of the said gravel truck a few well-chosen thoughts concerning his parentage and sexual habits.

At the intersection of Farnsworth Avenue and East Indian Trail Road, Fred gleefully departed the former and headed west on the latter. Indian Trail Road was so named because that was what it was, before there ever was a Cythera or before there ever were settlers from the East bent on escaping congestion and lack of opportunity and seeking new horizons and a better life. When they arrived in the area which eventually became Cythera, they were warmly greeted by the indigenous population – affectionately but mistakenly called "Indians" – who traveled hither and yon on a well-worn path which eventually was paved over and became Indian Trail Road in honor of the settlers' hosts.

If Farnsworth Avenue was a major north-south thoroughfare on the east side of Cythera, then Indian Trail Road was its east-west counterpart on the north side, and whatever has been said about the former also pertains to the latter (according to the aforementioned writer well-known for his flammatory style of writing and his controversial subject matter which garnered an equal measure of respect and disrespect). Fred had as much difficulty navigating this street as he had the other one. For one thing, he soon encountered the aforementioned city bus again and had to follow it for longer than he cared to, because it delighted in stopping every fifty feet to pick up and drop off passengers; for another thing, he could not turn into a passing lane because of the large number of people hurrying hither and yon to be somewhere.

While he was proceeding very slowly, he had the time (if not the inclination) to observe in minute detail Cythera's brand new police station. From the dank and dark confines in the basement of City Hall, the CPD, a.k.a. the "Keystone Kops," who arrested first and asked questions later, removed to an imposing gray-and-white monolith, looking for all the world like a fortress (which, if truth be told, was precisely what the architect had in mind). Here was the new domain of one Colonel Luther Ozymandias Oglesby, USMC (ret.) – "Chief Ozzie" as he was affectionately called by friend and foe alike – who had sworn to clear the streets of Cythera of the scum, vermin, riff-raff, and animals which infested them and, to this end, had sent his officers hither and yon to harass, detain, and otherwise crimp the activities of as many of the scum, vermin, riff-raff, and animals as they could get their hands on (and they had gotten their hands on quite a few).

Fred, the driver of taxi #65 of the Cythera Cab Company, had once been one of those scum, vermin, riff-raff, and animals who had infested the streets of Cythera. In his misbegotten youth, he had been one of Tommy Russell's Commandos; and he, like the other members of that organization, had been fortunate not to have been gotten hold of by the "Keystone Kops." Eventually, he had decided not to push his luck any further than it had already been pushed (which was quite far, if he said so himself) and to become a respectable citizen of Cythera. To this end, he had taken employment at the Cythera Cab Company, simply because he knew the ins and outs of the City better than most citizens.

At the moment, however, he had the bad luck to have been caught behind a city bus where he had the further bad luck to gaze upon the fortress known as the Cythera Police Department, the domain of Chief Ozzie, who had sworn to clear the streets of Cythera of the scum, vermin, riff-raff, and animals which infected them and sent his officers hither and yon to harass, detain, and otherwise crimp the activities of as many of the scum, vermin, riff-raff, and animals as they could get their hands on. As long as he (that is, Fred) was in the mood, he sent Chief Ozzie a few well-chosen thoughts concerning *his* parentage and sexual habits.

Eventually, the city bus turned off of Indian Trail Road at Ohio Street, and Fred believed he was in the clear at last. Fred, however, believed falsely. As soon as he reached Indian Trail Road and State Route 25, he (and many other motorists) was (were) halted by a funeral procession heading north to a nearby cemetery. Either the deceased had been a very popular person in life or (s)he had had a very large family, because (s)he headed a very long procession. There must have been at least fifty vehicles in the procession, all moving at a ponderous pace. *[Author's note: the Author wishes to apologize to the Reader for this uncharacteristic piece of purple prose. He could not think of any other descriptive phrase which would have done justice to the scene.]* Eventually, the final vehicle of the procession passed through the intersection, and all of the stalled traffic moved forward at a ponderous pace. *[Author's note: oops! Sorry again.]*

Now, Fred believed he was in the clear. He truly believed. Except, he was wrong.

"Dispatch to 65."

"65 here. Go ahead, dispatch."

"Where you at? The hospital just called back. That pick-up is urgent."

"I got caught up in traffic, Uncle Gordy. I'm two minutes from the hospital."

"10-4."

Honk you, poohead!

Listlessly, taxi #65 of the Cythera Cab Company pulled up in front of the Provisional Medical Center located at the northern edge of Cythera. Taxi #65 of the Cythera Cab company did not, of course, pull up in front of the hospital by itself; it had a driver (identified as one Fred) who did the actual pulling up. The driver also applied the brake and stopped; otherwise, taxi #65 would not have stopped (even by itself) and most likely would have proceeded into the lobby of the Provisional Medical Center, unnerved the hospital staff and patients, caused considerable injury to said hospital staff and patients and damage to the hospital, taxi, and taxi driver, moderately to severely, thereby providing the hospital with more people to be healed or die trying, and elicited fainting spells by the administration.

Fred exited his cab, went inside, identified himself to the receptionist (who gave him a "Visitor" badge and a dirty look), signed the guest register, asked for directions to the package pick-up office (a formality since he had been there many times before), and marched at a brisk pace to the said office.

At the package pick-up office, he was greeted by the aforementioned pretty little blonde technician with dimpled cheeks, sparkling blue eyes, an hour-glass figure, and an infectious smile. He was instantly re-smitten and again wished he weren't otherwise occupied. Reluctantly, he re-identified himself, stated his business, and waited patiently while the pretty little blonde technician with dimpled cheeks, sparkling blue eyes, an hour-glass figure, and an infectious smile retrieved the desired package. She returned in a trice-and-a-half with the desired package and handed Fred a transfer form for him to sign. Fred signed the form, accepted the desired package, and gave the pretty little blonde technician with dimpled cheeks, sparkling blue eyes, an hour-glass figure, and an infectious smile a smile of his own designed to send provocative signals and to raise certain hopes.

With the desired package in hand, he marched at a brisk pace back to the receptionist, returned the "Visitor" badge (and the dirty look), exited the hospital, jumped back into his cab, and continued on his merry way.

As Fred was leaving the grounds of the Provisional Medical Center, he spotted another familiar sight, an avocado-green van, entering the said grounds. The logo on the side of the van was an image of a pelican on roller skates carrying a large sack in its pouch. The wording underneath the image read: "Cythera Parcel Service – We Deliver (Eventually)." As he passed the van, he gave the driver a thumbs-up as a sign of professional courtesy. The driver of the van returned the thumbs-up and nearly side-swiped another vehicle and a tree in doing so. The CPS had a laughable reputation for doing just about everything a parcel service should *not* do, and Fred did laugh, uproariously, and continued on his merry way.

THE INTERVIEW
PART III

So, where was we, Blondie? Oh, yeah. Yer question was, did I ever get into a serious accident? Lots o' near misses, lemme tell ya, no thanks to all them honkin' pooheads who think they own the honkin' streets. I did have one semi-serious accident – on New Year's Day, wouldja believe?

I had just dropped off a fare at a laundromat at Lake Street and Indian Trail Road and was pullin' outa the parking lot when this woman driver comes roarin' up the street outa honkin' nowhere on my blind side and honkin' rams me on the left-front fender. Spun me around, she did. Rang my chimes, she did. I got honkin' whiplashed, but that was all. The worst part was *I* got a honkin' ticket – *me!* – fer failin' to yield the honkin' right-of-way. Can ya believe that, Blondie?

Which reminds me of some more "Crackerjacks" I've encountered over the years. *[Author's note: this is obviously a non-sequitur. Uncle Gordy always lacked the ability to segue from one topic to another in a proper fashion. Of, course, pointing this out to him usually earned the pointer-outer a sharp rebuke liberally peppered with colorful expressions which cannot be printed here.]*

They's a special kind o' weaver I call the "short-cutters." Since they're always in a honkin' hurry, they make left turns sooner'n they should and cross over the left lane of the cross-street. And, sometimes, if they're in a *super* honkin' hurry, they take a little bit o' the right lane as well. Any on-coming traffic has got to stop halfway down the honkin' block, or else they lose their honkin' left-front fender and maybe part o' their grill-work. Why do the honkers do it? Because they feel like it, that's why, Blondie.

Here's another poohead fer ya: "blind-siders." Man, oh, man! How I hate them honkers! You think honkin' gaters are bad? You ain't met the blind-siders yet. They don't sit on yer honkin' rear bumper. Oh, no! They sit on yer honkin' left-rear *fender* where they're hidden from view, and they just stay there – like honkin' *forever!* You can't switch lanes, 'cause you don't know they're there, and yer liable to take off their honkin' right-front fender. Then they sue yer honkin' butt. So, you got to slow down a bit and see if the honker will pass you, or you got to hit yer honkin' gas pedal and get far enough ahead of 'im so you can get into his lane. It don't work sometimes, 'cause the honker tries to keep up with ya. Honkin' pooheads!

And then they's the honkin' "high-beamers." Ya don't hafta put up with 'em in the daytime, of course. But, at night – look out! Those honkers must have honkin' eye problems, Blondie, and they need a lot o' light to see where they're goin' – even on a well-lighted street. No honkin' low beams fer them. Nope. Gotta go straight to the honkin' floodlight mode! Ya meet 'em, and it's instant blindness. So, you play their honkin' little game and give the high beams right back. Serve 'em right. Heh-heh-heh.

Hang on a minute, Blondie. Got another call.

[There is a brief conversation as Uncle Gordy obtains important information germane to the well-being, i.e. the revenue, of the Cythera Cab Company. When the conversation concludes, he notifies a taxi which is available for duty. That is to say, he notifies the *driver* of a taxi who is available for duty, since taxis do not speak except in private when no humans are around. Uncle Gordy does not notify taxi #65 – that is to say, the *driver* of taxi #65 – because it – the driver – is not available for duty. Instead, he notifies taxi #23 – that is to say, the *driver* of taxi #23 – and sends it – him—on its – his – merry way. *(Author's note: the Reader will encounter taxi #23 – that is to say, the* driver *of taxi #23 – further on in this narrative but is forewarned that the said encounter may not be entirely enlightening.)*

[At this point in time, Uncle Gordy would *really* like to take a long pull from the pint of Jack Daniels and a long drag from the Marlboro, belch, fart, and scratch his privates (not necessarily in that order) and then nod off. He cannot do so, of course, because he is still in the presence of one Harriet Methune Beiderbeck, star reporter (in her humble estimation) of the Cythera *Clarion-News*, and therefore must suffer all the torments of Hell until the interview has concluded.]

11:00 am
(or thereabouts)

Once upon a time *[Author's note: the Reader is assured that (s)he will not be told a fairy tale here – which literary form generally begins with this much revered expression – but will continue to read the narrative (s)he bought/borrowed/stole this book to do. The Reader is therefore encouraged to continue to read for his/her edification.]*, Randall Road, the route that Fred, the driver of taxi #65 of the Cythera Cab Company, took as he went his merry way from the Provisional Medical Center to Dunlap Hospital, was a simple rural county highway which ran from Cythera's northwest region north to a small municipal airport (which may or may not be located on a lake). For most of this route, the alert driver beheld nothing but farmland for miles and miles on both sides of the highway. One might be tempted to use the descriptive term "bucolic," but one will not be so tempted here. Nevertheless, the drive along Randall Road tended to be peaceful, relaxing, and joyful – the ideal place for a Sunday drive for those given to such activity.

On the day that Fred, the driver of taxi #65 of the Cythera Cab Company, was traveling on that simple rural county highway, that highway had long since ceased to be simple and rural. Rather, it had become a congested, four-lane county highway, bounded for miles and miles on both sides by strip malls and subdivisions. If Fred had had his druthers in the matter, he might have chosen an alternate route, one more peaceful, relaxing, and joyful *[Author's note: the Reader will excuse the use of the archaic term "druthers." Since (s)he has excused all the others so far, (s)he therefore is stuck with it.]*; but, inasmuch as Randall Road was the most direct route between the Provisional Medical Center and Dunlap Hospital and inasmuch as Fred wanted to keep his operating costs at a minimum, he was forced to ignore his druthers and stay the course.

There is one point on Randall Road which is the crest of a hill where one may view the scenery for five miles in all directions. One must be quick, however, to view this scenery for five miles in all directions because one is driving a motor vehicle and one must be aware of what one is driving at all times lest one becomes a customer at either of the aforementioned medical facilities (which may or may not be one's good fortune). Once upon a time *[Author's note: sorry – force of habit.]*, the view from the crest of that hill was, uh, bucolic and lent itself to the peaceful, relaxing, and joyful quality of the aforementioned Sunday drive. Nowadays, the view from the crest of that hill is anything but bucolic, and one will take anything but a peaceful, relaxing, and joyful Sunday drive; one is more likely to be a customer at one of the aforementioned medical facilities (which may or not be one's good fortune).

Fred, the driver of taxi #65 of the Cythera Cab Company, ignored his surroundings as best he could and concentrated on his driving – not an easy task as he had to battle traffic and burn up costly gasoline.

Feloniously, taxi #65 of the Cythera Cab Company pulled in front of Dunlap Hospital located in a community north of Cythera. Taxi #65 of the Cythera Cab Company did not, of course, battle traffic, burn up costly gasoline, and pull up in front of Dunlap Hospital by itself; it had a driver (identified as one Fred) who did the actual battling, burning up, and pulling up. The driver also applied the brake and stopped; otherwise, taxi #65 would not have stopped (even by itself) and most likely would have proceeded into the lobby of the hospital, annoyed the hospital staff and patients, caused considerable injury to the said staff and patients and damage to the hospital, the taxi, and the driver, moderately to severely, and invited a vigorous protest from all concerned.

Fred exited his cab, went inside, identified himself to the receptionist (who gave him a "Visitor" badge and a dirty look), signed the guest register, asked for directions to the package drop-off office (a formality since he had been there many times before), and marched at a brisk pace to said office.

At the package drop-off office, he was greeted by the gorgeous little red-headed technician with dimpled cheeks, sparkling green eyes, an hour-glass figure, and a come-hither smile. He was instantly re-smitten and again wished he was not otherwise occupied. Reluctantly, he identified himself, stated his business, and waited patiently while the gorgeous little red-headed technician with dimpled cheeks, sparking green eyes, an hour-glass figure, and a come-hither smile accepted the package and wrote out a receipt. Fred accepted the receipt and gave the gorgeous little red-headed technician with dimpled cheeks, sparkling green eyes, an hour-glass figure, and a come-hither smile a smile of his own designed to send provocative signals and to raise certain hopes.

With the receipt in hand, he marched at a brisk pace back to the receptionist, returned the "Visitor" badge (and the dirty look), exited the hospital, jumped into his cab, and continued on his merry way.

As Fred was nearing Cythera, his radio crackled (as radios often do, especially when they are in a foul mood).

"Dispatch to 65," the radio crackled.

"65 here," the radio crackled. "Go ahead, dispatch."

"Where you at?" Uncle Gordy crackled.

"Coming up on Randall Road and Oak Street," Fred crackled.

"Great timing, 65," the radio crackled. "Pick up our 'friend' at Courtyard Villages. He's ready for his 'lunch' at his 'club.'"

"Him again?" the radio crackled.

"Yeah, and he asked fer you specifically," Uncle Gordy crackled.

"Why me?" Fred crackled.

"Dunno, 65," the radio crackled. "Some people got all the luck."

"10-4, Uncle Gordy," the radio crackled.

Honk you, poohead!

INTERLUDE THE THIRD

The Visitor has arrived at the site of one of the most marvelous sights he (or any of his kind) has ever seen: the shopping mall.

[In times long ago, Americans shopped in a centrally-located business district. America was then clusters of small towns with only a few large cities where the major industries resided. Americans in these small towns could walk or ride in the family auto and reach the business district with ease; and, once there, they could shop until all of their needs/desires were satisfied. And all the while, they would greet each other with a practiced familiarity. As towns grew slowly but steadily with an increase in population, neighborhood stores -- the so-called "mom-and-pop" establishments – popped up like mushrooms to provide more immediate, more specialized services. They did not, however, take away from the central business district but rather supplemented it.

[After the close of World War II, American society underwent a radical change. The country was now acknowledged as the world's dominant political and economic force; prosperity increased, and so did the population. Many small towns became medium- and large-sized cities, and the once large cities burgeoned into metropolises. Soon, it was realized, a shopping trip "downtown" entailed a more complex, more time-consuming enterprise. The "mom-and-pop" stores could not fill the void because of the increased costs. Something had to be done if Americans' needs/desires were to be satisfied quickly and efficiently.

[And so the shopping mall was created – large clusters of retail/service outlets conveniently located in outlying areas far from the central business district. The malls had everything – from grocery stores to clothing stores, from restaurants (mostly "fast-food" establishments) to theaters, from banks to book stores – and all one had to do was to hop into the family auto and go from one end of the mall to the other. The major difference between the central district and the outlying ones was that the former were family-owned and –operated, while the latter were chain stores controlled by faraway conglomerates. Little by little, Americans traded small-town-ness for convenience, and the shopping mall became a permanent fixture on the scene.

[The City of Cythera had not been immune to this transformation of American society. If anything, it embraced the change whole-heartedly. The old industries and the family-owned and –operated stores disappeared one by one – either through assimilation by out-of-town business interests or through bankruptcy – and the good folk of Cythera thought nothing of it, did not care, and/or shrugged their collective shoulders. Then they went shopping.

{As the City burgeoned in all directions, every segment desired a shopping mall, and every segment got one. Some segments merited more than one because of their demographics, and these were either crammed together or separated by only a block or two. Where the Visitor now stood, there were no fewer than four malls in close proximity, and none of them duplicated the outreach of another (more or less). They were not Cythera's first malls, nor were they its first cluster, but they were definitely not the last on either score.]

The Visitor stares in wonder at this complex and shakes his head.

How primitive! *he thinks.* This species must be at least four centuries behind mine.

Immediately, he chides himself for his non-rational reaction. How would his superiors regard his snap, emotional judgment? What would they write up in his personnel file? He is here to record the accoutrements of this civilization, not to judge it; he is obliged to make as objective a report as he can, devoid of personal asides. If his superiors want his opinion – and they are not likely to want it under the current circumstances – they will ask for it in their own good time and certainly not in a formal report. Advancing personal opinions without authorization might jeopardize his chances for promotion.

Having properly chided himself, the Visitor resumes his task of observing and recording this unusual complex – primitive though it may be. The first thing he observes is the increase in the number of vehicles here. The increase must be at least five-fold. Yet, even though the numbers have increased, the operators of the vehicles do not seem inclined to slow the said vehicles down significantly; rather, they appear to be rushing hither and yon at a velocity certain to incur collision and injury to themselves and others. Frequently, he notes, there are near misses, particularly at intersections of cross-streets, which result in the activation of the noise-making mechanisms, the gesticulations of arms and hands, and a barrage of vocalization. These, he recalls, are the same greetings which had been directed at him upon his arrival here; apparently, the indigenous population exhibit a high level of civility toward one another and strangers alike.

He has not been neglected on that score. Since he has remained in the center of the street, following the white lines all the way, his share of the greetings has increased even though he is not indigenous to this civilization.

Why is that? *he wonders.* Can it be due to my present circumstances whereby I have arrived at a time when the indigenous populace are in a festive mood?

He must make further observations in order to verify this postulate.

He now stands in the middle of an intersection of streets, and the cacophony is almost deafening – or would be if he had neglected to modulate his listening devices. The noise-making mechanisms, the gesticulations, and the vocalizations assault him from all directions, even as the vehicle whiz by him at great velocity. Some of the vehicles come close to striking him; he receives a few gentle brush-backs as the operators skillfully perform what must be a special greeting ritual. He is at once confused and elated. His superiors had stated that the indigenous population were an untrustworthy lot, given to frequent and unprovoked acts of violence. But, here, they do not show any tendency toward violence but greet him as if he were in kinship to them.

What a perplexing situation! *he muses.* More observation is called for.

The second thing the Visitor observes is a selective system of traffic control. Some of the vehicles are at rest while others are in motion, and the flow of traffic is directional; first, the traffic moving in one direction and its opposite proceed, then halts as the traffic in the other two directions are given their turn. And the controlling factor appears to be the sets of multi-colored lights set upon metal poles. All traffic in a given direction is halted when the top light in the set is bright and moves when the bottom one is bright. What function the center light performs, he is at a loss to understand; some traffic moves while this light is bright, posing an apparent contradiction.

There are notable exceptions to this pattern, and these occur when the top light is bright. Some vehicles do not come to a rest position but continue on at very high velocities. Perhaps the operators of these vehicles have been given special leave to break the pattern of traffic flow. Even so, he observes one or two near-collisions, followed by the activation of the noise-making mechanisms, the gesticulations, and the vocalizations. It is all very confusing. Perhaps his superiors can provide some insight when he reports back.

He now leaves his position in the center of the street and crosses to one side as soon as the bottom light signals that it is permissible to move in that direction. He crosses in the midst of more activations of the noise-making mechanisms, more hand gestures, and more vocalizations to which he responds accordingly.

Enough pleasantries, *he says to himself.* I have serious duties to perform and limited time to perform them.

He approaches the nearest set of structures beyond what is obviously a storage area for vehicles (as there are many of them lined up in row after row after row) and makes his third observation: a mixture of foot and vehicular traffic. The operators of the vehicles are obviously seeking a vacancy in the storage area; and once they are successful, they will join the foot traffic. The latter is nearly as brisk and heavy as the former; the units of this species travel to and from the storage area and in and out of the structures. They enter the structures empty-handed and exit heavy-laden with packages, and more often than not, they wheel out wheeled metal carts because of the heavy loads. Clearly, the structures are supply depots where the units receive the necessaries for their survival, although it appears that some of the units require more supplies for their survival than others of their species. In a rational society (such as his), every unit would receive an equal number of supplies.

Ah! there I go again! *he chides himself for the second time.* I'm making judgments when I should be making observations.

As the Visitor wanders through the vehicle storage area, he makes note of the identities of the supply depots. He recognizes many of the labels:

"tools," "groceries," "furniture," and "toys." Some he does not: "liquor," "jewelry," "bank," and "music." No, wait! That is not entirely true. Now he recalls what a "bank" is; it is a supply depot where the units obtain a supply of the local medium of exchange which they exchange for the necessaries. But why do they need a medium of exchange at all? Why do they not simply requisition what they need in a straightforward fashion without any complications?

It is all very confusing, *he thinks.* I am certainly glad I am not a data analyzer. I would not last a tenth of a cycle with the data I'm collecting now.

Presently, he spies a most curious scenario. At one of the supply depots – one which issues a mixture of supplies – an unusually large number of units are entering and exiting, but they are strangely garbed. Until now, he had seen the units garbed in drab-looking clothing which almost resembles a uniform. Not so here. Here, the units wear gaudily-colored clothing, and the individual pieces do not complement each other. Some of these units also wear several layers of clothing, and few of the top layers cover the lower layers completely. Some of the units wear clothing which is either too small or too large for their physiques. Some of the units wear animal hides/furs in profusion, and some wear actual animals – live and dead? – and stroke them continuously.

What in the name of the Almighty Spirit is this structure that it should attract so many bizarre units? Are these units not of the same species as the others and therefore require special supplies which only this depot can supply? Here is a great conundrum, indeed, one which might stump even a data analyzer.

Ah, well, time to move on, *the Visitor thinks.* I have much more to observe.

He returns to the street and continues along the white line, amidst a fresh round of activation of the noise-making mechanisms, hand gestures, and vocalizations. He luxuriates in this friendly environment and returns the greetings in the accepted fashion.

THE INTERVIEW
Part IV

Where was we, Blondie? Oh, yeah. Have I ever been cheated out of a fare? Huh! I been honkin' stiffed more times in forty years of drivin' than I care to honkin' think about. Most of it was in my early years when I wasn't too honkin' smart. Got lots o' honkin' smarts now, I wanna tell ya. Ain't nobody can honkin' pull a fast one on me nowadays.

Lemme tell ya, Blondie, they's a lot o' honkers out there who ain't ashamed of honkin' beatin' a cabbie outa his fare. Yer first clue when the honker is goin' to stiff you is when he sez I ain't got no money on me at the moment, wait here, and I'll go inside and get some. That's when the honker disappears on ya.

My biggest stiff was when I picked up a honker downtown who wanted to go to an apartment building in Bartonville. That's $15, flat rate. So, I take 'im there, he gives me the honkin' spiel, and that's the last time I see 'im.

Then there's the honker who stiffed me *twice*. I was just startin' out as a cabbie, and I wasn't payin' no honkin' attention to faces. This young honker wanted to go visit his honkin' girlfriend; he disappears on me after givin' me the honkin' spiel. A few months later, a young honker wants to go visit his honkin' girlfriend, and he disappears. I stop and think, this is the same honkin' address as before and that musta been the same young honker too.

Well, I'll tell ya, Blondie, they's an old sayin': 'Fool me once, shame on you; fool me twice, shame on me.' I learned real quick to look at honkin' faces – and rememberin' them.

Got some more Crackerjacks fer ya. And some more o' my more memorable fares.

Huh? Lunchtime already? Well, you come back, and I'll give ya all the honkin' juicy details.

[Harriet Methune Beiderbeck, star reporter (in her humble estimation) for the Cythera Clarion-News, *who had won several awards for her reporting which (in her humble estimation) she had deserved and who was generally referred to (though not to her face) as "Harry the Hatchet," thanks to her reputation for sniffing out and pursuing a story until (1) it became old news or (2) some other story needed to be sniffed and pursued, departs the premises of the Cythera Cab Company, but not before she had to promise Uncle Gordy that, yes, she would return and finish the interview.*

[For his part, Uncle Gordy sighs a huge sigh of relief over being left alone for a while. Whereupon he takes a very long pull from the pint of Jack Daniels and a very long drag from the Marlboro, belches prodigiously, farts prodigiously, and scratches his privates prodigiously (not necessarily in that order). As soon as the amenities are taken care of, he nods off.]

11:11:11:11 am
(approximately)

Courtyards Village was a collection of two-story brick buildings lined up in a single row. Shade trees, shrubbery, and flower beds abounded from one end to the other for the edification of the residents. Whether or not the said residents were duly edified is not germane to this narrative; suffice it to say that the potential for edification was present. A main walkway ran the whole length of the property, and branch walkways extended to each building. Wooden benches which could accommodate four slender residents or two obese ones had been placed at the junctions of the main walkway and the branch walkways for the enjoyment and comfort of the residents. Whether or not the said residents were duly joyful and comforted is also not germane to this narrative; suffice it to say that the potential for enjoyment and comfort was present.

Nonchalantly, taxi #65 of the Cythera Cab Company pulled into the parking lot of Courtyards Village and selected a space in front of the third building in the row. Taxi #65 of the Cythera Cab Company did not, of course, pull into the parking lot and select a space in front of the third building in the row by itself; it had a driver (identified as one Fred) who did the actual pulling in and selecting. The driver also applied the brake and stopped; otherwise, taxi #65 would not have stopped (even by itself) and most likely would have proceeded into the third building in the row, caused annoyance, indignity, and discomfort (not necessarily in that order) to the owners of the property and considerable damage to the building, residents, taxi, and taxi driver, moderately to severely, and precipitated a great deal of whooping and hollering.

When Fred, the driver of taxi #65 of the Cythera Cab Company, pulled into the parking lot and selected a space in front of the third building in the row, his fare was already waiting for him, sitting on the wooden bench in front of the third building in the row, placed there for the enjoyment and comfort of the residents. Whether the fare was duly joyful and comforted is also not germane to this narrative; suffice it to say that the potential for his enjoyment and comfort were present.

Fred knew that this individual sitting on the wooden bench at the junction of the main walkway and the branch walkway was his fare because the said individual was a "regular." That is to say, he called for a cab nearly every day, sometimes oftener. Cab drivers liked "regulars"; they were a prime source of revenue and could be counted on to keep the wolf from the driver's door. *[Author's note: the Reader should be aware that this expression is little more than a metaphor and not a literal one. Otherwise, there would be fewer cab drivers in the world and fatter wolves.]* In the case of the said individual sitting on the wooden bench in front of the third building in the row, he called for a cab twice a day, every day of the week, once going to his chosen destination and once returning home from his chosen destination.

"Hi, Fred," Fred greeted him cheerily.

"Hi, Fred," Fred responded slightly less cheerily. "You're two minutes late."

[Author's note: the Reader will undoubtedly think that the Author is trying to pull a fast one on him/her with this duplication of names. The fact of the matter is, however, that the fare's name was also Fred and that is why he preferred to ride with Fred (the driver).

"Would you believe I was out of town when I got the call to pick you up?"

"I don't believe anything a taxi driver tells me."

"Uh-huh. Anyway, long time no see."

"Yeah, right. Not since the day before yesterday."

"Yesterday was my day off."

"Uh-huh."

This little repartee continued for another minute and a half after which Fred (the fare), anxious to get to his chosen destination and drink his lunch, signaled to Fred (the driver) to be on his merry way. Taxi

#65 of the Cythera Cab Company duly pulled out of the parking lot at Courtyards Village and headed south again on Randall Road. Taxi #65 of the Cythera Cab Company did not, of course, pull out of the parking lot of Courtyards Village and head south again on Randall Road by itself; it had a driver (identified as one Fred) who did the actual pulling out and heading south again. The driver released the brake and applied a foot (the right one, as it happened) to the taxi's accelerator. Otherwise, taxi #65 would not have gone anywhere (even by itself) and remained in front of the third building in the row for all of Eternity (more or less).

Fred (the driver) would have lost a "regular."

When Fred (the driver) reached Indian Trail Road, he turned left, headed east, crossed State Route 31, and crossed the river which split Cythera in two on the bridge placed there for the convenience of motorists. Whether or not said motorists were duly convenienced is not germane to this narrative; suffice it to say that the potential for convenience was present. He stopped abruptly five yards shy of State Route 25.

Although there were traffic signals at Indian Trail Road and State Route 25, they were not the reason why Fred (the driver) stopped abruptly. He stopped abruptly because there was a freight train in front of him -- moving no faster than freight trains usually do – and he might have had reason to regret not stopping abruptly. In fact, this particular freight train was moving slower than freight trains usually move because it was coming to a rail spur whereupon it would either divest itself or accumulate one or more freight cars (neither of which is relevant to this narrative) at a local manufacturing concern (it matters not which one). The abrupt stop was, moreover, a rare one because Fred (the driver) could count on one hand (it matters not which one) the number of freight trains he had seen in his short lifetime on this particular track.

Eventually, the freight train either divested itself or accumulated (neither of which is relevant to this narrative) one or more freight cars at a local manufacturing concern (it matters not which one) and continued on its merry way to the next stop on its itinerary (it matters not which one). Fred (the driver) turned right onto State Route 25 and continued on his merry way to Fred's (the fare) chosen destination where he was scheduled to drink his lunch.

Fred's (the fare) chosen destination where he was scheduled to drink his lunch was a small watering hole on State Route 25 aptly (and simply) named the "North End Tap." The North End Tap was an odd-looking building, having originally been a railroad car which served as the temporary headquarters of a railroad construction crew in the early days of Cythera. Surprisingly, when whatever construction the construction crew did had been completed, the construction crew forgot to deconstruct the temporary headquarters, and the former railroad car remained there forlornly. Years later, a gentleman of Scandinavian extraction purchased the building and converted it into a watering hole which catered to workmen of Scandinavian extraction who had immigrated to Cythera. With changing demographics, the North End Tap eventually catered to persons of non-Scandinavian extraction, but the owner didn't care as long as the new clientele spent their money there.

Fred (the fare), although not of Scandinavian extraction (his extraction is not relevant to this narrative), did spend his money there every day for as long as anyone – especially Fred (the driver) – knew. Fred (the driver) did not care how much money Fred (the fare) spent there as long as he called a taxi every day until the end of Time. *[Author's note: "the end of Time" is perhaps sheer hyperbole as Fred's (the fare) lifetime was as finite as anyone else's, but the Reader should understand the true significance of the expression.]*

Uneasily, taxi #65 of the Cythera Cab Company pulled up in front of the North End Tap. Taxi #65 of the Cythera Cab company did not, of course, pull up in front of the North End Tap by itself; it had a driver (identified as one Fred) who did the actual pulling up. The driver also applied the brake and stopped; otherwise, taxi #65 would not have stopped (even by itself) and most likely would have proceeded into the North End Tap, upset the owner and his clientele, caused considerable injury to the said owner and his clientele and damage to the building, taxi, and taxi driver, moderately to severely, and sobered up some the clientele.

Fred (the fare), having arrived at his chosen destination where he was scheduled to drink his lunch, paid his fare and paid Fred (the driver) a fond farewell. Fred (the driver), aglow with the addition to his day's income, reached for the two-way radio.

"65 to dispatch."

"Dispatch here. Go ahead, 65."

"I'm clear, Uncle Gordy."

"Wonderful. Got nothin' fer ya at the moment. Head on down to the depot and wait for the next commuter train."

"10-4."

Honk you, poohead!

Uncle Gordy flipped the bird even though Fred (the driver) could not see him. Then he took a short pull from the pint of Jack Daniels and a short drag from the Marlboro, belched, farted, and scratched his privates (not necessarily in that order). As soon as the amenities were taken care of, he nodded off.

11:15 am
(minus two-and-one-half seconds)

Harriet Methune Beiderbeck, a.k.a. Harry the Hatchet," star reporter (in her humble estimation) for the Cythera *Clarion-News*, did not exactly lie to Uncle Gordy, dispatcher and all-around *bon vivant* of the Cythera Cab Company, when she told him she was going to lunch at her favorite eatery, the Cythera Pancake House. She fully intended to go to lunch at her favorite eatery, the Cythera Pancake House, where she would indulge herself – not in pancakes as those were strictly for Sunday brunch, if and when she could pry Max away from his laptop – but in a big juicy steak burger with tomato, onion, lettuce, and mayo with a dill pickle and a portion of French-fried onion rings on the side, all washed down with a tall, frosty mug of root beer. She would rather have washed the big juicy steak burger with tomato, onion, lettuce, and mayo with a dill pickle and a portion of French-fried onion rings on the side with a bourbon or two, but the Cythera Pancake House was a family-style eatery and therefore did not have a liquor license.

Before going to the Cythera Pancake House, then, she fully intended to go to Mcgillicuddy's Tavern, where she could indulge herself in a bourbon or two. Ordinarily, she might have waited until late afternoon to fully indulge herself in a bourbon or two, but today she believed she was entitled to advance the time. After spending the past two hours listening to the reminiscences of a smelly old goat and being called "Blondie" repeatedly, she needed to fully indulge herself in a bourbon or two.

McGillicuddy's Tavern was an unassuming one-story building in the heart of a lower-middle-class neighborhood. There were no signs on it to proclaim its identity, but there was no need for signs. Everyone knew what it was and who it was for. Mcgillicuddy's was a strictly word-of-mouth establishment; and, if one were not attuned to the grapevine, one might have found oneself in an environment (s)he would likely not be caught dead in, much less alive. Not that the tavern was dangerous. Rather, it was just...*strange* (as the Reader will soon learn).

The interior of Mcgillicuddy's was just as unassuming as the exterior – some wag had gone as far as to describe it as nondescript – and resembled any other bar in any other city in any other time period. It differed from any other bar in any other city in any other time period in only one respect in that it possessed certain features which were just... *strange* and lent the establishment a certain ambience (unwanted or otherwise). *[Author's note: these features will be described in more detail as the occasion warrants.]*

Into this strange, nondescript establishment enters one Harriet Methune Beiderbeck, a.k.a. "Harry the Hatchet," star reporter (in her humble estimation) for the Cythera *Clarion-News*.

She sauntered in and walked across the nondescript tile floor past three nondescript wooden tables (each possessing four nondescript wooden chairs) and up to the nondescript wood-and-plastic bar. She sat down on one of the nondescript metal-and-leather stools -- the third one from the nondescript wooden entrance which was the only one she sat on when she was fully indulging herself in a bourbon or two – and swiveled around to regard the nondescript far plastered wall. Something seemed different about it today, making it somewhat less nondescript. But what? Oh, yes, some of the paint was peeling off, making the former bright interior of the tavern dingy-looking (more or less). Somehow, she thought, it was a great improvement on the place.

Having examined and given grudging approval of the new "décor," Harriet next surveyed the room to see who else lacked the propriety of patronizing a bar at 11:01:49 am (and perhaps a little bit more). Not that she really cared – she preferred to have the place to herself – but perhaps she might find a tidbit or two to pass on to the Cythera *Clarion-News'* gossip columnist. *[Author's note: the gossip columnist for the Cythera* Clarion-News *does not call herself that. Her column is titled "Our Fair City," and it purports to inform the readership about who's who and what's what which may or may not interest said readership. Anything which may or may not smack of scandal is wholly incidental.]*

As it happened, three other patrons inhabited McGillicuddy's. Two of them – one of them a professor of mathematics, the other a professor of philosophy, both from nearby Cythera College – she recognized as being "regulars." In fact, she had never seen either of them sitting in any other location than at their nondescript wooden table in the nondescript corner nearest the nondescript wooden front door where they now sat. They were playing chess and sipping wine – of all things! – or at least that was what they seemed to be doing. So intense was their concentration on their match that, had neither of them made a move to push a chess piece across the board or to pick up a wine glass to sip from it, one might have mistaken them for statues (which tableau would have been appropriately captioned as "The Chess Match."

The third patron was also a "regular." He also did not sit in any other location than where he was now sitting which was the far end of the nondescript wood-and-plastic bar. He was busily scribbling in a notebook; he would scribble briefly, gaze off into the distance, and then scribble some more. Harriet snorted in derision (which she often did) at this poor sap (her words) who was nothing but a hack writer with delusions of grandeur (her words).

"You wish to order, Mrs. Biteback?"

She swiveled on her nondescript metal-and-leather stool and peered at the bartender who had sidled in on little cat's feet and taken her completely by surprise (which, in her case, was not an easy task to do as she was a past master of surveying her surroundings minutely with a reporter's eye for detail no matter where she was). The bartender was a slender young man, clearly of Southeast Asian extraction, dressed in a faded green sweater and equally faded blue jeans. His most noticeable features were an engaging smile and gleaming black eyes, the surest signs of a stranger in a strange land trying to make the best of his situation, i.e. a naif. His name was Tranh, and he was a fish out of water in McGillicuddy's (or any other place for that matter).

"That's *Beiderbeck*, Tranh."

"Yes, madam. Tranh remember you."

"Fine. I'll have my usual – straight bourbon."

"Yes, madam. One bubbin coming up."

Tranh sidled away on his little cat's feet, and Harriet eyed the other patrons again. The statues in the nondescript corner had come to life again, more or less, as one of the players pushed a pawn forward ever so lightly with the tip of his finger (it matters not which one); in reaction, his opponent hummed a hum of interest and took a sip of wine. Then all was stillness again. Harriet shook her head in disbelief. When did those characters teach their classes? she wondered idly. And were they any more animated then than they were now? The scribbler was still scribbling. He glanced at Harriet, frowned in thought, and scribbled some more. Harriet rolled her eyes toward the nondescript ceiling.

"Here you are, Mrs. Biteback. One bubbin."

"That's *Beiderbeck*," she muttered pointedly and swiveled around again.

"Yes, madam. Enjoy your drink, madam."

"Oh, I certainly will."

She picked up the glass, brought it slowly to her lips, and took a small sip. Tranh was known to grab the wrong bottle on occasion, and one would never be sure if (s)he was getting what (s)he had ordered. Case in point: the small sip was *not* bourbon, but Scotch. She rolled her eyes toward the nondescript ceiling and began counting the cracks in it.

Decision time: should she call Tranh back and point out the error of his ways? Or should she just drink the damn Scotch and leave? The Scotch wasn't all that bad – not as good as bourbon, of course, but tolerable. Her gynecologist would have advised her not to drink any alcoholic beverage during her pregnancy. But, after spending two hours listening to the reminiscences of a smelly old goat and being called "Blondie" repeatedly, she was really entitled to indulge herself in something alcoholic, pregnancy or no pregnancy. OK, so she'd drink the damn Scotch – slowly – and leave.

A movement at the nondescript wooden front door caught her eye then, and she swiveled on her nondescript metal-and-leather stool to observe the newcomer. At the sight of the newcomer, her stomach knotted up, and her pregnancy had nothing to do with it. She recognized the newcomer and wished she were somewhere else. It was really bad timing on her part to be in McGillicuddy's at the moment the newcomer had decided to drop in.

The newcomer was one June East. No one knew if that was her real name or if it was just a put-on on her part. She always insisted on being addressed as "June East," and no one cared one way or the other. What she did for a living no one knew or cared. [Author's note: one cynical individual (whose identity is not germane to this narrative) suggested that she was a member of the world's oldest profession, although he could never produce a witness to her propositioning anyone.] Be that as it may, why she was in McGillicuddy's was to cadge a drink or two (or three). Whether she was too cheap to buy her own or too self-important to buy her own, no one knew or cared, but she always managed to impose herself on anyone within shouting distance.

June East was a commanding figure, however. Aloof and soft spoken, she stood over six feet tall in her stocking feet. She had jet-black eyes, and looking into them was like looking into two deep wells. She wore her equally jet-black hair in a page-boy bob which glistened in the light. She wore what seemed to be a "uniform" for her, consisting of a blue-and-red pinstriped suit (with padded shoulders), an off-white silk shirt, a monogrammed lavender tie, black-and-white wing-tipped shoes (highly polished), a turned-down white fedora (with a lavender band), and a white carnation in the lapel of the suit. No one could have missed her in a crowd, and that was all to her advantage. [Author's note: the aforementioned cynical individual (whose identity is not germane to this narrative) suggested that she was not a woman but a female impersonator in drag, although he could never produce a witness to her actual gender.]

When she sauntered into McGillicuddy's, she assumed a slow measured pace and a regal bearing as if she were the Queen of Sheba and padded across the nondescript tile floor toward the nondescript metal-and-leather stool nearest the nondescript wooden door. She slid smoothly onto it and sat quietly at the nondescript wood-and-plastic bar acting like the Queen of Sheba, slumming.

Ordinarily, Tranh would have sidled over on his little cat's feet and asked June East what she wanted to drink. But after the umpteenth time of sidling over on his little cat's feet, asking her what she wanted to drink, and getting only umpteen Mona-Lisa smiles and holes stared through him, he had decided to wait until she signaled him for service (which she never did). *[Author's note: the Reader might protest the use of the terms "umpteenth" and "umpteen" as either vague or exaggerated. The Author hastens to point out that many reputable mathematicians whom he has consulted have, in their expert opinion, consider that "umpteenth" and "umpteen" are actual numbers and therefore legitimate mathematical expressions. They have also informed him that the symbol used to represent them in any mathematical equation is "?."]*

Harriet pointedly ignored the Queen of Sheba – that is to say, June East – and sipped her Scotch. She sipped and sipped and sipped until the glass was empty, at which time she stopped sipping and signaled to Tranh for another round. He sidled over on his little cat's feet, snatched the empty glass away, and sidled away on his little cat's feet to fill the new order. The new order arrived in record time. Harriet took a sip and was pleasantly surprised to learn that it was actual bourbon she was sipping this time. Whereupon she downed half of it in one gulp.

While she was gulping down half a glass of bourbon, another individual entered McGillicuddy's and lumbered across the nondescript tile floor toward one of the nondescript metal-and-leather stools at the nondescript wood-and-plastic bar. This individual lumbered because that was the only way he ever walked; this individual was, in point of fact, one Professor Merfelman, who taught history at nearby Cythera College and who was a bear of a man, being six-feet-three-inches tall in his stocking feet (which he sometimes affected in class and always affected in the privacy of his own home and in the privacy of other people's homes who insisted that their guests remove their shoes whether or not they were Japanese) and three hundred pounds (more or less) in weight which resulted in his lumbering manner of walking.

Merfelman was also as hairy as a bear. His hyperpilosity had bestowed upon him a rather magnificent foliage of jet-black hair on top of his head and a very bushy moustache and beard. (One presumed that his hairiness extended to the rest of his body, but no one had ever stepped forward to verify that presumption – whether out of lack of knowledge or of curiosity, no one knew or cared.) Out of this brush, one could discern a pair of gray eyes staring at one with all the intensity of a laser beam and a long Roman nose which protruded like a sign post.

He possessed a mouth as well that could be seen only when he opened it (which was often).

Merfelman was also the unintended and unwanted sparring partner of Professor Maxwell Beiderbeck, who taught economics at nearby Cythera College, husband of one Harriet Methune Beiderbeck, star reporter (in her humble estimation) for the Cythera *Clarion-News*, and more recently the father of her unborn child. Merfelman was the Quintessential Liberal and Beiderbeck (the professor, not the reporter) the Quintessential Conservative, and their intellectual sparring matches were legendary – both on and off campus – but fruitless and pointless.

When Harriet saw him lumbering in her direction, she grimaced, gnashed her teeth, and gulped the other half of her glass of bourbon. And then she signaled to Tranh for a third round – her gynecologist be damned!

Merfelman halted at the nondescript metal-and-leather stool adjacent to the one upon which Harriet sat. He halted because, despite his great bulk, he was not strong enough to push aside the nondescript wood-and-plastic bar which was bolted to the nondescript tile floor – even if he had had a desire to push aside the nondescript wood-and-plastic bar bolted to the nondescript tile floor (which, presumably, he did not, for reasons known only to him which are not relevant to this narrative).

"Why, it's Mrs. Beiderbeck," Merfelman boomed. "What a pleasure to see you."

"Hello, Professor," Harriet responded with great effort. "I'm surprised to see you here."

"Ah, well, I thought I'd see how the other half of humanity entertains itself." He heaved his great bulk onto the nondescript metal-and-leather stool adjacent to the nondescript metal-and-leather stool upon which Harriet was sitting without waiting for an invitation to join her. "And how is 'Max, Jr.'?"

"You're assuming it's going to be a boy."

"'Maxine' then," he stated with a shrug.

"'Max/Maxine' is doing just fine. He/she is starting to kick up a storm."

"Perhaps he/she is protesting the fact that he/she is going to be a Beiderbeck. When is your due date?"

"Another nine weeks, more or less."

"I shall have to buy the little tyke an appropriate gift. The complete works of George Orwell, perhaps."

"Don't put yourself out, Professor."

"No trouble at all, dear lady."

"You seem to be in an ebullient mood today."

"Indeed. I'm getting married."

"Married? I can scarcely believe it. What woman would want –" She bit her tongue and buried the thought which was oozing out of her brain. "Oh, wait, Max told me that you and, uh, the woman in Dr. Silliphant's office –"

"Maria Running Deer Winkelman," Merfelman supplied.

"Right. You and she are an item. When's the happy day?"

"The end of the school year. And we'll be honeymooning on her tribe's reservation – in their casino/hotel actually."

Harriet and Merfelman were suddenly aware of the presence of Tranh, who had sidled over on his little cat's feet and was waiting for an opportunity to get a word in edgewise. Tranh smiled professionally.

"Would the gentleman like to order?"

"The gentleman would," Merfelman responded professionally. "I'll have a claret."

"A clear-it? Tranh regrets to say that he is not familiar with that drink."

"It's a wine, dear fellow. Let's see." He peered over Tranh's shoulder to inspect the array of bottles on the nondescript plastic counter behind the nondescript wood-and-plastic bar. He spied the bottle he was hoping to see and pointed at the said bottle. "That bottle there. That's a claret – or a reasonable facsimile thereof."

Tranh turned, following the pointing finger (it matters not which one), and pointed at the said bottle himself. Merfelman nodded. Tranh took down the said bottle, opened it, and poured a hefty amount into the nearest glass available (which, as it happened, was a beer glass). He placed it before Merfelman.

"There you are, sir. One clear-it."

"Thank you, my good man." He raised his glass to Harriet. "Cheers, dear lady."

He took a sip of his claret and began choking and gagging.

"*Godfrey!*" he yelped. "This wine has turned to vinegar! How long has it been on the shelf?"

"I should have warned you, Professor," Harriet said with a smirk. "Things at McGillicuddy's are not always what they seem."

"Indeed? What are you drinking?"

"Bourbon. A real man's drink, or so Max claims."

"He suffers from delusions of grandeur. Nevertheless, I'll join you." He turned to Tranh, who was still smiling professionally. "I'll have a bourbon, my good man."

"Yes, sir. One bubbin coming up."

As Tranh sidled away on his little cat's feet to fill the order, Merfelman was aware of a movement next to him and swiveled around on his nondescript metal-and-leather stool to confront the source of the movement. June East, a.k.a. the Queen of Sheba, had bestirred herself and, seeking a new prospect for cadging a free drink, had swiveled around on her nondescript metal-and-leather stool in order to make her pitch. She did not swivel around on her nondescript metal-and-leather stool quietly as that particular nondescript metal-and-leather stool squeaked with a squeak which could be heard everywhere in McGillicuddy's. It squeaked so loudly that the chess players sitting at the nondescript wooden table in the nondescript corner nearest the nondescript wooden front door sat up straight in their nondescript wooden chairs in utter shock, their concentration on their chess match broken beyond repair. It squeaked so loudly that the scribbler at the far end of the nondescript wood-and-plastic bar gritted his teeth in agony and dropped his pencil and notepad on the nondescript tile floor. Harriet, working on her third drink, felt nothing. Merfelman, still dealing with the taste of vinegar in his mouth, was too irate to care.

"Would you buy a lady a drink?" June East purred in a soft, silky tone of voice.

Merfelman looked her up and down and backward and forward more than once and examined his options as to the nature of a response. His first choice usually was sarcasm of which he was a past master.

Yet, as this was his first encounter with June East, he hesitated. He was ever the connoisseur of fine feminine pulchritude, and he was observing a choice specimen of feminine pulchritude. He thought a more sophisticated approach was apropos.

But then, June East made a *faux pas*: she batted her eyelashes (although, on close examination, the action seemed more like a muscle spasm than a deliberate attempt at seduction). She did not believe she was making a *faux pas*, however; to her, it was her standard operating procedure for cadging a free drink. Sometimes it worked, and sometimes it didn't. This time, it didn't. Merfelman regarded batting eyelashes as a *faux pas* and, therefore, his choice of response was made for him.

"I would indeed buy a lady a drink," he responded smoothly. "And, if I chance to meet one, I shall."

It is a safe bet that that was not the response June East expected. It is an even safer bet that that was not the response June East cared for.

June East stared a hole through Merfelman with narrowly slitted jet-black eyes, while smoke – thick, black, and smelly – emanated from her entire being. *[Author's note: the Reader will pardon the hyperbole, but the Author couldn't resist making it. Continue reading.]* Tension was in the air. The chess players sitting in the nondescript corner nearest the nondescript wooden front door prepared to make a mad dash toward the said nondescript wooden front door. The scribbler at the far end of the nondescript wood-and-plastic bar prepared to hide behind the said nondescript wood-and-plastic bar. Harriet prepared to guffaw. Merfelman took a sip of his freshly arrived bourbon. Tranh smiled professionally.

"*Honk you!*" June East murmured through clenched teeth in a most unladylike tone of voice. "You honking fat, hairy honker!"

"'Fat'? 'Hairy'? Oh, my, I've been cut to the quick! As for your proposal, let me consult my appointment book and see if I can pencil you in."

Merfelman reached into his coat pocket and produced an imaginary appointment book. He began turning imaginary pages, stopped when he had reached the day's date, and studied the imaginary page carefully. After a moment, he shook his head and turned more imaginary pages. He stopped at one, and his face brightened.

"Ah, I have an opening a week from tomorrow, at 3:30 pm. Shall I pencil you in?"

The smoke emanating from the entire being of June East grew thicker, blacker, and smellier. She slid off the nondescript metal-and-leather stool upon which she was sitting and marched in quick-step across the nondescript tile floor toward the nondescript wooden door.

At this point, the jukebox squatting in the nondescript corner nearest the nondescript wooden door to the back room came to life entirely on its own. It had a mind of its own and played music at the oddest times when people least expected it to or wanted it to. The jukebox (the only descript item in McGillicuddy's) was a gaudily-colored pink-and-pastel-green affair complete with multi-colored flashing lights, and it came with a large and varied assortment of 45-rpm records which played music from the 1940's and 1950's. Except when it played entirely on its own, most patrons at McGillicuddy's ignored it because (1) said patrons had no taste for 1940's/1950's music and (2) said patrons did not patronize McGillicuddy's for the purpose of cultural enhancement but for the purpose of forgetting their woes and numbing themselves to the outside world in general.

The said descript jukebox played a few bars of "Dancin' in the Dark" and turned itself off at the same time June East opened the nondescript wooden door at the front of the building and slammed it shut behind her.

"A better put-down I have never witnessed," Harriet declared. "You do have your moments, Professor."

"Thank you, my dear. I often surprise myself at how easy it is to create ripostes on the spur of the moment."

"Wait'll I tell Max about this. He won't believe it." She consulted her watch. "Well, it's time for lunch. I must be going."

"Ta-ta. Give my regards to Max."

Harriet Methune Beiderbeck, star reporter (in her humble estimation) for the Cythera *Clarion-News*, who had won several awards (which, in her humble estimation, she deserved) for her reporting, slid off the nondescript metal-and-leather stool upon which she was sitting and sauntered across the nondescript tile floor toward the nondescript wooden front door. Her next port of call was the Cythera Pancake House where she intended to indulge herself – not in pancakes as those were strictly for Sunday brunch, if and when she could pry Max away from his laptop – but in a big juicy steak burger with tomato, onion, lettuce, and mayo and a dill pickle and a portion of French-fried onion rings on the side, all washed down with a tall, frosty mug of root beer.

After that, being well fortified, she'd finish her interview with the smelly old goat at the Cythera Cab Company.

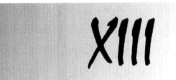

XIII

11:46 am
(three minutes before the next train arrival

Fred headed for the train depot via Broadway. He took his time getting there, not because he wanted to but because the noon-day traffic wanted him to. Taking an alternate route was not an option as it would have taken him out of his way and added miles to the taxi's odometer. A taxi driver had to pay for the miles he drove as part of his daily lease, and it behooved him to minimize his miles as best he could. In point of fact, that was the foundation of Rule #2 of the taxi driver's code of conduct.

Fred could not do so this time and thus had to head for the train depot via Broadway and endure the noon-day traffic with forbearance. *[Author's note: long years of observation have led to the conclusion that neither endurance nor forbearance counted for anything in the collective mind of noon-day traffic. It is a "dog-eat-dog-and-everything-else" world out there.]* At the intersection of Broadway and Illinois Avenue, the noon-day traffic was stalled (as it usually was), and Fred had to wait his turn to pass through. While he waited his turn to pass through, he observed the traffic signals in order to keep his mind occupied.

He observed that new changes to the traffic signals had been made in selected locations, Broadway and Illinois Avenue being one of them. Eventually, the City would change all of them – or not, depending upon the level of outrage the changes in the traffic signals produced in the general population. Most cities in America operated the standard "Walk" and "Don't Walk" cautions on their traffic signals to warn pedestrians of a possible risk to their well-being. Not so in Cythera, whose current Administration believed in nitty-grittiness, i.e. hard reality. Therefore, the traffic-signal cautions to pedestrians read "Run" and "Run Like Hell." Fred shook his head in bemusement. Pedestrians had it easier than motorists.

An age later, the traffic signal regulating Fred's direction of travel changed to green, and a dozen or more other vehicles were able to pass through the intersection before the signal turned to red again. Three of the dozen or more vehicles passing through the intersection passed through *after* the signal turned to yellow, and one of the dozen or more vehicles passing through the intersection passed through *after* the signal changed to red. *[Author's note: taxi #65 of the Cythera Cab Company was* not *one of the three nor one of the one. The driver of taxi #65 of the Cythera Cab Company (identified as one Fred) had an exemplary record – well,* almost *exemplary, but the exceptions are not relevant to this narrative and must be reserved for a different narrative (if a different one is necessary).]* Fred chuckled to himself as he thought about how Uncle Gordy enjoyed cataloguing motorists into derogatory categories.

As he approached the intersection of Broadway and New York Street, he spotted a familiar figure waiting for the traffic signal to change to green and the pedestrian caution to signal "Run" or "Run Like Hell." This was his second sighting of the familiar figure today – a rarity for him. The familiar figure was none other than "Uncle Bert," he of the bright red shirt, blue trousers, and trademark rainbow suspenders without which he never went anywhere. When Fred, the driver of taxi #65 of the Cythera Cab Company, spotted the familiar figure of "Uncle Bert," he tooted his horn, as everyone who spotted "Uncle Bert" did when they passed by him out of respect for him. And, since "Uncle Bert" did not like tooting horns, he shook his fist, as he did at anyone who tooted their horns (not that his shaking his fist prevented anyone from tooting). Fred laughed uproariously at "Uncle Bert's" eccentricities and continued on his merry way.

Formidably, taxi #65 of the Cythera Cab Company pulled into the taxi stand at the depot. Taxi #65 of the Cythera Cab Company did not, of course, pull into the taxi stand by itself; it had a driver (identified as one Fred) who did the actual pulling into. The driver also applied the brake and stopped; otherwise, taxi #65 would not have stopped (even by itself) and most likely would have rolled forward, crossed the tracks, caused a great deal of considerable inconvenience to the passengers and potential passengers of the arriving train, injury to said potential passengers, and damage to the arriving train, taxi and driver, moderately to severely, and fomented a blistering retort from the engineer of the said arriving train.

When taxi #65 – that is to say, Fred – pulled into the taxi stand at the depot, it – that is to say, he – discovered that it – that is to say, he – discovered that it – that is to say, he -- was fourth in line waiting for a fare. This discovery put a frown on Fred's face – one he kept handy for situations like this one – because the odds of picking up a fare were lessened. A taxi driver learned to be stoical in such situations; otherwise, he might (1) lose his temper, (2) lose his job, and/or (3) lose his mind (not necessarily in that order).

Two of the three taxis ahead of him belonged to a rival taxi company (which shall go nameless in this narrative). The third was taxi #23 of the Cythera Cab Company, and its driver was named Chuck. Chuck had a habit of switching cab companies when he became bored with one or another one. This day, he was driving (again) for the Cythera Cab Company; how long he would drive for Cythera Cab Company before he switched to another taxi company (which shall go nameless in this narrative) was anybody's guess. Chuck liked to surprise people.

Fred exited his cab, walked over to taxi #23, and ignored the taxis of the rival cab company (which shall go nameless in this narrative). When he arrived at taxi #23, he grinned hugely and said in a booming voice:

"Chuck-a-luck-make-a-buck!"

This was Fred's standard greeting to Chuck whenever he spotted him, regardless of whatever cab company he was driving for at the moment. It was meant to be a humorous chiding of Chuck's habit of switching cab companies. Whether Chuck recognized the humor of the greeting was of no interest to Fred; he used the greeting because he had a wicked sense of humor.

Chuck peered at him, smiled perfunctorily, and said:

"Hi, Fred. How the honk are you?"

That was Chuck's standard greeting whenever he heard Fred's standard greeting. He used that greeting to let Fred know that he could care less about Fred's wicked sense of humor. Chuck's standard greeting deterred Fred not in the least, and Fred maintained the jibe.

"Keepin' busy?" Fred said by way of small talk.

"So-so," Chuck replied. "You?" [Author's note: taxi drivers never talk about how much they earn. One, it's none of anybody's business but their own. And two, it's embarrassing to say how much a taxi driver earns, because most of the time he doesn't earn very much.]

"Well, I've already made my lease, and I'm only halfway through my shift." [Author's note: Fred, driver of taxi #65 of the Cythera Cab Company, was the lone exception to the previous Author's note. He believed in complete candor (more or less).]

"Today's your lucky day."

"Uh-huh."

"Pam is in love with you, Fred. She's told Gordy to steer the good fares your way."

"You keep sayin' that, Chuck. You really believe it?"

"Sure. The way she looks at you. The way she talks to you. She wants your body."

"Yeah, right. She's had so many husbands and boyfriends, I've lost count. I really need to be one in a series."

"You might be 'Mr. Right' for her."

"And I might be 'Mr. Stupid,' getting mixed up with my boss."

This observation elicited a smile from Chuck, the driver of taxi #23 of the Cythera Cab Company, one much less perfunctory than the previous smile. If Fred knew his sore spot, he knew Fred's sore spot.

"Dispatch," Chuck's radio crackled. "Who's up first at the depot?"

Fred's radio also crackled, but Fred was not in his cab to hear it crackle. Therefore, no crackle existed.

"23, Gordy," Chuck answered the call.

"Oakie-doakie, Chuckie. Got a hot one fer ya. Our buddy Keith is through drinking the Spider's Web dry and wants to go to the Mill."

"10-4, dispatch," Chuck responded through clenched teeth.

Chuck hated to be called "Chuckie" even more than he hated to be called "Chuck-a-luck-make-a-buck." "Chuckie" was what one called a small child, and Chuck at age 32 was hardly a small child. Also, he never called Uncle Gordy "Uncle Gordy" because he didn't have Fred's wicked sense of humor.

"There you go, Chuck – a real hot one!"

"Yeah, right."

If there was a fare worse than a laundry run, it was a bar run. Putting up with drunks who talked gibberish non-stop, made cracks about your parentage and your sexual habits, peed/pooed/vomited in the cab, fell asleep on you and wouldn't wake up long enough to give directions, and/or forgot to tip the driver in a proper fashion for putting up with the above was not on a taxi driver's top ten list of welcome passengers. The "regulars" were the worst of the lot as they thought they owned the driver and therefore could behave any way they pleased. And some of the "regulars" were especially disgusting – the fellow named "Keith," for instance, who drank from a bottle in the taxi and never failed to slobber all over himself.

As Chuck pulled away from the taxi stand, Fred observed a smattering of passengers debarking from the train which had just arrived. [Author's note: a "smattering" is a special term which describes a specific number of things in a collection. A smattering is larger than a bunch but smaller than a gathering. Most people tend to confuse the term with other expressions and confound their listeners endlessly.] One party of three individuals piled into one of the taxis of a rival company (which shall go nameless in this narrative) and was whisked off to parts unknown or cared about. A party of one piled into the other taxi of a rival company (which shall go nameless in this narrative) and was whisked off to parts unknown or cared about.

An elderly couple approached taxi #65 of the Cythera Cab Company, and Fred knew instantly that they were going to pile into his cab and ask to be whisked off to the casino. Fred had driven a taxi long enough to recognize the type. This couple – husband and wife? man and girlfriend? woman and boyfriend? (who knew these days when loose arrangements were pursued by senior citizens as vigorously – or as vigorously as possible given their age – as younger people) – were on an outing to blow their Social Security checks on the slot machines or the roulette wheels or the Keno tables (but they never played poker or blackjack for some unfathomable reason). Fred thought the prospect of whisking this couple off to the casino was sad, but a fare was a fare and he was obliged to take it.

Sure enough, the elderly couple piled into taxi #65 of the Cythera Cab Company and asked to be whisked off to the casino. Fred sighed.

Casino runs were only three dollars (four for a couple), and one did not get rich on casino runs.

"65 to dispatch."

"Dispatch here. Go ahead, 65."

"I have two going to the casino, Uncle Gordy."

"10-4, 65."

Honk you, poohead!

Taxi #65 whisked off to parts known but not cared about. Taxi #65 did not, of course, whisk off by itself; it had a driver (identified as one Fred) who did the actual whisking off. The driver released the brake and applied a foot (the right one, as it happened) to the accelerator. Otherwise, taxi #65 would not have gone anywhere (even by itself) and would have remained at the taxi stand at the depot for all of Eternity (more or less).

Fred would have lost a fare when the elderly couple died of old age.

INTERLUDE THE FOURTH

The Visitor leaves the realm of the supply depots and enters one of a completely different function. The one-story structures here are smaller than the former structures; they have smaller entrances and smaller viewing panels. Moreover, they are surrounded by various species of vegetation. He recognizes some of these species from previous reports: "grass," "trees," and "bushes." Some few of these structures possess multi-colored vegetation, and he recalls that they are called "flowers" which serve as a decorative accoutrement. What the purpose the other species of vegetation serve is not immediately clear to him; they are, apparently, personal preferences by the units which occupy the structures.

These structures are habitations, he recognizes, and they vary in the number of units who occupy them – two adult units and a number of juvenile units. None of the structures are uniform in size or shape or coloring. Interspersed among the small structures are multi-story ones. From previous reports, he identifies them as dwelling places for adult units who do not yet possess juvenile units and dwell here until such time that they do acquire them. These taller structures, he believes, actually make more sense than the smaller ones; in his own society, they are the normal dwelling places for most of his kind, whether or not they possess juvenile units. Smaller structures are reserved for high officials because the nature of their functions in society require that they dwell in them.

Someday, the Visitor muses, if I am diligent enough and faithful enough, I too shall dwell in one of those smaller structures. But I must not waste time in idle thinking. I must work hard, as my superiors have admonished me, and all will come to pass.

All of a sudden, he spots an anomaly. It has not been mentioned in previous reports, and he is at a loss to understand its function. He must now make a closer inspection. The new data will provide the data analyzers a fresh puzzle to solve and, not incidentally, find him favor in *the eyes of his superiors. He approaches the anomaly with all deliberate speed.*

A portion of the grassy area around the structure where the anomaly exists seems to have been set aside for the purpose of growing small species of vegetation. These species are arranged in rows, one species in each row; as much as the structures in this area, they differ in size, shape, and coloring. What purpose they serve is unclear; they obviously are not decorative in nature. He is moved to make a video recording as his superiors may not believe an oral account.

While he records this anomaly, the Visitor becomes aware of the fact that he himself is under observation. He is shocked that, due to his curiosity over the strange species of vegetation, he has failed to avoid personal interaction with the indigenous populations. The unit which is observing him is a juvenile female dressed in colorful garments; it also wears a brightly-colored ribbon in its hair. From his training, he remembers that the ribbon is a cultural symbol, but he cannot remember which symbol. This culture has many such symbols, and he has had difficulty in the past in sorting them out. His superiors will surely suspect that he had been sleeping in that particular training session.

He now has a further, and more embarrassing, problem which overrides the cultural one. The juvenile female unit is speaking to him in its own language. He has not been given advanced training in the local language as he is here to observe, not to communicate. What then should he do? He has not finished recording the anomaly, and his superiors will not be pleased with an incomplete report. On the other hand, if he continues to record, the juvenile female unit may be prompted to summon one or more of the adult units in this habitation. They may, in turn, attempt to communicate with him; and failing that, they may be disposed to summon the local authorities who will attempt to communicate with him and/or detain him for an indefinite period of time. This would be highly unacceptable as he might not ever be able to return home.

Given the choice of an incomplete report and indefinite detainment, the Visitor opts for the former. He returns to the street as quickly as he can. The juvenile female unit continues to speak to him, and its voice becomes louder and more strident.

Should he include this incident in his report? His superiors will obviously question him about the incomplete report and will learn about this failure to follow instructions. On the other hand, if he does not report fully and the incident comes to light by other means, he will be severely punished for filing a false report. He now wishes he had not been given this assignment. His future seems dark.

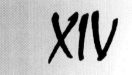 

1145 hours UT
(for those Readers who are reading
this narrative in Antarctica)

Harriet Methune Beiderbeck, star reporter (in her humble estimation) for the Cythera *Clarion-News*, who had won several awards (which, in her humble estimation, she deserved) for her reporting, had just been served at the Cythera Pancake House her order of a big juicy steak burger with tomato, lettuce, onion, and mayo with a dill pickle and a portion of French-fried onion rings on the side, plus a tall, frosty mug of root beer to wash it all down with, and she was contemplating the said order's color patterns, aromas, and shapes before masticating it into little pieces when she was rudely interrupted.

If she were nothing else, Harriet Methune Beiderbeck was a creature of habit. Once she fell into a comfortable routine, she rarely deviated from it. Only a massive external force, e.g. a hydrogen bomb or a planet crashing into the Earth, could disturb her immovable object. One of her many comfortable routines was sitting in the Cythera Pancake House at lunchtime, munching on a big juicy steak burger with tomato, lettuce, onion, and mayo with a dill pickle and a portion of French-fried onion rings on the side, and washing it all down with a tall, frosty mug of root beer. Rumor had it that whenever one of her comfortable routines was disturbed, she would fix said disturber with such a menacing glare that an army of rats would flee for their very lives, and she would hold that menacing glare until said disturber vacated the premises (presumably fleeing for his very life). This rumor was disturbingly true.

The flags went up, not so much because Harriet Methune Beiderbeck's routine was being disturbed as because the disturber was the last person she wanted to see – her cameraman, Ichabod.

Ichabod stood out like a sore thumb, no matter where he was or whom he was disturbing. He was a rail-thin person of average height with tufts of hair jutting out from behind each ear with shiny baldness in between. His equally thin face was punctuated by two blue, bulging, watery eyes, a nose which put one in mind of a water faucet, and a perpetual puckered-up, thin-lipped mouth. He resembled somewhat like the figure in "The Scream." A frayed white shirt and faded brown trousers hung on him in the same manner as they would on a scarecrow (which was as succinct a description of him as one could get).

"There you are!" the Scarecrow screeched with a nasal twang. "I've been going *ca-razy* looking for you. It hasn't been *ca-razy* enough that Mister McNamara thought I knew where you were. But, when I tell him I don't know, he goes *ca-razy* and runs out of his office like a *ca-razy* man! I never saw so much *ca-raziness* in all my life! So, I go *ca-razy* too!"

"What did McNamara want?" Harriet asked as patiently as she could.

"He wanted to know when you were going to file your story."

"He did, did he? Well, you go back and tell him I'm still working on it."

"If I tell him that, he'll go *ca-razy* again! *Everybody* will go *ca-razy!*" Ichabod turned and scurried toward the door. "It's just *ca-razy*, I tell you!"

Harriet Methune Beiderbeck, star reporter (in her humble estimation) for the Cythera *Clarion-News*, who had won several awards (which, in her humble estimation, she deserved), simply shrugged and returned her attention to her order of a big juicy steak burger with tomato, lettuce, onion, and mayo with a dill pickle and a portion of French-fried onion rings on the side, plus a tall, frosty mug of root beer to wash it all down with. She would take her time, indulging in the feast. The smelly old goat at the Cythera Cab Company wasn't going anywhere.

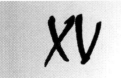 

High Noon
(to coin a phrase)

"65 to dispatch."

"Dispatch here. Go ahead, 65."

"I'm clear at the casino."

"Whoopee-doo. Back to the Provisional Medical Center for another package goin' to Dunlap Hospital."

"Again? Wow! Money in the bank. Thanks, Uncle Gordy."

"Honk you, poohead!"

Since Harriet Methune Beiderbeck, star reporter (in her humble estimation) for the Cythera *Clarion-News*, had not yet returned from her lunch break to complete her interview with him, Uncle Gordy felt safe enough to voice his commentary aloud. He also felt safe enough to take a very long pull from the Jack Daniels and a very long drag from the Marlboro, belch prodigiously, fart prodigiously, and scratch his privates prodigiously (not necessarily in that order). And, as soon as the amenities were taken care of, he felt safe enough to nod off.

Taxi #65 of the Cythera Cab Company pulled away from the casino and headed toward the Provisional Medical Center. Taxi #65 of the Cythera Cab Company did not, of course, pull away and head toward by itself; it had a driver (identified as one Fred) who did the actual pulling away and heading toward. The driver released the brake and applied a foot (the right one, as it happened) to the accelerator. Otherwise, taxi #65 of the Cythera Cab company would not have gone anywhere (even by itself) and most likely would have remained at the casino for all of Eternity (more or less).

Fred would have lost a valuable fare.

Delicious thoughts of having his daily lease paid for him by the special medical assignments and rendering all of his other fares as a great deal of take-home pay danced merrily in his head. Taxi drivers wished that every day would be as profitable; but it was usually a forlorn wish, and they learned to be stoical (more or less) about it. Still, when The Day of the Big Pay-off arrived, they allowed the delicious thoughts to dance merrily in their heads.

From the casino, Fred headed north up Lake Street, past "Restaurant Row." Every city had a "Restaurant Row" – a long stretch of fast-food joints on both sides of a street all clamoring for the same customers – which hawked every conceivable type of cuisine in the world, and Cythera was no exception. Some cynical persons insisted that the City had more than one "Restaurant Row," that every neighborhood had one, and that one did not need to drive all over town looking for one's favorite cuisine of the moment. The only thing which set off "Restaurant Row" on Lake Street was that it had been the first of its kind in the City and therefore it had taken on an "Old World" atmosphere (more or less).

Fred had availed himself from time to time of the cuisine to be had on Lake Street when he wasn't feasting on peanut-butter-and-jelly sandwiches. In fact, he had two specific eateries he frequented the most when he could afford them (which two are not germane to this narrative). As he approached "Restaurant Row," he began to plan on frequenting one of the two specific eateries he frequented the most when he could afford them (which one is not germane to this narrative), because he was certain he could afford to frequent it once he totaled up his take-home pay for the day.

His delicious thoughts dancing merrily in his head were interrupted by an improbable disturbance ahead of him. *[Author's note: the term "improbable disturbance" is usually reserved, in the conventional sense, for any locale other than Cythera (where, if anything can go wrong, it invariably does), and the Reader must understand that it is used in the present instance for the sole purpose of calling his/her attention to an improbable disturbance in Cythera, which would be considered probable for any other locale than Cythera.]* A traffic signal had just turned red, halting north-south-bound traffic. From the second vehicle from the signal in the north-bound lane, five male teenagers emerged and began running around their vehicle like squirrels on steroids. These exertions were greeted by the tooting of many horns and not a few shouted references to one's parentage and sexual habits, all of which were studiously ignored and/or laughed at by the said teenagers. As soon as the traffic signal started to change and allow north-south-bound traffic to proceed, the said teenagers piled back into their vehicle and zoomed away.

Fred laughed uproariously at the antics of the said teenagers. What he had witnessed was a teenaged prank he hadn't seen since his own teenage years but had participated in himself more than once: a "Chinese fire drill." Why it was called that no one knew (or cared); and, if anyone did know (or cared), (s)he kept the information to him/herself. The purpose of a Chinese fire drill was to get out of one's vehicle while waiting at a traffic signal and circle the said vehicle as many times as one could before the traffic signal changed. Teenagers found the exercise to be the most uproarious thing to do; and, if it annoyed other motorists in the process, so much the better.

Fred proceeded to move on and, when he came to Indian Trail Road, where he would make a left turn and head toward Provisional Medical Center, he spied the said teenagers again conducting a fresh Chinese fire drill (amid fresh beeping of many horns and not a few fresh shouted references to one's parentage and sexual habits) for their amusement and other motorists' annoyance. As he came abreast of the pranksters, he gave them the thumb's-up gesture which signified – in some circles anyway – universal brotherhood. Two of the said teenagers who were closest to him returned the gesture. When the traffic signal changed, Fred made his left turn while the said teenagers continued north, and he never saw them again. He laughed uproariously again, however, at the memories the prank had evoked of his own youthful follies.

Crankily, taxi #65 of the Cythera Cab Company pulled in front of the Provisional Medical Center located on the northern edge of Cythera. Taxi #65 of the Cythera Cab Company did not, of course, pull in front of the Provisional Medical Center by itself; it had a driver (identified as one Fred) who did the actual pulling in front of. The driver also applied the brake; otherwise, taxi #65 would not have stopped (even by itself) and most likely would have proceeded into the lobby of the

Provisional Medical Center, caused curiosity in the staff and patients and considerable injury to said staff and patients and damage to the lobby, taxi and taxi driver, moderately to severely, and provided the hospital more customers to be healed or die trying.

Fred exited his cab, went inside, identified himself to the receptionist (who gave him a "Visitor" badge and an exceptionally dirty look), signed the guest register, asked for directions to the package pick-up office (a formality since he had been there many times before), and marched at a brisk pace to said office.

At the package pick-up office, he was again greeted by the pretty little blonde technician with dimpled cheeks, sparkling blue eyes, an hour-glass figure, and an infectious smile. He was re-smitten and wished he weren't otherwise occupied. Reluctantly, he identified himself, stated his business, and waited patiently while the pretty little blonde technician with dimpled cheeks, sparkling blue eyes, an hour-glass figure, and an infectious smile retrieved the desired package. She returned with the desired package and handed Fred a transfer form for him to sign. Fred signed the form, accepted the desired package, and gave the pretty little blonde technician with dimpled cheeks, sparkling blue eyes, an hour-glass figure, and an infectious smile a smile of his own designed to send provocative signals and raise certain hopes.

"We have to stop meeting like this," he said provocatively.

"How should we meet?" she said, raising certain hopes.

"After work, in a restaurant of your choice," he said provocatively.

"I get off at 5 o'clock," she said, raising certain hopes.

"I'll pick you up at 5:15," he said provocatively.

"I'll be waiting," she said, raising certain hopes.

With the desired package in hand (and lust in his heart), Fred marched at a brisk pace back to the receptionist, returned the "Visitor" badge (and the exceptionally dirty look), exited the hospital, jumped into his cab, and continued on his merry way.

INTERLUDE THE FIFTH

The Visitor trudges onward. And, as he trudges, he formulates a new theory about all of the dwelling structures that he has observed. His own society is heavily populated, and there is little room for expansion – hence, dwelling structures for the general population (such as himself) tend to be multi-story ones in order to accommodate everyone. Here in this society, however, the population must be very less dense to allow for such a wide-spread construction of smaller dwelling structures. Or, alternatively, the bureaucracy here must be exceptionally large.

He reviews his observations so far and instantly sees a flaw in his theory. If the population is smaller or the bureaucracy larger, how then to explain the existence of the tall, multi-story structures in the first place? Can it be that they serve a different purpose? Are they, perhaps, dwellings for criminals or the insane and the occupants are confined close together in order to facilitate the eradication of their criminal or insane behavior? This is how it is done at home. But, can he extrapolate the familiar to the unfamiliar setting? He must ponder these questions further and, more importantly, make more observations. If this new theory holds up, then this society must have a large number of criminal and insane units.

He hopes he can reach the administrative center of the city before sunset. While he has had no time restrictions placed upon him, and he is free to take as much time he requires in order to complete his mission, his desire is more personal in nature. He is afraid of the dark and has been since childhood. He has been counseled concerning this phobia, but he still cannot shake the fear. Perhaps he should increase his pace...

Just then, he is aware of a vehicle approaching him, and it is slowing down. The vehicle is colored black-and white, and it has a red light on its upper surface. From previous reports, he realizes that this vehicle is operated by the local law-enforcement personnel. His own society has such personnel, although they do not travel in vehicles like this one; rather, they use the same moving walkways everyone else does, and one may see a hundred or more each rotational period as they monitor the activities of the population at large and halt those individuals displaying anti-social behavior.

The Visitor has no reason to fear law-enforcement personnel. His kind has been taught from the time they were able to grasp the concept of law enforcement that these personnel perform important duties and that they must be respected because of those duties. If the law-enforcement personnel here require his attention, he is obliged to render it.

The law-enforcement vehicle pulls up beside him and comes to a complete stop. Two personnel are inside – a driver and his superior. They wear what his kind would deem peculiar – called locally a "uniform." Law-enforcement personnel in his society do not wear such peculiar clothing bur wear the same garb everyone else does. They are distinguished only by the wearing of yellow, conical headgear.

As a sign of respect for these law-enforcement personnel, he greets them by holding his nose, the gesture used in his society. For good measure, he also uses the hand gesture that he has learned is the preferred greeting here. The law-enforcement personnel react in a surprising manner. Both of them exit their vehicle quickly and roughly push him against the vehicle. The driver touches every part of his body, which act offends him. At home, only family members are allowed to touch one in such a manner. Law-enforcement personnel do not behave in this fashion; instead, they politely ask the subject for his identification, his destination, and his purpose for being on the street. Once they are satisfied that the subject is a law-abiding person, they wish him a safe and pleasant journey and go on their way.

All the while, these law-enforcement personnel are speaking to him in their own language (which he does not understand) very loudly and very rapidly. The face of the superior of the two has turned a bright red, a sign the Visitor would recognize if he were at home as a sign of sexual attraction. He is naturally alarmed by this development. He does not understand why this individual is sexually attracted to him when he and the individual have not been properly introduced and have not completed the ritual for engagement. Obviously, sexual situations are quite different here. Nevertheless, he experiences embarrassment by this treatment.

It is clear to him that he must disassociate himself from this *impropriety. He is torn, however, between showing respect for law-enforcement personnel and observing correct social mores. He is, after all, here to observe, not to participate. What he chooses to do then is to follow an emergency procedure that he has been taught to employ only in extreme situations. He reaches into a pocket of his garment and produces a shiny silver disc. Each of the field operatives carry with him a number of these discs, each of which perform a specific function. Each of them possesses a single charge and therefore can be used only once and then taken back to headquarters for re-charging. He presses a blue button located at its center.*

The disc emits a blue aura which envelopes the law-enforcement personnel. At once, they cease their embarrassing behavior and look at each other in a bewildered manner. The disc has erased their short-term memories, and they have no idea of where they are or what they are doing there or why they are standing in the middle of the street. Slowly, they enter their vehicle and drive away.

The Visitor is greatly relieved by their departure. Though he feels bad about having to treat law-enforcement personnel in such a disrespectful fashion, he knows that it has been essential for the satisfactory conclusion of his mission. Now free of obstruction, he continues toward the city center.

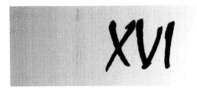

XVI

12:15 pm
(and not a second more)

Harriet Methune Beiderbeck, star reporter (in her humble estimation) for the Cythera *Clarion-News*, who has won several awards (which, in her humble estimation, she deserved), swallowed the last bit of her big juicy steak burger with tomato, lettuce, onion, and mayo (the pickle and portion of French-fried onion rings on the side having already disappeared down her gullet) and washed it down with the last dregs of the tall, frosty mug of root beer. She then proceeded to belch a most unladylike belch, grinned foolishly for the benefit of any nearby diners who might have been annoyed by her belch, and belched another most unladylike belch for good measure.

She really didn't want to rush her lunch – especially in light of the fact that a smelly old goat at the Cythera Cab Company was waiting for her to return in order to regale her with more of his unamusing anecdotes and to call her "Blondie" repeatedly. But her publisher, the redoubtable Michael John McNamara was having another of his hissy fits, and he would not be happy – and perhaps not even then – until Harry the Hatchet filed her story. She paid the check, requested a receipt (McNamara would rue the day he had given her an expense account!), and walked back to the Cythera Cab Company.

The smelly old goat was nodding off and slumping in his chair. In point of fact, he was slumping so much that he was sliding off the chair in preparation to falling to the floor like a sack of potatoes. If Harriet had been her usual self, she would have let the smelly old goat fall to the floor like a sack of potatoes. But that would delay the rest of the interview for who knew how long. What if her baby decided to enter the world in the meantime? To be born in the office of a cab company with a smelly old goat for a midwife was something not to be wished upon anybody.

And so, she nudged the smelly old goat on the shoulder. In response, he mumbled some obscenity and shifted his weight which served to propel him further toward the floor like a sack of potatoes. She nudged him again and provoked more obscenities. Exasperated (Harriet exasperated easily), she used the only method which would gain his attention.

"Hey! I need a cab!"

Uncle Gordy's eyes snapped open. They were quite glazed, and he spent the better part of minute focusing them. Eventually, he became aware that there was another human being in the office.

Well, honk! *What does this honker want?*

He studied the human being for another better part of a minute. It seemed to him that he had seen it before – but where and when? He'd seen hundreds, if not thousands, of human beings during his lifetime, and it could have been any one of them. Or it could be a new human being who only looked like an old human being. That was usually the case in his line of work. He continued to study this human being for another better part of a minute until a memory cell in his brain clicked on. He struggled to sit upright and nearly fell to the floor like a sack of potatoes.

"Hey, Blondie, yer back! Have a seat. Got some more honkin' Crackerjacks fer ya."

Harriet sighed in resignation and sat down in the only other chair in the office. The said chair hadn't improved its comfortability one iota. She took out pad and pen and waited patiently (or as patiently as she was accustomed to – which was very little) for the smelly old goat to regale her with unamusing anecdotes and to call her "Blondie" repeatedly.

XVII

12:15:01 pm
(or thereabouts)

Quietly, taxi #65 of the Cythera Cab Company pulled up in front of the Dunlap Hospital located in a community north of Cythera. Taxi #65 of the Cythera Cab Company did not, of course, pull up in front of Dunlap Hospital by itself; it had a driver (identified as one Fred) who did the actual pulling up. The driver also applied the brake and stopped; otherwise, taxi #65 would not have stopped (even by itself) and most likely would have proceeded into the lobby of Dunlap Hospital, caused fear and loathing amongst the hospital staff and patients and considerable injury to said hospital staff and patients and damage to hospital, taxi, and taxi driver, moderately to severely, and provided the hospital with more customers wanting to be healed or die trying.

Fred exited his cab, went inside, identified himself to the receptionist (who gave him a "Visitor" badge and an exceptionally dirty look), signed the guest register, asked for directions to the package drop-off office (a formality since he had been there many times before), and marched at a brisk pace to the said office.

At the package drop-off office, he was again greeted by the gorgeous little red-haired technician with dimpled cheeks, sparkling green eyes, an hour-glass figure, and a come-hither smile. He was instantly re-smitten and again wished he weren't otherwise occupied. Reluctantly, he identified himself, stated his business, and waited patiently while the gorgeous little red-haired technician with dimpled cheeks, sparkling green eyes, an hour-glass figure, and a come-hither smile accepted the package and wrote out a receipt. Fred accepted the receipt and gave the gorgeous little red-haired technician with dimpled cheeks, sparkling green eyes, an hour-glass figure, and a come-hither smile a smile of his own designed to send provocative signals and to raise certain hopes.

"We have to stop meeting like this," he said provocatively.

"How should we meet?" she said, raising certain hopes.

"After work, in a restaurant of your choice," he said provocatively.

"I get off at 5 o'clock," she said, raising certain hopes.

"I'll pick you up at 5:15," he said provocatively.

"I'll be waiting," she said, raising certain hopes.

With the receipt in hand (and lust in his heart), Fred marched at a brisk pace back to the receptionist, returned the "Visitor" badge (and the exceptionally dirty look), exited the hospital, jumped into his cab, and continued on his merry way.

[Author's note: the astute Reader will observe that Fred, the driver of taxi #65 of the Cythera Cab Company, could not possibly have kept both of the aforementioned trysts. The Reader will thus conclude that he kept only one of the aforementioned trysts (it matters not which one) and abandoned the other (it matters not which one). There is, however, one possible explanation for Fred's seemingly impossible tryst-making. Fred could have been in possession of a time machine as described by that wizard inventor, H.G. Wells. (How he could have come into the possession of this marvelous machine is not germane to this narrative.) With said marvelous machine in his possession, he could have kept one tryst (it matters not which one), had a most delightful evening, returned home, gotten into the said marvelous machine, gone back in time, kept the other tryst (it matters not which one), and had another delightful evening. The Reader may make of this explanation as (s)he will.]

THE INTERVIEW
PART V

Ya got another question first, eh? Have I ever tossed anyone outa my cab?

I tell ya, Blondie, some days I wanted to toss out all o' them honkers who got in. Biggest honkin' gripers in the whole honkin' world, people who call fer a cab. Mebbe I shoulda put 'em in a special category of Crackerjacks. That's where the honk they belong, yessiree.

One o' my first customers accused me of tryin' to jack up the honkin' fare by drivin' slow. That ain't the way it works. The meter is based on the rotation of the wheels, and nothin' else. Ya go slow, and the meter goes slow; ya go fast, and the meter goes fast. Ain't no two ways about it. I wanted to tell that honker how'd he like to walk the rest o' the honkin' way. Couldn't do that though – city rules, doncha know? – got to pick up every honker who calls a cab.

They's one exception, however. Honker gets rowdy or belligerent, you can give 'im the honkin' boot. I had one just like that. It was early in the morning, and the honker musta got out o' the wrong side o' the bed. He starts raggin' on me about this 'n' that, and I honkin' took as much as I could, which wasn't much. I told 'im to get the honk outa my cab and call another honkin' cab company. That answer yer question?

Did I ever have any customers I did like? Yeah, one. A little old lady – a real sweetheart if there ever was one. I picked her up at a local nursing home and took her to the Provisional Medical Center fer emotional counseling. She hated to go there, but her son and daughter-in-law forced her to go. She claimed they was stealin' her blind. Anyways, we'd talk all the way to the hospital and sometimes, she'd recite some poetry to me from memory. Amazing! The downside was she was tired o' livin' and wanted to die. Made me feel like poo when she talked like that. Dunno what happened to her. I reckon she got her wish, eventually. Real sad, Blondie, real sad. She was a class-A sweetheart.

So, some more Crackerjacks.

"Yakkers." Talk about honkin' pooheads! They love to talk up a honkin' storm to anyone who'll listen to 'em 'stead o' payin' attention to the honkin' street. They's two varieties: unassisted and assisted. The unassisted honkers wave their honkin' arms and hands while talkin' to whoever's in the honkin' car with 'em; if they're alone, they honkin' talk to themselves. The assisted honkers use a cell phone or a honkin' smartphone; they got themselves the honkin' need to call up someone on the honkin' spur o' the moment, and they do so 'cause they honkin' can. They yak and yak until they honkin' run out o' things to say, which is usually never. Ya gotta give these honkers a wide berth, Blondie, 'cause they're in a honkin' world o' their own.

Then they's the honkin' "pretties." They're a new bunch o' Crackerjacks, but they're just as bad as the honkin' yakkers when it comes to not payin' attention to where the honk they're at. You seen 'em all o' the time. They're late fer work – no time to put on their honkin' faces – so they do it in the honkin' car. The guys are shavin', doin' a quick comb-out, brushin' their teeth; the gals are puttin' on lipstick, mascara, eyeliner, etc., doin' a quick comb-out. I wanna tell ya, Blondie, some o' them honkers need a whole new face 'stead o' honkin' tryin' to pretty up the old one, ya know what I mean?

Right along with them two kinds o' honkers are the "sightseers." Would ya believe they's actually some honkin' drivers who stay under the speed limit? Ya know why? They're honkin' gawkin' at ever'thing under the sun, lookin' this way and that way. Don't make no honkin' difference *what* they're lookin' at – a tourist attraction, some funny sign on the side of a building, an auto accident, some honker on the street who looks strange – they lose all honkin' track o' their surroundings. They need to get a honkin' grip and pull over to the curb if they wanna honkin' gawk.

Another question, Blondie?

XVIII

12:30 pm
(according to the atomic clock
in Fort Collins, Colorado)

"65 to dispatch."

"Dispatch here. Go ahead, 65."

"I'm back in town, Uncle Gordy, and rich as Croesus."

"Whoopee-doo, 65. Head for the library, goin' to Plum Street."

"10-4."

Honk you, poohead!

Fred smiled broadly. A fare to Plum Street meant only one thing: Russell the Rat was ready to go home. But what was he doing at the library? When the two of them were in the Commandos, leading the "Keystone Kops" – that is to say, the Cythera Police Department – on a merry chase and causing ulcers and gray hair in Chief of Police Colonel Luther Ozymandias Oglesby, USMC (ret.) – "Chief Ozzie," as he was affectionately called by friend and foe alike – Tommy used to say that libraries were for prima donnas and that a *real* education could be had on the streets. And Tommy Russell was *very* "educated"!

So, why was he haunting the library all of a sudden? Was he a closet book reader? And, if he was, how long had he been in the closet? That stint at Cythera College had to have something to do with it, Fred believed.

Fred, the driver of taxi #65 of the Cythera Cab Company, took Randall Road to Downer Place, turned left, and headed downtown. On the way, he spotted another fixture in Cythera, none other than Chesterfield Landis, reputedly the *second* oldest man in town. He was pushing one-hundred years of age; and in all that time, he had ridden nothing but a bicycle (or so he claimed). He was riding his old blue-and-white bicycle (a contraption which was nearly as old as he was) at the time and wearing his usual yellow coat and black hat (both of which were also nearly as old as he was). *[Author's note: the word "contraption" is archaic in the extreme, but it is apropos here, given what it describes – not to mention who was operating it.]*

As Fred approached Chesterfield Landis, he tooted his horn, as both a gesture of warning and of greeting. The tootee waved at Fred, and the distraction caused him to lose control of his contraption temporarily, at which point he began to weave back and forth across the street. Fred was obliged to apply the brake on taxi #65 of the Cythera Cab Company; otherwise, he would have rendered the tootee flatter than the proverbial pancake. Chesterfield Landis eventually regained control of his contraption and realized the awkward position he had put himself in, at which point he laughed and laughed and laughed and continued on his merry way. Fred did likewise, i.e. laughed and laughed and laughed and continued on *his* merry way.

Dispiritedly, taxi #65 of the Cythera Cab company pulled up in front of the Cythera Public Library, located on Benton Street on the island in the river which divided the City. Taxi #65 of the Cythera Cab Company did not, of course, pull up in front of the Cythera Public Library by itself; it had a driver (identified as one Fred) who did the actual pulling up. The driver also applied the brake and stopped; otherwise, taxi #65 would not have stopped (even by itself) and most likely would have proceeded into the Library and down the stairs to the Young People's Department, disconcerted the staff and the young people, caused considerable injury to the said staff and the young people and damage to the Library, taxi, and taxi driver, moderately to severely, and elicited righteous wrath from the management.

The Cythera Public Library, located on Benton Street on the island which divided the City, was a venerable old building possessing an incongruous modern façade. The façade was the sole sop to changing times and demographics that the then management cared to make and/or could afford. Once inside the building, however, one could easily discern the age of the building. It moaned and groaned and creaked and muttered with each step one took across the floor; moreover, if many people took many steps across the floor, the said floor undulated and threatened to collapse; moreover, the wind whistled through the cracks and made hearing difficult; moreover, the musty odor of old books and the dinginess of the walls and ceiling and the dim lighting testified to old age. Nonetheless, the Library was still a popular place to visit and browse and commingle and learn a thing or two.

The address of the Library – 1 East Benton Street -- was something of a misnomer. The building had been constructed at the south end of the island at the end of Island Avenue and straddled said avenue which marked the dividing line between East and West Cythera; only because the administrative offices were located on the east side of the building did the library have its current address. Some cynical residents said that it should have been designated as "0 Benton Street," but no one listened or cared.

Tommy Russell, a.k.a. "Russell the Rat," was waiting for Fred at the main entrance and quickly jumped into the cab.

"Hey, Fred, they sent you again!"

"Yeah. I've been a busy little boy today. Sometimes, we get days like this and make good money. You going home?"

"Yep. Back to the little woman."

"Not so little – if you catch my drift. She got a sister?"

"Nope. But she's got a cousin who's just as gorgeous. Want an introduction?"

"Sure. By the way, what were you doing *here*? The library is the last place I expected to see you at."

"I was gettin' some information on how to run a political campaign. I'll need it if I'm goin' up against an old pro like Mayor Dork. I'll have to lose my old Commando persona and look and speak respectably."

"Russell the Rat – respectable. Who'da thunk it? If you win – and I hope you do – this town won't be the same again."

"You better believe it, pal. Let's go, huh?"

"Right." Fred reached for his radio. "65 to dispatch."

"Dispatch here. Go ahead, 65."

"Heading for Plum Street, Uncle Gordy."

"10-4, 65."

Honk you, poohead!

THE INTERVIEW
PART VI

Ya haven't run outa questions, have ya, Blondie? Didn't think so.

Would I ever recommend drivin' a cab fer a living to anyone? *Honk, no!*

Drivin' a cab is long, hard work. It's mostly wear and tear on the mind. Ya hafta know where yer goin', which means ya hafta carry a map around with ya. Oh, you can ask the honkin' dispatcher fer directions to a pick-up or drop-off point, but I don't trust dispatchers more'n I can honkin' throw 'em – 'especially one who ain't never driven a cab.

So, why am *I* a dispatcher? I got the experience and the know-how – forty honkin' years of drivin', that's why. I carry a map with me – in my head where it won't get lost – and that gives me the honkin' edge, Blondie.

Then they's havin' to deal with all sorts o' people. Most of the honkers who get into the cab don't know what the honk they want, so ya hafta honkin' babysit 'em and tell 'em the best way to get to where they're goin'. Most o' the time, they know only one way to go to a particular place, but a taxi driver who's got the honkin' experience has several ways to go. And that makes the difference between a satisfied customer and a dissatisfied one, doncha know?

So, why did I choose to be a taxi driver in the first place?

Circumstances, Blondie, circumstances, and nothin' else.

They was a time when I was down on my luck, and nobody was hirin'. I grabbed at the first honkin' thing what was available. I was born and raised in Cythera, and I thought I knew this town pretty well to be a taxi driver.

Huh! I soon found out that I didn't know Cythera as well as I thought I did. Man, was that a rude honkin' wake-up call! I learned how to get around in a honkin' hurry, 'cause my income depended on givin' the impression that I knew what the honk I was doin'.

Anyways, I fell into a comfortable rut. The more I drove, the more I knew about drivin'. And the more I knew about drivin', the less interested I was in doin' anything else.

But, like I said, I wouldn't recommend it to anyone. Ya hafta be desperate to take on a job like taxi-drivin'.

Now, I got more Crackerjacks fer ya, Blondie. I saved the worst o' them fer last, 'cause they're the biggest menaces on the streets.

First menace: bikers. They're as bad as motorists. These honkers pedal on the wrong side o' the street or go the wrong honkin' way on a one-way street. They don't stop fer honkin' stop signs or traffic lights but sail on through the honkin' intersection if they's no traffic comin'. And they weave back and forth across the honkin' street as if they owned it. They must have a honkin' death wish or somethin'.

The worst of the bikers are the honkin' adults. Kids I understand 'cause nobody taught 'em the honkin' rules of the road. But you'd think adults would know better. Yeah, I know what yer thinkin', Blondie; bikers ain't bound by the rules of the road. But they are; they's a special honkin' rule book just fer them. Fact o' the matter is, those honkers don't give a honk.

Second menace – and the worst o' the honkin' worst: "runners." You see 'em all the time, Blondie. Ain't got time to stop at a honkin' traffic signal, so they keep on truckin.' Mostly, they run the yellow light, 'stead o' slowin' down and stoppin.' But many o' them honkers – too many o' them – like to run the red light. Why the honk they do it is 'cause they honkin' can. You'd need a honkin' traffic cop on every corner, doncha know? So, they meet another honker who's in a honkin' hurry too. WHAMMO! I'd like to have one o' them honkin' ray guns like they got on 'Star Trek.' I see a honkin' runner. *Zap!* The honker won't be runnin' no more, ya know what I mean? Heh-heh-heh.

One last question? Hang on, Blondie. Got another call here.

(somewhere between 12:30 and 12:45)

Ring-ring! says the telephone joyfully. *Ring-ring!*

Honk you! says Uncle Gordy [to himself, of course, as it wouldn't do to say it out loud in front of Harriet Methune Beiderbeck, star reporter (in her humble estimation) for the Cythera *Clarion-News*, who has won several awards (which, in her humble estimation, she deserved) for her reporting and who more than likely would have included such remarks in her interview just to spite her publisher, the aforementioned Michael John McNamara].

"Cythera Cab Company. Service with a smile."

"I need a cab to go to Elmont."

"Where you at?"

"At the Howard Johnson's, #48."

"OK. Be fifteen minutes." *Give or take an hour.* Uncle Gordy reaches for the radio. "Dispatch to 65."

"65 here. Go ahead, dispatch."

"You clear on Plum Street?"

"Another minute, Uncle Gordy."

"OK. When you clear, head for Howard Johnson's. The fare is goin' to Elmont."

"This is my lucky day. Money in the bank! 10-4."

Honk you, poohead!

Taxi #65 of the Cythera Cab Company dropped off its fare at 543 Plum Street and headed east. Taxi #65 of the Cythera Cab Company did not, of course, drop off and head east by itself; it had a driver (identified as one Fred) who did the actual dropping off and heading east. The driver also released the brake and applied a foot (the right one, as it happened) to the accelerator. Otherwise, taxi #65 would not have gone anywhere (even by itself) and most likely would have remained in front of 543 Plum Street for all of Eternity (more or less).

Fred would have lost a big fare.

At Plum Street and Pennsylvania Avenue, Fred turned left and headed toward Indian Trail Road. He instantly regretted his action. He had been following the taxi driver's dictum of taking the shortest route possible to pick up a fare and temporarily forgotten what was at Pennsylvania Avenue and Illinois Avenue. What was at Pennsylvania Avenue and Illinois Avenue was an elementary school (one of the oldest on the west side of Cythera), and today only a half day of classes had been scheduled. That meant that all of the students would be waiting outside to be picked up by either a school bus or a guardian which meant that the intersection would be jammed with vehicles in all four directions, and traffic would be reduced to a snail's pace. Unfortunately, Fred was committed, and he gritted his teeth for the ordeal to come. *[Author's note: for the sake of the Reader's sanity, details of the snail's pace through the intersection at Pennsylvania Avenue and Illinois Avenue will not be related here. Suffice it to say that Fred was bored to tears and frustrated beyond belief, and he muttered incoherently to himself.]*

Disgruntledly, taxi #65 of the Cythera Cab Company pulled up in front of Howard Johnson's, #48. Taxi #65 of the Cythera Cab Company did not, of course, pull up in front of Howard Johnson's, #48, by itself; it had a driver (identified as one Fred) who did the actual pulling up. The driver also applied the brake and stopped; otherwise, taxi #65 would not have stopped (even by itself) and most likely would have proceeded either into #48, angered the occupants, caused considerable injury to the said occupants and damage to #48, taxi, and taxi driver, moderately to severely, and provoked the owners into filing a lawsuit against the Cythera Cab Company, or over an embankment, crashed onto the tollway below, caused a great inconvenience to any oncoming traffic and considerable injury and damage to the motorists in the said oncoming traffic, taxi, and taxi driver, moderately to severely, and forced the owner of the Cythera Cab Company (the aforementioned Pam) to replace taxi #65 and its driver (identified as one Fred) at considerable expense.

Two ladies exited #48 at once, and Fred was greatly surprised to see them. One was a striking redhead wearing a maroon knit dress which both complemented her hair and emphasized certain physical features; the other was a striking strawberry blonde wearing a yellow T-shirt which complemented her hair and tight jeans which emphasized certain physical features. Fred was surprised because they were the same two striking young women he had picked up at the YMCA earlier in the day and dropped off at the train depot. Being a self-avowed connoisseur of the female form, he again took his best smile out of his tote bag, put it on, and adjusted it for maximum effect.

"Good afternoon, ladies," he greeted the two striking young women lecherously.

"Well, look who's here," one of the striking young women (it matters not which one) murmured. "It's the cabbie with the breathing problem."

"Well, *honk!*" the other striking young women (it matters not which one) grumbled. "Just our luck."

The fact that he had two striking young women in his cab notwithstanding, Fred had a second reason for putting on his best smile. They were going up the river to Elmont, a twenty-dollar fare *each*.

"Where to, ladies?"

"You know where Club Ronnie is, on Route 25?" one of the striking young women (it matters not which one) responded.

"Sure do." Fred reached for the radio. "65 to dispatch."

"Dispatch here. Go ahead, 65."

"On my way to Elmont, Uncle Gordy."

"10-4, 65."

And don't come back, poohead!

Taxi #65 of the Cythera Cab Company pulled away from #48 at Howard Johnson's and headed for Route 25. Taxi #65 of the Cythera Cab Company did not, of course, pull away and head for by itself; it had a driver (identified as one Fred) who did the actual pulling away and heading for. The driver released the brake and applied a foot (the right one, as it happened) to the accelerator; otherwise, taxi #65 would not have gone anywhere and most likely would have remained in front of #48 for all of Eternity (more or less).

Fred would have lost a sizeable fare and a spectacular view.

No sooner had taxi #65 – that is to say, Fred – pulled out of Howard

Johnson's than the two striking young women fished cigarillos out of their purses, lit up, and began puffing away. Fred wisely rolled down his window which action elicited a giggle out of one of the striking young women (it matters not which one). As soon as the air cleared (more or less), he remarked:

"You ladies didn't leave town after all."

"Oh, we left town all right," one of the striking young women (it matters not which one) replied. "We went to Leland to see if the gentleman's club there had an opening. The owner doesn't nickel-and-dime us like honking Ronnie does. There weren't any openings, so we came back here."

"Lucky me."

"Yeah, lucky you," one of the striking young women (it matters not which one) snorted.

The remainder of the trip was spent in silence as Fred concentrated on the spectacular view through the haze of cigarillo smoke.

Fitfully, taxi #65 of the Cythera Cab Company pulled in front of Club Ronnie. Taxi #65 of the Cythera Cab Company did not, of course, pull in by itself; it had a driver (identified as one Fred) who did the actual pulling in. The driver also applied the brake and stopped; otherwise, taxi #65 would not have stopped (even by itself) and most likely would have proceeded either into Club Ronnie, bothered the staff and patrons, caused considerable injury to said staff and patrons and damage to Club Ronnie, taxi, and taxi driver, and provoked fisticuffs at the hands of the bouncer, moderately to severely, or rolled over an embankment, splashed into the river below, caused considerable injury to the fish and the passengers and damage to taxi and taxi driver, moderately to severely, and forced the owner of the Cythera Cab Company (the aforementioned Pam) to replace taxi #65, its driver (identified as one Fred), and its passengers at considerable expense.

Club Ronnie was a small weathered building at the side of Route 25 overlooking the Wolf River on the eastern outskirts of Elmont. In a former life, it had been a roadhouse where food was sometimes served, liquor was often served (illegally), and gaming devices and activities were offered (also illegally). The county sheriff paid weekly visits to the establishment – not to be served food, but to serve warrants and collect the liquor, the gaming devices, and the owners and employees -- in a futile attempt to maintain the morals of the county. As the twentieth century rolled on toward more liberal climes, the liquor became legal, but the gaming devices and activities did not. The county sheriff paid infrequent visits to the establishment only if some moralistic individual complained about the goings-on at the establishment. The current owner of the building removed all of the gaming devices and activities when he took possession in order to demonstrate that he was a moralistic person too and substituted a more lucrative draw, i.e. exotic dancers (that is to say, strippers). The county sheriff continued to pay visits to the establishment, both on and off duty.

"Here we are, ladies," Fred announced. "The fare is forty dollars."

"You must be honking kidding," one of the striking young women (it matters not which one) growled.

"No, ma'am. The Company has established that amount as the fare to Elmont, based on mileage and wear and tear on the vehicle."

"Well, *honk!*" the other striking young women (it matters not which one) fumed.

The striking young women paid up, exited the taxi, and slammed the door behind them. Fred got a sizeable fare and revenge for the cigarillo smoke. He reached for his radio.

"65 to dispatch."

"Dispatch here. Go ahead, 65."

"I'm clear in Elmont, Uncle Gordy."

"Whoopee-doo. Come on back."

"10-4."

Honk you, poohead!

THE INTERVIEW
PART VII

So, ya wanna know how to deal with taxi drivers, eh, Blondie?

Heh-heh. I got an earful of advice on that subject.

Tip #1: stay out of a taxi driver's way, if yer a honkin' motorist, bicyclist, motorcyclist, skateboarder, or whatever. Cabbies don't stop fer nobody or nothin'. Get in their way, and they'll run ya over.

Tip #2: always give the taxi driver the honkin' right-o'-way. His business is more important than yers, and he needs his honkin' space. Don't make no honkin' difference who or what the honk ya are – just stop and pull over.

Tip #3: don't ever beep yer honkin' horn at a taxi driver fer any reason. Just be friendly and courteous and don't give 'im no honkin' poo.

Tip #4: save yer honkin' hand signals – 'specially them involvin' fingers – for someone else, like a honkin' Crackerjack. Give a cabbie the honkin' bird, and he'll see yer one and raise ya one.

Tip #5: don't ever park in the honkin' taxi stands. The taxi driver has enough honkin' competition as it is. He just might give ya a little nudge, if ya know what I mean.

Tip #6: if yer a fare, don't ever give a taxi driver a honkin' twenty-dollar bill (or higher), 'specially if it's early in the day. A taxi driver ain't a honkin' bank; he don't carry a whole lot o' cash. Of course, if ya wanna tip 'im big, lay them big bills on 'im.

Tip #7: keep yer honkin' mouth shut when yer ridin' in the cab – unless yer providin' information on yer destination. A taxi driver has got to concentrate on his drivin', what with them honkin' Crackerjacks out there. Besides, he ain't interested in yer honkin' medical problems, marital woes, political views, or family affairs. If ya wanna hear his in return, then, yeah, prepare yerself fer a honkin' earful.

Tip #8: don't complain about a taxi driver's drivin'. He knows what the honk he's doin' and knows the best way to get ya where ya wanna go. Complain, and you'll find yerself walkin' the rest o' the way.

Tip #9: don't get honkin' feisty with the taxi driver. You definitely will get the heave-ho.

Tip #10: keep yer honkin' brats and pets quiet at all times. Better yet, leave 'em at home. The taxi driver has enough to worry about in front o' him without havin' to put up with honkin' screechin', cryin', barkin', growlin', or any other kind o' noise behind 'im.

Tip #11: absolutely NO smokin', drinkin', or eatin' in the cab – unless ya wanna share with the driver. Otherwise, it only reminds 'im of the honkin' hard times he hasta endure, what with the honkin' Crackerjacks, odd workin' schedules, and the constant demands of his passengers and his dispatcher.

Tip #12: NEVER, EVER honkin' stiff a taxi driver. If ya do, make honkin' sure in the future you see him before *he* sees *you*, if ya know what I mean.

Here's a friendly tip fer *you*, Blondie. Next time yer on the street, avoid as many traffic signals and stop signs as ya can. You'll get around town a whole lot faster if ya do. Take it from one who knows. That's what forty honkin' years o' drivin' will teach ya.

Well, that's all I got to say. It's been a slice talkin' to ya. I'll be waitin' fer yer piece to appear in the *Clarion*. Gonna show it to ever'body I know. Mebbe they won't give a cab driver no honkin' poo from now on, huh?

Have a nice day, Blondie.

[Harriet Methune Beiderbeck, star reporter (in her humble estimation) for the Cythera *Clarion-News*, who has received several awards (which, in her humble estimation, she deserved) for her reporting, left the Cythera Cab Company hastily, happy to be rid of the smelly old goat of a dispatcher and breathe fresh air. She headed straight for her place of employment in order to wave her interview in the face of her esteemed publisher, the aforementioned Michael John McNamara.

[Once he was left to his own devices, Uncle Gordy took a very long pull from the pint of Jack Daniels and a very long drag from the Marlboro, farted loudly, belched loudly, and scratched his privates repeatedly (not necessarily in that order). When the amenities had been taken care of, he nodded off.]

01:01:01:01:01 pm

Ring-ring! says the telephone cheerfully. *Ring-ring!*

Uncle Gordy looks at the telephone with one bleary eye. His other eye is half-closed, and it is too much of an effort to open it fully.

Ring-ring! says the telephone happily. *Ring-ring!*

"Honk you!" says Uncle Gordy unenthusiastically.

Ring-ring! says the telephone joyfully. *Ring-*

"Cythera Cab Company," says Uncle Gordy unenthusiastically. "Service with a smile."

Even though the caller cannot see him, he still exposes a mouthful of yellowed teeth in a grotesque facsimile of a smile.

"Fred here, Gordy. I'm ready to go home."

"Oakie-doakie. Be about fifteen minutes." *Give or take an hour.*

"Thanks, Gordy."

Click.

"Honk you, poohead!"

Uncle Gordy takes a short pull from the Jack Daniels and a short drag from the Marlboro, belches, farts, and scratches his privates (not necessarily in that order). As soon as the amenities are taken care of, he reaches for the radio.

"Dispatch to 65."

"65 here. Go ahead, dispatch."

"How close are you to town?"

"I'm just leaving Barterville."

"OK. Pick up Fred and take 'im home. He's through with his 'lunch.'"

"10-4, Uncle Gordy."

Uncle Gordy flips the bird, even though the driver of taxi #65 of the

121

Cythera Cab Company cannot see him. Then he takes another short pull from the pint of Jack Daniels and another short drag from the Marlboro, belches, farts, and scratches his privates (not necessarily in that order). As soon as the amenities are taken care of, he nods off.

INTERLUDE
THE SIXTH

The Visitor is now suffering from hunger pangs. Ordinarily, he would have had a leisurely morning meal of sponjes and greem, which he has enjoyed every morning since childhood. His birth-units had never understood why he enjoyed those foodstuffs so much when he could have had all of the pungas he wanted. (Pungas were their favorite morning meal.) The simple fact of the matter was that he just liked the taste of sponjes and greem, and nothing they could say or do would dissuade him from asking for them.

This morning, his superiors had called him at an early hour, waking him out of a sound sleep, and told him that changing circumstances had dictated an earlier departure for his current assignment. Therefore, he had had to forego his sponjes and greem and settle for a quick snack of fruzz. The fruzz had not been very satisfying, and now he is hungry again.

He is also tired. All this walking – how do the indigenous units endure it? Perhaps that is why there are so many of the vehicles he has seen so far. The indigenous units prefer to travel in those vehicles – even though the vehicles clutter the streets – rather than walk long distances as he is doing.

He spies a very large – a "tree," he recalls its designation – with abundant foliage, makes for it, and plunks himself down. He reaches into his travel pouch and fishes out his ration pack, a metallic box no larger than two hand spans. The ration pack is standard issue for field investigators; unfortunately, they contain a very limited choice of rations. One has a choice of three different food bars – ching, bufor, or swas – the Visitor has tasted all three and found none of them very satisfying. Bufor comes close to appealing to his taste buds, but the way it is prepared for use in the field leaves something to be desired.

He opens the ration pack gingerly, as it is still warm, and peers at the bufor food bar. He sighs in resignation and begins eating it. Oh, how he would love to have a large dish of sponjes and greem!

As soon as he has finished eating all he cared to eat – about half of the food bar – he leans back against the tree and relaxes. And, before he knows it, he dozes off.

He is abruptly, and rudely, awakened by one of the indigenous wild-life forms, a creature his orientation had labeled a "dog." This dog is now licking his face from one side to the other with a long, wet tongue. It is disgusting! Only one's mate was allowed to do that, and then after they had been mated for eleven cycles. He has no desire to mate with any of the indigenous units here, least of all with any of the wild-life! Did the dog wish to mate? How disgusting!

The Visitor rises to his feet and begins to walk again toward the city center. The dog follows him, even into the street, and makes crude, unintelligible sounds. The drivers of the vehicles which pass him by activate their noise-making mechanisms repeatedly. He simply greets them as before and continues walking. The dog continues to follow while dodging the traffic but eventually gives up the chase and runs away. He shakes his head in disbelief. What a weird society this is!

I surely won't put *that* in my report! *he thinks.* No one would believe me. My superiors would accuse me of making a joke at their expense (best case scenario) or of falsifying the record at the target society's expense (worst case scenario). Better to be accused of filing an incomplete report than a false one.

He trudges onward, his mind entertaining misgivings about this mission. It has been a disaster so far. This society has defied all logic; no rational beings could live like this. Is it so primitive, despite the few modernistic elements he has seen so far, that the indigenous units prefer living like this?

One possible explanation comes instantly to mind: this has been a test. He has been placed in a virtual reality in order to learn how he would react to such societies before being sent out into the field. If he observes as he should in a true reality and files a faithful report, he would likely pass the test and be given a real assignment; if, however, he could make no sense of what he observes and files a disjointed report, he would surely fail the test and therefore be denied any real field missions.

Now that he thinks it through, he realizes that his supervisor is precisely the sort who would concoct such a test. His supervisor has always displayed a sadistic side, and he –

Ah, no! don't think what you're thinking, *he tells himself.* That way leads to suspicious behavior, and suspicious behavior will result in disciplinary action and/or dismissal.

Best to treat this scenario as a real one and file a report based upon straightforward observation. Let my superiors make of it what they will. I'll have performed as I should.

Thus bolstered, the Visitor continues on.

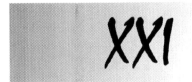
XXI

02:15 pm
(Eastern Daylight Savings Time)

Noisily, taxi #65 of the Cythera Cab Company pulled up in front of the North End Tap. Taxi #65 of the Cythera Cab company did not, of course, pull up in front of the North End Tap by itself; it had a driver (identified as one Fred) who did the actual pulling up. The driver also applied the brake and stopped; otherwise, taxi #65 would not have stopped (even by itself) and most likely would have proceeded into the North End Tap, caused some alarm to the patrons and the owner, considerable injury to the said patrons and owner, and damage to the building, the taxi and driver, moderately to severely, and provoked a lawsuit by the owner.

Fred (the driver) did not spot Fred (the fare) immediately. More than likely, Fred (the fare) had decided to order "one for the road" and lost track of time – which was easy to do if one understood Fred (the fare). Fred (the driver) decided to wait a full ten minutes for Fred (the fare) to put in an appearance. *[Author's note: it is standard practice for taxi drivers to wait a full ten minutes for a fare to put in an appearance – longer if the fare is a "regular" – after which the driver calls his dispatcher and have him call the fare (if feasible) and jiggle said fare's memory. A failure by the fare to respond permits the driver to leave and seek out a different fare.]* Fred (the driver) decided that, in this case, precipitate action was necessary; he exited his cab and entered the North End Tap.

He immediately spotted Fred (the fare) near the end of the bar, looking desultorily over his "one for the road." Fred (the driver) thought that, if Fred (the fare) were hunched over the said bar any further, he would most likely bang his head against it, resulting in considerable damage to Fred (the fare) and possibly having to rush him to the nearest hospital at his (Fred the driver) own expense. Fred (the driver) could not let that happen, not when a fare was at stake. Fred (the driver) then quietly walked up behind Fred (the fare) and said in a nasal twang:

"Hey, buddy, are you buying?"

There were other patrons in the North End Tap at the time, and all of them chuckled over the question. Fred (the fare) was notoriously miserly and seldom bought a round for anyone else. The question, however, broke through his looking desultorily over his "one for the road," and he sat up straight (and almost fell off his stool).

"Huh?" he exclaimed in a slurred voice. "Me buying? Hell, no!"

Fred (the fare) then swiveled around to see who was trying to cadge a drink from him. After five seconds of focusing his eyes, he recognized Fred (the driver) and wrinkled his nose.

"Oh, it's you. 'Bout time you got here."

Fred (the fare) slid off his stool and nearly lost his balance. Amid more chuckling from the other patrons, he righted himself after half a minute of struggling and followed Fred (the driver) toward the door. Being the courteous fellow that he was, Fred (the driver) opened the said door, held Fred (the fare) tightly as he maneuvered down the steps. Further, Fred (the driver) opened the door of the taxi and shoved Fred (the fare) inside. He jumped into the taxi himself.

Taxi #65 of the Cythera Cab Company pulled away from the North End Tap and headed north toward Oak Street. Taxi #65 of the Cythera Cab Company did not, of course, pull away and head north by itself; it had a driver (identified as one Fred) who did the actual pulling away and heading north. The driver released the brake and applied a foot (the right one, as it happened) to the accelerator; otherwise, taxi #65 would have remained at the North End Tap for all of Eternity (more or less).

Fred (the driver) would have lost a fare and a "regular."

"65 to dispatch."

"Dispatch here. Go ahead, 65."

"On my way to Courtyard Village, Uncle Gordy."

"Whoopee-doo! Let me know when you clear."

"10-4."

Honk you, poohead!

Uncle Gordy then took a short pull from the pint of Jack Daniels and a short drag from the Marlboro, belched, farted, and scratched his privates (not necessarily in that order). As soon as the amenities were taken care of, he nodded off.

01:36 pm
(on the dot)

"65 to dispatch."

"Dispatch here. Go ahead, 65."

"I'm clear at Courtyard Village, Uncle Gordy."

"Whoopee-doo! Head for Cythera College, Dannon Hall, at Randall and Marseillaise. A young lady will be waiting for you. Take her to 461 North Avenue – and nowhere else. Got it?"

Fred was puzzled by Uncle Gordy's instructions. He was not to take the young lady at Cythera College, Dannon Hall, at Randall and Marseillaise nowhere else but 461 North Avenue? Did he think he (Fred) would kidnap the said young lady for some unsavory reason? Oh, well, a fare was a fare.

"Got it. On my way."

Honk you, poohead!

Taxi #65 of the Cythera Cab Company pulled out of Courtyard Village and turned left onto Randall Road. Taxi #65 of the Cythera Cab Company did not, of course, pull out and turn left onto by itself; it had a driver (identified as one Fred) who did the actual pulling out and turning left onto. The driver released the brake and applied a foot (the right one, as it happened) to the accelerator; otherwise, taxi #65 would not have gone anywhere (even by itself) and most likely remained at Courtyard Village for all of Eternity (more or less)

Fred would have lost a fare and disobeyed Uncle Gordy.

It was a straight shot to Dannon Hall at Cythera College, and Fred would have made good time in arriving there, if it hadn't been for one minor problem. The one minor problem was that it was the "noontime rush hour," that time of the day when all of Cythera went shopping at all of the strip malls on Randall Road. Traffic was therefore heavy and travel was slow, and Fred cursed all the way to Cythera College.

Carefully, taxi #65 of the Cythera Cab Company pulled up in front of Dannon Hall eventually. Taxi #65 of the Cythera Cab Company did not, of course, pull up by itself; it had a driver (identified as one Fred) who did the actual pulling up. The driver also applied the brake and stopped; otherwise, taxi #65 would have proceeded into Dannon Hall, caused delays in the business of education, considerable injury to students, faculty, and damage to Dannon Hall, taxi, and taxi driver, moderately to severely, and provoked the Administration of Cythera College into running about like squirrels on steroids.

The said young lady was waiting for him at the door. She was studying her watch at the time and frowning deeply. Fred groaned when he spotted her, because he recognized her all too well. She was the oldest child of the owner of the Cythera Cab Company (the aforementioned Pam), and she was Pest #1 as far as he was concerned. She liked to come around to the office and pester the dispatchers and the drivers. No one liked her, and Fred now understood why Uncle Gordy had given the instructions he had given. Take the kid home and be done with her.

The kid piled into the cab and gave Fred the biggest poo-eating grin he had ever seen. It was also the most evil grin he had ever seen. It was typical of the kid. She was up to no good – again.

"Hello, Felicia," Fred said mock-courteously.

"Hello," Felicia purred. "Fred, isn't it?"

"Uh-huh."

"Could you stop at McGillicuddy's for a minute so I can get a can of pop?"

"No can do. I've got orders to take you straight home. Besides, you're underage."

"Well, *poo!* Look, I'll make it worth your while."

"Yeah?"

"Yeah. How long has it been since you've had a woman?"

"Too long. But, you're still underage. I'm not about to risk my job and my freedom doing you. You're going straight home!"

"Well, *poo!*"

"65 to dispatch."

"Dispatch here. Go ahead, 65."

"I've got the fare, Uncle Gordy. Heading for 461 North Avenue."

"Oakie-doakie. Have her sign a charge slip."

"10-4."

Have fun, poohead. Heh-heh-heh!

Uncle Gordy then took a short pull from the pint of Jack Daniels and a short drag from the Marlboro, belched, farted, and scratched his privates (not necessarily in that order). As soon as the amenities were taken care of, he nodded off.

Taxi #65 of the Cythera Cab Company pulled away from Dannon Hall at Cythera College and headed east on Marseillaise Street. Taxi #65 of the Cythera Cab Company did not, of course, pull away by itself; it had a driver (identified as one Fred) who did the actual pulling away and heading east. The driver released the brake and applied a foot (the right one, as it happened) to the accelerator; otherwise, taxi #65 would not have gone anywhere and most likely remained in front of Dannon Hall at Cythera College for all of Eternity (more or less).

Fred would have lost a fare, displeased his boss (the aforementioned Pam), and listened to Felicia's bitching endlessly. *[Author's note: the Reader may look askance at the use of the word "bitching" in this context and think that it should be used in some other context. The Author hastens to point out that the word "bitching" is in common usage in this context and therefore is the proper word to use in the said context. Besides, that was the word Fred, the driver of Taxi #65 of the Cythera Cab Company, used to describe the incident, and the Author was obliged to quote him faithfully.]*

INTERLUDE THE SEVENTH

In due time, the Visitor sights the first signs of the central city of this society. There are many tall buildings here, each of them obviously housing a specific function of governance – the many departments, bureaus, divisions, offices, and so forth – in which the important decisions are made. And see! that very tall structure – so slender and majestic – has to be where the Administrator and his staff hold court and oversee all the functions of governance. Now, he was getting somewhere. This mission would not be a total disaster after all!

Filled with self-confidence, he quickens his pace until he arrives at an intersection at the very edge of the city center.

And that is where everything goes wrong.

No sooner has he entered the intersection than he spies a potentially dangerous situation. There are many vehicles at this intersection, including three oddly-colored ones which cause him to wonder what their function is. Why else would they be so oddly-colored if not to call attention to themselves in order to disseminate important information?

One of the vehicles in the vicinity is heading in his direction. In point of fact, it is heading straight for him. This causes him to wonder why the driver of the vehicle should choose to drive at him. Was he following a natural instinct, the purpose of which is to defend his territory? The Visitor knows about territoriality in primitive societies. But, surely, from the mass of government buildings in plain view, this society could hardly be labeled "primitive."

Perhaps, on certain days, natural instincts which these units were powerless to avoid comes to the fore and governs their reckless behavior. Or, perhaps the driver is obeying a government edict concerning population control. In this case, a lottery might be held and units who drew the correct numbers were authorized to eliminate either themselves or another unit of his choice. This is a crude method, to be sure, but if the population had *reached a level of unsustainability, desperate measures might have been called for.*

In any event, he is being targeted for elimination. And, since he is not a member of this society, he is not bound by its governmental edicts and therefore must remove himself from this potentially dangerous situation. He looks about for an avenue of escape and finds none.

Think fast, fool! *he admonishes himself.* Time is short!

After examining all of his options (which number less than the digits on one hand), he makes his decision. He takes one step to his left and waits for the driver to make a counter-move. The driver's counter-move is quick in coming; he veers to his left (the Visitor's right) and continues his travel.

Having being spared a rather unpleasant consequence, the Visitor takes advantage of the fact that all of the attention of all of the units in the vicinity is focused on the said driver by reaching into his garment and pulling out another silver disc. This one has a red button on it. He presses the button, and the disc emits a red aura creating an illusion. Where once the units in the vicinity might have seen a being they do not recognize, they now see a local wild-life form that they do recognize – a "red squirrel." They see this "red squirrel" scamper away toward the nearest tree.

The "red squirrel" – that is to say, the Visitor – decides that he has seen enough of this topsy-turvy society. He will file his report and let his superiors puzzle it out. He then reverses direction and heads back the way he had come in order to retrieve his own vehicle and return to headquarters. He looks forward to discharging his duty and relaxing with a large bowl of sponjes *and* greem.

Hopefully, his next assignment won't be so traumatic.

XXIII

01:51:01 pm
(if anyone cares)

"65 to dispatch."

'Dispatch here. Go ahead, 65."

"I'm clear at North Avenue, Uncle Gordy."

"Whoopee-doo! Did you have a nice trip?"

"Oh, peachy-keen. Did you know there are only three taverns in all of the southwestern part of Cythera? My fare is an expert on taverns."

"I'll bet. Got nothing fer ya right now. Why -- Oops! Hold on a sec."

Ring-ring! says the telephone cheerfully. *Ring-ring!*

"Honk you!" says Uncle Gordy unenthusiastically.

Ring-

Cythera Cab Company. Service with a smile."

"I'm at the casino. I'm going to the 'Y'."

"OK. Be about fifteen minutes." *Give or take an hour.* "Dispatch to 65."

"65 here."

"Pick-up at the casino. Goin' to the 'Y'."

"10-4, Uncle Gordy."

Honk you, poohead!

Uncle Gordy takes a short pull from the pint of Jack Daniels and a short drag from the Marlboro, belches, farts, and scratches his privates (not necessarily in that order). As soon as the amenities are taken care of, he nods off.

Taxi #65 of the Cythera Cab Company pulled away from 461 North Avenue and headed downtown. Taxi #65 of the Cythera Cab company did not, of course, pull away and head downtown by itself; it had a driver (identified as one Fred) who did the actual pulling away and heading downtown. The driver released the brake and applied a foot (the right one, as it happened) to the accelerator; otherwise, taxi #65 would have remained at 461 North Avenue for all of Eternity (more or less).

Fred would have lost a fare and would have had to listen to Felicia bitching endlessly.

Fred took the non-scenic route to the casino – North Avenue to Broadway to New York Street – saving the scenic routes for the benefit of fares who were not familiar with Cythera. As long as the ride was smooth and pleasant and uneventful and as long as the taxi driver did not bore him with small talk, the fare was usually happy. Fares who were familiar with Cythera would have realized that he was taking the long way around in order to jack up the meter

At the intersection of North Avenue and Broadway, he encountered the "lemon car" again, traveling west. As before, he pointed at it, laughed uproariously, and nearly ran over a pedestrian trying to cross the street who shook her fist and cursed a blue streak. Fred ignored the fist-shaking and the cursing, because Taxi Rule #3 – ignore the petty concerns of others (motorists and pedestrians alike) because the taxi driver's business is more important than theirs – was a time-honored obligation, and Fred was exceptionally diligent in this regard. He continued on his merry way.

At the intersection of Broadway and New York Street, he encountered the "Pepto-Bismol" car again, also traveling west. As before, he put one of his fingers (it matters not which one) in his mouth and made a gagging motion. He believed he was being quite clever. How the driver of the "Pepto-Bismol" car responded to this bit of cleverness – if (s)he responded at all – was unknown and may or may not be relevant to this narrative. Fred continued on his merry way.

Zealously, taxi #65 of the Cythera Cab Company pulled up in front of the Cythera Classic Casino. Taxi #65 of the Cythera Cab Company did not, of course, pull up by itself; it had a driver (identified as one Fred) who did the actual pulling up. The driver also applied the brake and stopped; otherwise, taxi #65 would not have stopped (even by itself) and most likely would have proceeded into the lobby of the casino, caused a tad of consternation amongst the staff and customers and considerable injury to said staff and customers and damage to casino, taxi, and driver, moderately to severely, and provoked some harsh language from the owners.

Eventually, the fare walked/strolled/weaved/stumbled/staggered out of the Cythera Classic Casino and peered at/stared at/focused on/gazed at/regarded/re-focused on taxi #65 and approached it gingerly. The fare was an elderly, white-haired male whose appearance could charitably be called "non-descript." *[Author's note: the Reader may find the use of the term "non-descript" extremely denigrating. It was not used in that way, however; it was used because the person in question* was *non-descript, and no other term could have been apropos.]* Said non-descript fare entered/ wiggled into/squeezed into/wormed into/threw himself into/fell into taxi #65 and gave Fred a toothy smile.

"Good afternoon, sir," Fred greeted him politely while holding his nose.

"Is it really?"

"Yes, sir. Where to, sir?"

"The 'Y', my man. I'm going to take a swim."

"Right. Off we go."

Taxi #65 of the Cythera Cab Company started to pull away from the curb at the Cythera Classic Casino and head west but thought better of it. Taxi #65 of the Cythera Cab Company did not, of course, start to pull away, head west, and think better of it by itself; it had a driver (identified as one Fred) who did the actual starting to pull away, heading west, and thinking better of it. The driver almost released the brake and applied a foot (the right one, as it happened) to the accelerator; otherwise, taxi #65 would not have remained at the casino for all of Eternity (more or less).

Fred thought better of it because, as he was about to pull away and head west, a delivery truck from the Cythera Parcel Service – whose motto was "We Deliver – Eventually" – barreled down New York Street, weaving in and out of traffic, and nearly side-swiped taxi #65 as it passed by. Fred duly slammed on the brake (with his right foot, as it happened); otherwise, there would have cause for consternation, embarrassment, injury, damage, outrage, and harsh language.

"What the honk?" Fred muttered.

"What the honk?" the fare echoed.

As soon as it was safe to proceed, Fred proceeded. He headed west on New York Street until he reached Locust Street where he turned left and proceeded south. As he approached the intersection of Locust Street and Main Street, he observed a most remarkable sight.

The most remarkable sight was a humanoid figure, approximately five feet tall and thin as a rail. It had large bulging eyes, a nub of a nose, and a slit of a mouth set in a narrow face but no detectable ears. It wore a gray coverall and a black pouch around its waist. But the most remarkable part of this most remarkable sight was the bluish tinge of its skin. *[Author's note: the Reader will undoubtedly find this description rather fantastic and hard to believe. The Author is in full accord. But Fred, the driver of taxi #65 of the Cythera Cab Company, has sworn (although not on a stack of Bibles) that that was what he saw. No one, however, has stepped forward to corroborate his story.]*

What happened next was most remarkable as well.

When Fred spotted the most remarkable sight, his first immediate thought was, "what the honk is that honker doing in the middle of the street?" His second immediate thought was, "holy poo, he's right in my path, I've got to veer around him."

Taxi #65 of the Cythera Cab Company veered to the left. Taxi #65 of the Cythera Cab Company did not, of course, veer by itself; it had a driver (identified as one Fred) who did the actual veering. *[Author's note: this veering falls into the category of instinctual driving. That is to say, a driver will do the first thing which pops into his head. Quite often, instinctual driving is as unsettling as deliberate driving, and the Reader is advised against it if at all possible.]* The driver also pressed the brake (with the right foot, as it happened); otherwise, taxi #65 most likely would have obliterated the most remarkable sight and made the front page of the Cythera *Clarion-News*.

As Fred was veering to the left, he saw another most remarkable sight. The thin, blue humanoid figure suddenly disappeared and was replaced by a red squirrel which scampered toward the nearest tree. This further most remarkable sight caused him to veer to the left even further with unsettling consequences.

First, he sideswiped the "lemon car." The "lemon car" was a light-weight vehicle, and it proceeded to spin around and around and around until it slammed into a handy telephone pole and came to rest with one end (it matters not which one) up in the air. The driver of the "lemon car" duly screamed his head off, but no one was listening or cared. When Fred saw that he was going to sideswipe the "lemon car," send it spinning around and around and around, slam it into a handy telephone pole, and come to rest with one end (it matters not which one) up into the air, he instinctively veered to the right whereupon he sideswiped the "Pepto-Bismol" car. The "Pepto-Bismol" car was a medium-weight vehicle, and it proceeded to tip over and roll and roll and roll until it slammed into a handy light pole and came to a rest upside down. The driver of the "Pepto-Bismol" car duly screamed his head off, but no one was listening or cared. When Fred saw that he was going to sideswipe the "Pepto-Bismol" car, tip it over, send it rolling and rolling and rolling, slam into a handy light pole, and come to a rest upside down, he instinctively veered to the left again whereupon he sideswiped the Cythera Parcel Service delivery truck (whose motto is "We Deliver – Eventually"). The Cythera Parcel Service delivery truck was a heavy-weight vehicle and refused to move anywhere. The driver, however, duly screamed his head off, but no one was listening or cared.

"Hey-y-y, that was *fun!*" Fred's fare gushed. "Let's do it again!"

"Yeah, right. Oh, man, I feel funny all over." He reached for his radio. "65 to dispatch."

"Dispatch here. Go ahead, 65."

"You'll never guess what I just did, Uncle Gordy." Fred proceeded to tell Uncle Gordy what he just did and why. "I feel funny all over."

"Wait'll the cops show up, buster. You'll feel even funnier. I'm callin' 'em now."

You're honked now, poohead!

After he had called the cops, Uncle Gordy took a long pull from the pint of Jack Daniels and a long drag from the Marlboro, belched prodigiously, farted prodigiously, and scratched his privates prodigiously (not necessarily in that order). As soon as the amenities were taken care of, he chuckled over Fred's dilemma and nodded off.

In a matter of minutes (a record), Cythera's finest – also lovingly referred to as the "Keystone Kops," thanks to the reporting of one Harriet Methune Beiderbeck, star reporter (in her humble estimation) for the Cythera *Clarion-News*, who had won several awards (which, in her humble estimation, she deserved) for her reporting – arrived at the scene. The scene was full of gawking motorists and pedestrians, and the police officers had to play "dodge-'em" endlessly. The officers – who, as it happened, were the same two officers who not so long ago had no idea where they were or what they were doing there or why they were standing in the middle of the street – surveyed the scene, shook their heads in disbelief, and began asking the gawking motorists and pedestrians pertinent and impertinent questions. All who they asked pertinent and impertinent questions provided pertinent and impertinent answers. Finally, they asked Fred, the driver of taxi #65 of the Cythera Cab Company, the same pertinent and impertinent questions.

Fred proceeded to describe the most remarkable sight, and what he just did and why. The officers looked at him, then at each other, then back at him in disbelief. They proceeded to charge him with reckless driving, assault with a deadly weapon, conspiracy to commit assault with a deadly weapon, failing to yield the-right- of-way, two counts of failing to make a proper left turn, one count of failing to make a proper right turn, and, for good measure, driving under the influence. They handcuffed him, shoved him into their squad car, and hauled him off to police headquarters (amid a round of jeers, catcalls, and lewd suggestions from the gawking motorists and pedestrians).

For some unfathomable reason, the police officers, a.k.a. the "Keystone Kops," chose not to ask taxi #65 of the Cythera Cab Company any pertinent and impertinent questions – not that it would have done them any good as taxi #65 had no pertinent and impertinent answers to give. It remained where it was until someone told it where to go (even by itself).

Needless to say, Fred did not gain any more fares that day.

POSTSCRIPT

(because the Author does not like loose ends)

Fred is currently undergoing treatment at Cythera Mental Health Center.

Uncle Gordy retired from the Cythera Cab Company and now spends his days taking long pulls from pints of Jack Daniels and long drags from Marlboros, belches endlessly, farts endlessly, and scratches his privates endlessly (not necessarily in that order). And, when the amenities have been taken care of, he nods off for a long while.

Taxi #65 of the Cythera Cab Company retired as well. Taxi #65 of the Cythera Cab Company did not, of course, retire by itself; it had a tow truck which did the actual retiring – to a junk yard.

Chuck-a-luck-make-a-buck saved enough money to buy the Cythera Cab Company and has since turned the company into a reputable business (more or less).

Harriet Methune Beiderbeck, star reporter (in her humble estimation) for the Cythera *Clarion-News*, who has received several awards (which, in her humble estimation, she deserved) for her reporting, turned in her copy to her publisher, the aforementioned Michael John McNamara, who then edited it extensively and redacted the last part.

Maxwell and Harriet Methune Beiderbeck became the proud parents (more or less) of a bouncing baby girl. They did not, however, name it "Maxine." What they did name it is too horrible to mention.

Merfelman and Mrs. Winkleman finally tied the knot, and they are expecting sextuplets.

June East was arrested for soliciting, spent a year in jail (where she underwent a religious conversion), and can now be seen wearing a Salvation Army uniform as a Captain.

Ichabod still works at the Cythera *Clarion-News* despite all of the *ca-raziness* he sees daily.

Tranh still works at McGillicuddy's, and nothing more can be said.

[Author's note: for the insatiably curious Reader, it should be mentioned – needlessly and pointlessly, of course – that the Visitor, upon returning home, was charged with gross incompetence, falsifying an official document, and misusing government property. He has since been re-assigned to the street-sweeping division of the Sanitation Department.]

THE END

(until the next thrilling episode)

Tale the Second

"If elected, I promise…"

The Author wishes the Reader to know
that he had no personal knowledge
of the events in this narrative
but had to rely on second-hand information
given him by usually reliable sources.
All errors of fact should be assessed to the sources,
and the Author should be held blameless.

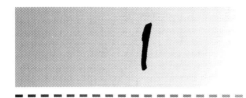

1

08:01 am
(on a warm day in late Spring)

The City Hall of Cythera squatted pretentiously at the intersection of Island Avenue and Downer Street on the south end of the island in the Wolf River, which divides the City in two. It was a colossal stone monument whose architecture imitated that of the government buildings in Washington, D.C. (whose architecture hailed back to the Late Roman period, when pretentiousness was all the rage on a grand scale for the purpose of impressing locals and foreigners alike with the importance of the City and its place in the cosmic scheme of things); and, if the Cythera City Fathers had had access to large quantities of marble rather than stone (of which there had been a large quantity), they would have given the Romans a run for their money (more or less).

The Hall – as it was affectionately called by the locals – thus affected a long, wide staircase rising to an equally wide portico upon which stood the central structure and the imposing row of columns with equally imposing cornices which stretched from one end of the portico to the other and held up the overhanging roof of the building. Behind the columns, the entrance to the Hall was a massive, yawning gap in the façade; above it had been inscribed a Latin phrase which completed the pretentiousness of the whole but which, in the present day, was quite incomprehensible (even to one who might be fluent in the language – and those in Cythera could be counted on one hand).

Cythera, in its early days, was actually two villages, East Cythera and West Cythera, the Wolf River dividing them as Nature had done in so many other places on Earth. The citizens of the separated villages existed in friendly rivalry, except when trade was involved; then, it was dog-eat-dog, and let the buyer beware. As both villages grew, geographically and demographically, and prospered, economically and pretentiously (more or less), the Powers-That-Be on both sides of the river began to think in terms of amalgamation; they believed that amalgamation would accelerate geography and demography, economy and pretentiousness *ad infinitum* and so put Cythera on the map of the world in a major way. And so it came to pass, as the Powers-That-Be formulated a political structure to govern both sides equally and *in toto*. This occurred shortly before the outbreak of the American Civil War – and not a moment too soon, in the humble opinion of the more progressive members of the City.

At once, the question arose: where to situate the seat of city government? If it were situated on one side of the river or the other, the side without a city hall would cry "foul" and "bias" and "hypocrisy" and other, less pleasant epithets which came to mind. The Powers-That-Be pondered once again, but wisdom eluded them, and they saw their fondest dream of pretentiousness evaporating like dew before the Sun. "You dolts!" (or words to that effect) cried the more progressive members of the City. "Why not situate the damned thing (or words to that effect) on the island that separates the City. Neither side could claim foulness or bias or hypocrisy or other, less pleasant epithets. City Hall would be on neutral turf (or words to the effect)."

And so it came to pass. The stone monument to pretentiousness was quickly erected, and the newly elected/appointed officials of the City of Cythera immediately occupied their pretentious offices with pretentious titles on the pretentious doors. (The more progressive members of the City, having done their civic duty, retired from the field and pondered other matters.)

The citizens of Cythera, through a popular referendum, had chosen to be governed by the mayor-commissioner form of government, having been convinced by the Powers-That-Be that this form was the most efficient one in terms of getting things done (or words to that effect). The more progressive members of the City snorted in derision but said nothing; they waited for the proper moment to say "we told you so" (or words to that effect). Both the mayor and commissioners were elected to four-year terms and held court (so to speak) once a week in a large central (and very pretentious) chamber to which everyone was invited to witness the exercise of democracy being played out on a grand (and pretentious) style. Seven commissioners there were, each of which had charge over a specific facet of city government and none of which had any practical experience in the inner workings of those facets; they were simply administrators who relied upon their underlings to manage the affairs of the City while they delivered pretentious public pronouncements and made pretentious public appearances to anyone who cared about such things.

The Office of the Mayor, which, naturally, was the most pretentious of all, was located, naturally, on the top floor of City Hall where His Honor could survey his kingdom to his heart's content as befitted his position. He had a large staff to handle the duties of the Office of the Mayor and to afford him ample time to survey his kingdom to his heart's content as befitted his position.

The current Mayor of Cythera was one Delbert Orville Richmond Kildare, who was as pretentious as they came. The son of a former Mayor of Cythera, the younger Kildare had grown up in the firm belief that he would follow in his father's footsteps, and so he never bothered to learn any other skills than the art of oratory. And he was a past master of the art of oratory; his admirers (the few) claimed that he could charm a miser out of all of his worldly goods, i.e. he was silver-tongued. His detractors (the many), on the other hand, claimed he could melt ice with his power of speech, i.e. he was full of hot air. All agreed, however, that he was a Political Animal of the first water. And, true to his beliefs, he rose through the political ranks and became Mayor as his father had done before him.

At the moment, Mayor Delbert Orville Richmond Kildare was not enjoying the fruits of his labor. True, he now stood at the large pretentious window of his large pretentious office from which he could watch the Wolf River flowing gently down the stream, surveying his kingdom to his heart's content as befitted his position. But, in his kingdom which he was surveying to his heart's content as befitted his position, there stalked a menacing dragon, and this menacing dragon was threatening to put His Honor out of a job – an unthinkable thing to think about inasmuch as he had no other skills than the art of oratory. He had to slay this menacing dragon by any and all means available – or else. *[Author's note: there are, of course, no real dragons in Cythera. The Reader will forgive the Author if he wallows in a bit of metaphoric excess as a means of spicing up an otherwise dull narrative.]*

The fact of the matter was that it was an election year for Cythera, and the citizenry were expected to do their civic duty and elect/re-elect a Mayor, his Commissioners, and a host of lesser officials. His Honor, Delbert Orville Richmond Kildare, had been Mayor of Cythera for the past twelve years, and he was looking forward to another twelve years in office. This time, however, a menacing dragon stalked the kingdom, and he was very worried; the dragon was acquiring a large following amongst the citizenry and threatened to put him out of a job. Having had an easy time of it the previous three elections, he was hard put to come up with a suitable strategy by which to slay this dragon. *[Author's note: the Reader is advised that this remark is strictly a figure of speech and not an incitement to violence.]* He needed to be assured that he could continue to survey his kingdom to his heart's content as befitted his position.

Now he stepped away from the large pretentious window in the large pretentious office, strode purposefully to his large pretentious desk, and pressed the "send" button on his large pretentious office intercom.

"Ms. Tix," he said authoritatively (and pretentiously), "please come into my office at once!"

Exactly ten seconds later, the large pretentious door to the Mayor's large pretentious office swung open, and in sauntered the Dream Woman of many a wretched male. She was Ms. Apollonia Tix, the Mayor's executive secretary, and she might have walked out of Greek legend. She stood exactly six-feet-two-and-one-half-inches tall in her stocking feet; and, since she was not in the habit of walking around in public in her stocking feet (or any other kind of feet), the shoes she wore when walking around in public added another half-inch to her stature. She weighed exactly one-hundred-and-thirty-five pounds which she maintained studiously through a rigorous program of exercises (including walking around in public); she was *not* overweight, however, but exceedingly statuesque, and she carried herself in a regal fashion as did the Greek goddesses of old. The other most striking features she possessed were a headful of long, flowing jet-black hair reaching down to her waist and a pair of gray eyes which hypnotized many a wretched male.

Ms. Apollonia Tix, the Dream Woman of many a wretched male, sauntered regally toward the Mayor's large pretentious desk, looked regally down upon His Honor from her lofty height, and smiled a Mona Lisa smile.

"You called, Mr. Mayor?" she asked regally.

"Indeed, I did, Ms. Tix. I want you to call Old Snake Eyes – uh, I mean, Chief Oglesby – and have him meet me here in" – he glanced at his large pretentious watch – "oh, say, half an hour. Tell him it's extremely urgent."

Ms. Tix regally produced a pen and notepad from a pocket in her slacks and regally made a notation. She regally gazed again at His Honor expectantly.

"Better get Commissioner Pisspot – uh, Philpott – in here as well."

Ms. Tix regally made another notation and regally gazed again expectantly. His Honor gazed back with a twinkle in his eye.

"And I'd like a back rub," he said lecherously.

Ms. Tix smiled another Mona Lisa smile.

Give me a moment while I hunt up some steel wool.

"I'll put that on my list of things to do, Mr. Mayor."

She regally pirouetted and sauntered out of the large pretentious office. Mayor Delbert Orville Richmond Kildare eyed her lecherously every step of the way. When the large pretentious door had closed behind her, he sighed a wretched-male sigh, then rose and returned to the large pretentious window where he resumed his surveying of his kingdom as befitted his position and evaluating his future (more or less).

 **11**

0835 hours
(precisely)

"Mr. Mayor," Ms. Tix announced regally over the intercom, "Chief Oglesby and Commissioner Philpott are here."

"Wonderful. Send them in."

The two individuals who entered the Mayor's large pretentious office and pulled up in front of his large pretentious desk couldn't have been more dissimilar if a Creator with a wicked sense of humor had planned it that way. And, given the randomness of human genetics, planning was out of the question; the said Creator with a wicked sense of humor merely rolled the dice and accepted whatever numbers turned up. In the present instance, the numbers were very odd.

Colonel Luther Ozymandias Oglesby, USMC (ret.), the Chief of Police of the City of Cythera, marched into the large pretentious office with military precision, came to a military halt, executed a military right-face, and finished with a military parade-rest – all the while murmuring the execution commands to himself in a military manner. One should not have been surprised if he had saluted His Honor in a military manner as one would to a superior officer. But he did not salute His Honor in a military fashion as one would to a superior officer, not because he was disinclined to do so, but because he believed the pipsqueak before him ought to have saluted *him* instead and because he had been annoyed by this interruption in his daily routine which was the harassing, arresting, detaining, and otherwise crimping the activities of as many of the scum, vermin, riff-raff, and animals which infected the streets of the City of Cythera as he could get his hands on (and he had

150

gotten his hands on quite a few). While he stood at parade-rest before His Honor, he smoldered in a military manner.

Chief Ozzie, as he was affectionately called by friend and foe alike (and there were more of the latter than there were of the former because of his harassing, arresting, detaining and otherwise crimping the activities of as many of the scum, vermin, riff-raff, and animals which infested the streets of the City of Cythera as he could get his hands on), was a hulk of a man. One could easily have fitted two Delbert Orville Richmond Kildares into him and still have room left over for a picnic basket full of food, drink, and utensils. *[Author's note: why anyone would want to do that is a mystery. In some circles, it smacked of sadism; in others, it smacked of buffoonery.]* He stood exactly six-feet-four-inches in his stocking feet; and, since he was not in the habit of walking around in public in his stocking feet (or any other kind of feet), the boots he wore when walking around in public added another inch to his stature. He weighed exactly two-hundred-and-forty-five pounds which he maintained studiously through a rigorous program of weight-lifting and quick-marches in public. The other most striking feature he possessed was a bald head – not shaved as was the fashion in military circles but absolutely hairless – which glistened in the light like a well-polished doorknob. It was rumored that he applied furniture polish to his head every day, but the rumor could not be confirmed.

This hulk of a man stood at military parade-rest and glared at the pipsqueak of a mayor with dark beady eyes and challenged him silently why His Honor was interrupting his daily routine of harassing, arresting, detaining, and otherwise crimping as many of the scum, vermin, riff-raff, and animals which infected the streets of the City of Cythera as he could get his hands on. His Honor winced before the dark beady eyes and looked away and toward the second visitor.

The second visitor, Phineas P. Philpott, Commissioner for Public Safety, was a sharp contrast to Chief Ozzie. Three of him could fit inside the Chief with enough room for the aforementioned picnic basket full of food, drink, and utensils. *[Author's note: why anyone would want to do that is another mystery, etc., etc..]* Commissioner Philpott stood exactly five feet in his stocking feet; and, since he was not in the habit of walking around in public in his stocking feet (or any other kind of feet), the shoes (with lifts) he wore when walking around in public added another three inches to his stature. He weighed exactly one-hundred-ten pounds soaking wet; and, since he was not in the habit of walking around in public soaking wet, he actually weighed only one-hundred-six pounds. The other striking feature he possessed was a carefully groomed, carefully waxed, and carefully shaped handle-bar moustache – which, as any number of casual (and not-so-casual) observers had remarked, made him look like Salvadore Dali in miniature.

Phineas P. Philpott, as Commissioner of Public Safety, was Chief Ozzie's nominal superior, although any number of casual (and not-so-casual) observers had remarked that it was clear to everyone – everyone, that is, except Phineas P. Philpott -- who the *real* boss was in the Commission. He stood before *his* nominal superior with an advanced case of the jitters. He hated to be called into the Office of the Mayor, because His Honor always wanted him to do something outrageous, like wearing loud ties or whistling Dixie.

Mayor Delbert Orville Richmond Kildare regarded his two visitors with all of the contempt he could muster (and that was considerable) in order to put them in their places. The practice worked well enough for the one, but not for the other, and so he stopped sneering at them and adopted an outwardly show of admiration (an act which he had inherited from his father and had perfected to a fine degree). Then he cleared his throat – which he did not only to gain attention but also to allay his own advanced case of the jitters, brought on by Chief Ozzie's continuous intense glare of annoyance with his dark beady eyes.

"Be seated, gentlemen," the Mayor said speciously.

Commissioner Philpott looked about for a chair his size, could find only large pretentious ones, and plopped down uncomfortably on one of them. Chief Ozzie continued to stand at military parade-rest.

"The reason I called you in here was to get an update on the security arrangements for the rally at eleven. You first, Commissioner."

Commissioner Pisspot – uh, Philpott – paled immediately and shrank several inches into the large pretentious chair. His breathing became erratic. Perspiration formed on his forehead, drizzled down the bridge of his nose, dripped off the tip of his nose, and splattered into his lap. He was evidently nervous, and he had good reason to be. His Honor had failed to explain the reason for this meeting beforehand, and he (the Commissioner) had failed to bring his notes on the matter at hand. He (the Commissioner) had therefore to rely on his memory which (1) he hated to do so and (2) he found unreliable most of the time – like now.

He (the Commissioner) glanced at Chief Ozzie for support. Chief Ozzie continued to stand at military parade-rest and stare at His Honor with dark beady eyes. He (the Commissioner) was on his own. He paled even further and shrank a few more inches into the large pretentious chair. More perspiration formed on his forehead, drizzled down the bridge of his nose, dripped off the tip of his nose, and splattered into his lap. In such situations, he (the Commissioner) had been known to speak in a whisper. He did so now.

"Well, Mr. Mayor," he whispered so low that His Honor had to strain to hear him, "everything that can be done has been done. I've ordered extra police officers to be stationed in the area of the rally – both uniformed and plain-clothes, especially the latter. I've also got a fire-department unit standing by with hoses in case things get out of hand. And I've instructed Chief Ozzie – uh, I mean Chief Oglesby – to employ any extraordinary measures he may deem necessary."

Commissioner Philpott stopped whispering then, having run out of things to say from memory and wishing he had his notes with him. He also stopped paling and shrinking into the large pretentious chair. Perspiration also stopped forming on his forehead, drizzling down the bridge of his nose, dripping off the tip of his nose, and splattering into his lap.

His Honor smiled insincerely.

"Thank you, Phineas. Well spoken." He turned to Chief Ozzie, who continued to stand at military parade-rest and stare at him with dark beady eyes. "What do you have to add, Chief?"

A big man generally had big lungs and therefore a big voice. Since Chief Ozzie was a hulk of a man, it stood to reason that he had a hulk of a voice. He did have one but elected not to use it on most occasions (more or less), because (1) it was deafening and tended to cause would-be listeners to run for cover, (2) its vibrations rattled windows and shook rooms, and (3) it hurt his own ears. Instead, on occasion, he cultivated a soft-spoken tone of voice which sounded almost feminine to the listener and raised certain suspicions in the said listener. Not that he cared how anyone reacted – because he was a hulk of a man, no one dared to find fault with the way he talked. Even to a pipsqueak like Delbert Orville Richmond Kildare, he spoke in a soft and feminine voice.

"The Commissioner has indeed given me extraordinary authority," he said softly and effeminately, "and I have implemented the following measures." He held up one finger (it matters not which one). "One, I have a SWAT team on stand-by alert, ready to take action if any scum, vermin, riff-raff, and animals should attempt to disrupt the rally." He held up a second finger (it matters not which one). "Two, I've positioned snipers on the rooftops of the nearby buildings in case the scum, vermin, riff-raff, and animals are armed." He held up a third finger (it matters not which one). "Three, I've ordered both of our gun-ship helicopters to monitor the area for signs of any scum, vermin, riff-raff, and animals from an hour before and an hour after the rally." He held up a fourth finger (it matters not which one). "And, four, I've requested the county sheriff's office and the district office of the state police to lend assistance in case the scum, vermin, riff-raff, and animals *really* get out of hand."

Chief Ozzie stopped talking in a soft and effeminate voice but continued to glare at His Honor with dark beady eyes.

"Well," His Honor said oily, "it appears that you gentlemen have the situation well in hand. There is one concern I have, however, and that is the tactics used by my political rival to besmirch my good name. Chief, have you been able to neutralize them?"

Somehow, Chief Ozzie managed to glare even more fiercely at His Honor with dark beady eyes. If looks could kill, then Delbert Orville Richmond Kildare should have been instantly disintegrated; moreover, part of the large pretentious office behind him should have disappeared, leaving a large gaping hole in the upper floor of City Hall.

It was a well-known fact throughout the City of Cythera that Colonel Luther Ozymandias Oglesby, USMC (ret.), had a personal grudge against His Honor's political rival and that therefore any spoken reference to said political rival was sufficient to trigger an apoplectic fit in the current Chief of Police of the City of Cythera.

In the first place, said political rival, one Thomas Albert Russell, had been the leader of the most notorious collection of scum, vermin, riff-raff, and animals ever to infect the streets of the City of Cythera. All efforts by him (Chief Ozzie) to put Mr. Thomas Albert Russell – known affectionately by friend and foe alike (of which there were many of the former and few of the latter) as "Russell the Rat" – behind bars where he belonged had failed utterly. The Commandos, the aforementioned most notorious collection of scum, vermin, riff-raff, and animals ever to infect the streets of the City of Cythera, had eluded the police at every turn and even managed to humiliate them on a regular basis – thus earning them the most distasteful epithet of "the Keystone Kops." This latter fact especially stuck in Chief Ozzie's craw, and he was continuously frustrated by the failure to put Mr. Thomas Albert Russell behind bars where he belonged.

In the second place, the aforementioned Thomas Albert Russell, a.k.a. "Russell the Rat," had during his non-illustrious college days managed to humiliate Chief Ozzie's son, Manfred Oglesby, during the latter's non-illustrious college days. Chief Ozzie was of the considered opinion that only *he* was allowed to humiliate his son (which he had done on a daily basis) and that anyone who dared to usurp his parental prerogatives was, *ipso facto*, scum, vermin, riff-raff, and an animal and ought to be immediately put behind bars where he belonged.

Now his tone of voice became noticeably less soft and feminine as he formulated his reply to His Honor.

"I have nothing new to report, Mr. Mayor," he grumbled.

"Nothing new? Nothing new? Russell the Rat has been running loose in this town for years. Now, he has the effrontery to challenge me for the Mayor's Office when he should really be put behind bars where he belongs. And you say you have 'nothing new' to report?"

"Yes, sir," Chief Ozzie grumbled. "Nothing new."

"Well, *honk!* Tell me *why* you have 'nothing new' to report."

"I'd've put the honker behind bars where he belongs long ago, if it weren't for his Number One, one Donald A. Brooke III."

"Where does he fit in?"

"He's the son of Donald A. Brooke, Jr., an old Marine buddy of mine. We both served in the Gulf War. 'Junior' knew military tactics inside and out; if anyone could out-think the Enemy, it was him. We would've won that war if the top brass had followed his advice.

"Somewhere along the line, he decided that what we were doing there was the wrong thing and we should get out. The brass went ballistic and re-assigned him to a desk job collecting statistics. He retired shortly afterward and joined the anti-war crowd. I'd say he taught his kid some of what he knew about military tactics, because the kid has been running circles around my boys for years. It's been like trying to catch the wind."

"I see," His Honor said unseeingly. "Well, you should re-double your efforts. I want to see Russell the Rat put behind bars where he belongs before the election is held. I'll be a shoo-in then."

"Yes, sir," Chief Ozzie grumbled.

"That's all, gentlemen. Carry on."

Commissioner Phineas P. Philpott instantly hopped off the large pretentious chair, made a dash for the large pretentious door, and exited the large pretentious office in the blink of an eye. [Author's note: the Reader will excuse the use of such a trite expression. But, the fact of the matter is that Commissioner Piss – uh, Philpott – was quicker on his feet than most people, and it was rumored that he could outrun a cat. The Author has interviewed several cats in order to verify this rumor, and all of them confirm the fact.] Chief Ozzie immediately came to attention, executed a military right-face, and marched toward the large pretentious door in a military manner, all the while murmuring the execution commands to himself in a military manner.

When the pair had departed, His Honor, Mayor Delbert Orville Richmond Kildare, returned to the large pretentious window and resumed surveying his kingdom as befitted his position and evaluating his future (more or less).

08.42.42.08 am
(maybe)

He glides through the large pretentious office door as if his feet were on rollers. (They weren't.)

He flashes a winning smile, revealing a perfect set of teeth which appear as if they were carved from ivory. (They weren't.)

He surveys the Office of the Mayor of the City of Cythera with deep-blue eyes which sparkle as if they reflect the firmament. (They don't.)

He stands exactly six-feet-four-inches tall in his stocking feet. And, since he is not in the habit of walking around in public in his stocking feet (or any other kind of feet), his Gucci shoes add another half-inch to his stature. He weighs exactly two-hundred-and-ten pounds which he studiously maintains by a rigorous program of exercises (including walking around in public).

Underneath his Brooks Brothers tailored, blue-and-yellow-pinstriped suit, his muscles ripple as if they have a life of their own. (They haven't.)

His skin is tanned from head to toe and might make George Hamilton green with envy. (It won't.)

His chestnut-colored hair is neatly barbered and coifed – not a hair out of place – and seems to be naturally curly. (It isn't.)

He comes across as the epitome of masculine pulchritude, a.k.a. God's gift to women. *[Author's note: the Author wishes to apologize to any Reader who does not believe in God for employing such a trite expression. It was the only one which seemed to fit the occasion. The Reader is free to substitute his/her own, more suitable trite expression.]*

This epitome holds until he opens his mouth and speaks. Then the illusion vanishes on the instant.

His name was Anthony Algernon Armstrong, and he was the Mayor's speech writer. When Ms. Apollonia Tix, the Dream Woman of many a wretched male, first laid eyes on him, she was instantly smitten and hoped to lay hands on him. He was one of the few men she had ever known to whom she could look up – literally – and dreamed of a happy life with him. Then he opened his mouth and spoke, and the illusion – and her dream – vanished on the instant.

Triple-A (for that was what he wished to be called) glided over to Ms. Tix's desk and flashed his winning smile while his eyes sparkled. Then he opened his mouth and spoke.

"Mith Tikth, would you pleathe announthe me to Hith Honor?"

"Certainly, Mr. A." She thumbed the intercom on and said regally: "Mr. Mayor, your speech writer is here."

"What the hell does he want so early in the morning? Oh, never mind. Send him in. And you come too. I need a neck rub."

Yes, sir. As soon as I find my hangman's noose.

Triple-A glided into the Mayor's large pretentious office and came to a rocking halt in front of the large pretentious desk. His Honor looked up at him with fish eyes and waited expectantly for him to open his mouth and speak. Triple-A chose not to open his mouth and speak first but allowed His Honor that honor. His Honor sighed in resignation.

"So, Triple-A, what's so urgent that it couldn't wait until, say, after lunch?"

"After lunch would've been too late, Del. I've got your thpeech for the eleven o'clock pep rally, and we need to go over it in order to work out the bugth."

"OK, let's have it. And don't call me 'Del'."

Triple-A reached into the inner pocket of his Brooks Brothers suit coat and produced two neatly-folded sheets of paper (length-wise, of course) and handed them over. His Honor unneatly unfolded the sheets and began to read them. With each passing second (more or less), his incredulity grew until it threatened to knock him to the floor. The floor was spared that indignity at the last moment, because His Honor stopped reading the sheets and started to wave them about.

"This *sucks!*" His Honor yelped ungraciously. "No one talks like this – not in this day and age! You would've made me sound like a nineteenth-century orator, full of flowery phrases, pious platitudes, and pathetic passion. Today's crowds would laugh me off the stage after the first paragraph. Tell me you're pulling my leg, Triple-A!"

Triple-A regarded His Honor with wounded innocence. A tear seemed to form in one of his ice-blue eyes. Or was it just a trick of the light?

"I am not pulling anyone'th leg, Delbert. You of all people thould know that. I'm deliberately making you thound like a nineteenth-thentury orator, becauthe the oppothithon ith making you look like a buffoon at betht and a wonk at wortht."

"I know what Russell the Rat is doing. But, couldn't you just make me out as, oh, say, an 'elder statesman" without all the florid prose?"

"Well, let'th thit down and work the thpeech over, thentith by thentith."

His Honor thumbed on the intercom.

"Ms, Tix, hold my calls for the next half hour, will you?"

"Certainly, sir."

"And do come in for just a minute. I could use a hug."

I'll call the City Zoo and have them send their gorilla over.

"Now, Triple-A, about this opening line. What am I supposed to make of 'Friends, citizens, Cytherans, lend me your ears'?"

ten minutes to nine
(for the benefit of the less precise clock-watchers)

Adjacent to a residential neighborhood in northwest Cythera once stood a bakery, the one positive element in an industrialized area. Why the owner had seen fit to site the bakery there might have made for an interesting story; but, no one had bothered to research the motive behind the siting. Be that as it may, when the wind was just right – and it was just right at least three days a week – the nearby residents woke up to the delicious aroma of freshly-baked bread. This was a life experience that no amount of prose or poetry could adequately describe. One had to be there to appreciate the full flavor of the experience.

Three-quarters of a block east of the former bakery – at 543 Plum Street – stood a typical two-story, wooden A-frame with an unattached garage and a small yard with one tree and some shrubbery. It was one of many such houses in the neighborhood with an enclosed porch (*screen-enclosed*, if you please). Said enclosed porch was an excellent place to relax and watch the neighborhood go through its daily routine – and to fill one's lungs with the delicious aroma of freshly-baked bread.

At the time of this narrative, this typical two-story, wooden A-frame with an unattached garage and a small yard with one tree and some shrubbery was the residence of one Thomas Albert Russell – affectionately called by friend and foe alike (many of the former and few of the latter) "Russell the Rat" – former leader of the Commandos, the most notorious collection of scum, vermin, riff-raff, and animals which had infected the streets of the City of Cythera and, currently, a candidate for the Office of the Mayor of Cythera.

After he had graduated from Cythera College (just barely), Tommy

Russell had held a number of jobs in an attempt to find something he liked. He had been a hotel clerk, a warehouseman, a taxi driver, and a liquor deliveryman (among other things), but none of these occupations thrilled him to the point of a life-long avocation. Always in the back of his mind, however, he remembered fondly the leadership qualities which had come to the fore during his college days; and the notion grew ever so slowly but steadily that he should seek out a career in politics and stand for office at the earliest opportunity. He started out as a precinct worker, then ran for the position of Commissioner (it matters not which one). He lost that election but ran again in the next one against an incumbent who had been involved in a kick-back scheme and defeated him handily. Two electoral cycles later, he set his sights on the Mayor's Office after listening to the growing criticism of the present office-holder who was looked upon as a milquetoast and deciding that the City of Cythera was ripe for a change in leadership.

It has often been said that, behind every successful man, there stood a strong-willed woman. In Tommy Russell's case, this could not be truer said. Behind him, next to him, and sometimes in front of him, stood one Amber Pembroke, a fellow alumnus of Cythera College, a fellow radical, and a fellow political animal. Amber had cut her political eye-teeth working alongside of her twin brother, Ambrose – a.k.a. Mohammed al-Sharif – during his stint with Operation PUSH, and she had continued to be a force to be reckoned with during the heady days of anti-war activism. Now, she was encouraging Tommy in his budding political career every step of the way. *[Author's note: it was rumored that she actually got behind him and* pushed *him every step of the way. But no one ever took into account Tommy's former experience as the leader of the Commandos, the most notorious collection of scum, vermin, riff-raff, and animals which infected the streets of the City of Cythera as an element in his determination to be the next Mayor of Cythera.]*

As the present narrative occurred on a Saturday morning, one might have expected to see (figuratively, of course) Mr. and Mrs. Thomas A. Russell sleeping in, which they had done on many Saturdays before. They did not have to jump out of bed, tend to their oblations, clean themselves up, eat a skimpy breakfast, and dash off to their respective jobs (he a hotel clerk, she the director of services for a local homeless shelter). They could, instead, wake up slowly and enjoy each other's company which they had done on many Saturday mornings. But that was before Tommy had thrown in his hat (figuratively, of course) as candidate for Mayor of the City of Cythera.

Now, Saturday mornings were devoted to mapping out campaign strategy. Actually, mapping out campaign strategy occurred every day as one exigency after another reared its ugly head and plans had to be altered, postponed, or cancelled altogether. But, on Saturdays, Tommy's campaign staff came to 543 Plum Street to update each other on the progress (if any) of their particular areas of endeavor on Tommy's behalf.

On this particular Saturday morning, however, said campaign staff was due to arrive at 543 Plum Street for the express purpose to go over the last-minute details of a political rally scheduled for 10:30 that morning (in counterpoint to a similar political rally on behalf of the current Mayor of the City of Cythera, one Delbert Orville Richmond Kildare, scheduled for 11:00 that morning). Therefore, Mr. and Mrs. Thomas A. Russell were up and about at what both of them considered to be an ungodly hour on a Saturday morning in preparation for the weekly staff meeting. [*Author's note: since Amber Russell-Pembroke was a militant agnostic, she was not inclined to use such phrases as "ungodly hour." The phrase had actually been uttered by Tommy, who was often given to hyperbole; and, whereas Amber adored him so much, she kept her silence when he used such phrases as "ungodly hour." She did, however, bestow upon him a disapproving frown.*]

For some unfathomable reason, the staff was late this morning, and Candidate Russell intended to inquire about this lapse of punctuality. The meeting was scheduled for 8:45, and it was now 8:50. He looked at his watch for the umpteenth time and fumed (figuratively, of course).

What's keeping those honkers? he fumed figuratively. *We've got to get this show on the road.*

He looked at his wife beseechingly. She merely shrugged her best I-don't-know shrug.

At that moment, as if on cue, the doorbell rang.

Ding-dong! said the doorbell engagingly. *Ding-dong!*

The ears of Mr. and Mrs. Russell perked up (figuratively, of course).

Ding-dong! said the doorbell energetically. *Ding –*

The breath of Mr. and Mrs. Russell caught in their throats (figuratively, of course).

Two seconds passed.

-- *dong!* said the doorbell earnestly.

"Donny's here," Tommy declared needlessly.

"Doesn't he ever get tired of announcing himself that way?" Amber growled needlessly.

"Nope. He's used that code since we were both in the Commandos." He started toward the front door. "Old habits die hard," he concluded needlessly.

Amber *humph*ed needlessly.

If anything, Donny Brooke (he of the unfortunate appellation) had changed very little from his appearance in a previous narrative. He still was a bleached blond hulk who towered over everybody. He still resembled an extra from an old Errol Flynn movie, and the casual observer would not have been surprised to see him wearing an eyepatch, a bandana, and seven-league boots and clenching a knife between his teeth. He still wore a gold-plated earring in one earlobe. He still bent his head low in the manner of a bull about to charge. And he still stared at one with pale blue eyes with uncomfortable intensity.

Where Donny Brooke differed from his appearance in a previous narrative was a sop to maturity. He no long wore long, stringy hair which cascaded haphazardly over his shoulders but now combed and brushed it in order to give it more body and luster and therefore a more pleasing appearance. And he no longer wore a thick moustache and beard which covered half his face but now trimmed and combed them in order to give them more luster and body and therefore a more pleasing appearance. In short, Donald A. Brooke III looked more like a businessman instead of a member of a street gang.

He was still roguish (as the Reader will soon learn) and given to acts of derring-do.

"You're late," Tommy grumbled needlessly.

"I was held up in traffic, fearless leader," Donny responded, grinning a wicked grin.

"Yeah? I've seen you drive, old buddy. You make race-car drivers look like kiddy-car pedalers in comparison."

"Nevertheless –"

"Never the mind. Amber is anxious to get this show on the road."

"As are we all."

Tommy's "campaign headquarters" was the dining room table, a commodious (if heavy) piece of mahogany furniture which took up most of the room's space. Six matching (equally heavy) chairs ringed the table. Seldom did any of these pieces see much use, since Tommy and Amber were accustomed to taking their meals in the kitchen at a small metal-and-vinyl table with two small matching metal-and-vinyl chairs. Mr. and Mrs. Russell did not use the dining room for entertaining guests either, because they (1) had few close friends, (2) their respective families had disavowed them for marrying beneath themselves, (3) none of the few friends they had cared to venture into the neighborhood, (4) the neighbors were apt to call the police if they spotted more than one vehicle parked in front of the house on the grounds that a large number of people at that address had to be up to no good, and (5) Mr. and Mrs. Russell liked their privacy. Hence, those who did come and go with the greatest frequency were the postman, the utility-meter reader, and the ubiquitous pair of Jehovah's Witnesses.

Until Tommy had thrown his hat into the ring (figuratively, of course). Now, each Saturday morning, Mr. and Mrs. Russell "entertained" three to four "guests" – the exact number depending upon whether or not one certain individual could screw up enough courage to enter the neighborhood – who, as it happened, were the "brain trust" (figurative, of course) of Tommy's bid for the Office of Mayor of the City of Cythera.

The first of the "brain trust" to have arrived was Tommy's constant companion (before and after his marriage to Amber Pembroke, who thereafter assumed a state of high dudgeon which state she assumed whenever the occasion warranted) since elementary school and his Number One in the Commandos, the most notorious of the scum, vermin, riff-raff, and animals which infected the streets of the City of Cythera; he continued to act as point-man, head of security, and intelligence gatherer for his "fearless leader," tasks he thoroughly enjoyed and hoped his father, Colonel Donald A. Brooke, Jr., USMC (ret.), would be proud of his accomplishments (not that he really needed his father's approval, but it was a plus).

Donny sauntered into the dining room, flashed Amber a huge lecherous grin, and gave her a light peck on the cheek. Amber in turn braced herself, gave Donny a polite smile, and pulled away as soon as he was through pecking. Donny plopped down on the chair at the foot of the table. *[Author's note: the "foot" of a table is not located at the ends of the "legs" of a table (if it were, then one would have had to refer to the "feet" of a table) but at the end of a table -- possessing a traditional set of chairs – which has a chair with no "arms." This "foot" is opposite the "head" of a table, the end of a table which has a chair with "arms" – the only chair with "arms" in a traditional set. The chair with "arms" is traditionally reserved for the head of the household, and the "foot" is given over to his spouse. This information has been thoughtfully provided to the Reader so that (s)he will not be confused on this point of table manners.]* Tommy took possession of the chair at the head of the table and relaxed. Amber, deprived of her rightful place at the foot of the table, took possession of the chair to Tommy's right and held herself stiffly. *[Author's note: traditionally, the chair at the right of the chair at the head of the table is reserved for one's special guest, not for one's spouse. Donny should have taken this chair instead; failing to do so showed poor table manners on his part.]*

Tommy was about to say something. But whether it was something of great pith and moment will never be known, because the doorbell rang again.

Ding – dong! said the doorbell enthusiastically. *Ding –*

Mr. and Mrs. Russell waited expectantly. Mr. Brooke grinned hugely. Three seconds passed.

-- dong! said the doorbell ebulliently.

"That'll be the Bookends," Donny declared thoughtfully.

"Brooke!" Amber declared exasperatedly. "Why did you give *everybody* a coded ring?"

"I'll tell you why as soon as everyone is here."

Tommy rose, went to the front door, opened it, and confronted the Bookends.

William and Wallace Nicholson, a.k.a. Willy and Wally, were identical twin brothers, and the number of people who could tell them apart could be counted on one hand. Two of those people were their parents, of course, who had an innate sense about such things but who also had a maddening sense of humor as they delighted in confusing the rest of humankind when it came to introducing their offspring.

Donny was a third person. He claimed he could tell them apart by the shape of their narrow noses. One of the Bookends – he wouldn't say which one in order to protect their privacy and/or their secret – had an indentation on his nose which was apparent only if one looked at the said nose at a particular angle. Ever the keen observer, Donny had spotted this difference upon his first encounter with them while on a foray to dream up support for Tommy. He instantly nicknamed them the "Bookends" but was the only person who ever referred to them in that manner.

Willy and Wally were tall and slender, and their clothes tended to hang loosely on their frames like tents. One of their narrow faces wore a perpetual mournful expression, while the other one wore a perpetual joyful one – emulating the ancient masks of Tragedy and Comedy. They had inherited their parents' maddening sense of humor by trading expressions periodically and thus confusing the rest of humankind even further. Despite this quirk, both were friendly and outgoing and could be trusted to lend support to a cause when they believed it was necessary.

And they believed that Tommy Russell needed their support, because the odds of his becoming Mayor of the City of Cythera were stacked against him. They knew, through their parents' connections, some Very Important Persons who could swing a considerable number of votes in Tommy's direction if they were asked to do so in the proper manner. These Very Important Persons – and Willy and Wally's parents – were part of a growing segment of the electorate who had become quite disgusted with the current Mayor's pretentiousness and wanted him out of office in the worst way – even if it meant electing somebody like Russell the Rat. Willy and Wally had volunteered to act as go-betweens for this disgusted segment of the electorate and the Russell campaign, but they had not bothered to inform the Russell campaign of their go-between-ness as the disgusted segment of the electorate wished to remain anonymous in case the pretentious Mayor won re-election.

Tommy blinked several times in confusion at the Bookends in a futile effort to tell them apart. In desperation (more or less), he said "Hi,

Willy!" to the left-hand brother who at this moment was wearing the mournful expression and "Hi, Wally!" to the right-hand brother who at this moment was wearing the joyful expression and hoped for the best.

Hope died aborning.

"I'm Willy," said the right-hand brother in a sepulchral tone of voice. "Hi, Tommy!"

"And I'm Wally," said the left-hand brother in a happy tone of voice. "Hi, Tommy!"

"Um, sorry, guys. C'mon in."

In the dining room, the Bookends greeted Amber and Donny cordially and took possession of the chairs to Donny's right.

"What kept you two?" Tommy inquired ungraciously. "Traffic?"

"We would have been here sooner," replied Willy (?).

"We would have been here sooner," echoed Wally (?).

"Except that we spotted Alice hiding behind a bush up at the corner of Highland –"

"—and Plum, and we had to talk her down in order to get her to come out of hiding."

Tommy furrowed his brow and looked off into the distance. He did not recall seeing Alice anywhere near the house.

"So, where is she?"

"Ah, well," replied Wally (?).

"Ah, well," echoed Willy (?).

"Since we did make it here safely, we're –"

"—sure that she'll be along any minute now."

At that moment, as if on cue, the doorbell rang once more.

"Ding – said the doorbell effervescently.

Mr. and Mrs. Russell waited expectantly. Mr. Brooke grinned hugely. The Bookends examined the ceiling with its elaborate pattern of cracks.

Four seconds passed.

—dong! said the doorbell excitedly.

"Alice," Donny declared needlessly.

"About time too," Amber declared exasperatedly.

Tommy rose, walked to the front door, opened it, and confronted the final member of the "brain trust."

Alice Monomoy was, to coin a phrase, a duck in a desert. That is to say, she no more belonged in the Russells' neighborhood than a cobra at a mongoose convention. She had been, and still was, a product of the southwestern quarter of Cythera, specifically that area which sported the largest houses with the largest garages and the largest yards with many trees and shrubs. Her family was Old Money, having lived in Cythera for seven generations; the Monomoys were not among the founders of Cythera, but they had been just one step behind and saw Opportunity all over the place. And they had wrung Opportunity for all it was worth (and it was worth plenty), amassing and losing and re-amassing a sizeable fortune.

Alice (whose uncle was on the faculty of Cythera College as a professor of economics) therefore did not have to work a day of her life. Daddy Monomoy gave each of his offspring a generous monthly allowance (with no strings attached), because (1) he could afford it; (2) he thought he could buy their love, and (3) he was an elitist of the first water. Alice took his money and secretly gave it to one charity or another. Meanwhile, she earned a living by owning and operating a local book store (specializing in literary works) and never talked about her family to anybody who didn't already know who she was (and those were few).

How she came to be involved in politics and, specifically, with the Russell campaign was an interesting story.

Some months before the mayoral campaign began, one Donald A. Brooke III happened to wander into the Cythera Book Shoppe looking for – of all things – a volume of French poetry. As he browsed the shelves, he ran into (quite literally) and knocked over the owner and operator who had been in the process of shelving some new acquisitions. Donald A. Brooke III (as the Reader knows) was a bleached-blond hulk who towered over everybody, but Alice Monomoy was a slightly-built young woman and therefore was susceptible to being knocked over whenever towering hulks – bleached-blond or otherwise – ran into her (whether or not they were looking for books of French poetry).

Alice soon found herself sprawled on the floor of her book store, looking up at a towering, bleached-blond hulk who looked down at her with great embarrassment. Then, remembering his manners, he offered his hand.

"*Pardonnez moi, mademoiselle,* [pardon me, miss]" he had said in a gentle tone. "*Je suis tres maladroit* [I'm very clumsy]."

Perhaps it was the French. Or perhaps it was the gentle tone of voice. Or perhaps it was the bleached-blond hulk-ness. Whatever it was, shock and discomfit gave way to – need we say it? – love at first sight. For his part, Donald A. Brooke III was indifferent to most women. *[Author's note: why this was so is a story for another time.]* But Alice was determined to snare him and began stalking him whenever she could. She could not have known that he was adept at losing anybody which was why she had to stalk him at great length.

Quite by accident, she learned that he was an integral part of the Russell campaign, and she took to wearing a "Vote for Russell" button. Then she volunteered to join the campaign, offering her business skills to pave the way. She had the least interest in politics and in Thomas A. Russell either as a candidate for political office or a human being, but she saw an opportunity to be near the man she loved. Donny took the pragmatic approach and accepted her for the money and the social connections she could provide.

Alice slipped by Tommy and made a bee-line for the dining room. *[Author's note: so far as anyone could determine, there were no bees in the Russell household which could make lines wherever they went. Alice would have had to make her own line.]* She plopped down on the only empty chair available which, by no mean co-incidence, was the chair to Donny's left. She smiled meaningfully at him. Donny examined the ceiling with its elaborate pattern of cracks. Tommy did not make a bee-line to his own chair; instead, he went as the crow flies and settled in smoothly. *[Author's note: so far as anyone could determine, there were no crows either in the Russell household, and Tommy could not fly.]*

"OK, troops" – he still used that trite expression as, apparently, it was the standard thing to say in these circumstances, i.e. doing battle against the forces of Evil and upholding the good name of Civilization – "let's get down to business. First, Donny, explain to everybody what the honk is with that doorbell code."

"Simply, fearless leader, that the word is out that Mayor Dork and Chief Ozzie are planning in infiltrate our organization with *agents provocateur.*" (A thrill coursed through Alice's body as she heard French coming out of his mouth.) "I've given specific codes to each of this group and to select members of our volunteer staff. If anybody rings your doorbell, and it's a standard ring, be forewarned that the caller may not be one of us."

"What if someone *knocks* on the door, Brooke?" Amber asked, playing devil's advocate.

"Same thing. I've instructed everyone to ring, not knock."

"Don't you just love all of this –"

"—intrigue? Right out of a spy novel!"

Both of the Bookends were temporarily wearing the Comedy mask. It would not last.

"You're so clever, Donny," Alice said in a husky, lust-filled voice, designed to send provocative signals and to raise certain hopes.

"All part of the service," Donny said in a steady neutral voice, designed to send non-provocative signals and to dash certain hopes. "There's more, fearless leader. I've also heard that some these *agents provocateur* will attempt to disrupt our rally this morning."

"Oh, man! Mayor Dork and Chief Ozzie aren't pulling any punches, are they?"

"The last resort of the incompetent, don't you know?"

"What can we do to prevent any disruptions?"

"Um, I hesitate to suggest a sure-fire way because there's a certain risk involved."

"And that is?"

"Calling on the Untouchables again."

"Oh, God, no!" Amber moaned. *[Author's note: the Reader must understand that "Oh, God, no!" was a reflex action on Amber's part due to her exposure to local habits. As a militant agnostic, she would not have willingly uttered such an expression.]* "That's 'Disaster City'!"

"I have to agree, and not just because I have to keep my wife happy."

"They got us out of a jam once before." *[Author's self-serving note: cf. a previous narrative for details.]* "Trouble is, I don't know if I can control them this time."

"Why not?"

"Well, Poohead seems to have gotten civilized lately, for some unfathomable reason. He's been taking baths on a regular basis. The others voted him out of the group because of it. I don't know who's in charge now. They're keeping a low profile."

"That's hard to do. I'll think about it. Let's move on to committee reports."

08:50
(approximately)

He strides through the door as if he owns the place. (He doesn't.)

He displays an authoritative expression on his face as if he were the most important person alive. (He isn't.)

He surveys his surroundings with a steely glint in his eyes as if he means to intimidate one and all. (He can't.)

He stands exactly five-feet-four-inches in his stocking feet – and since he is not in the habit of walking around in public in his stocking feet (or any other kind of feet), his Gucci wingtips add another half an inch to his stature – and weighs exactly two-hundred-fifty-five pounds. Underneath his off-the-rack, Sears-bought, blue-and-white pinstripe suit, rolls of fat ripple as if they have a life of their own. (They haven't.) His skin is flushed from hard exertion – walking from the pretentious elevator to the pretentious outer door of the Office of the Mayor of the City of Cythera – and would make George Hamilton highly bemused. His head is mostly hairless; the only trace of hirsuteness is a fuzzy ring of gray around the crown which seems to have been barbered that way. (It wasn't.)

His name was Spencer T. Augustus, and he was the Mayor's campaign manager. In fact, he had been the Mayor's campaign manager during all three previous bids in the mayoral election. It was rumored that he had been the campaign manager for the last bid in the mayoral election of the Mayor's father and that the elder Kildare had bequeathed "Augie" (for that was what he preferred to be called) to his son. Augie took the younger Kildare under his wing (so to speak) and guided him successfully through three campaigns. His Honor hoped that Augie would come through for him again.

"'Mornin', Ms. Tix," Augie said cheerfully. "Tell Himself that I've arrived."

Ms. Apollonia Tix, the Dream Woman of many a wretched male, regally flicked on the intercom.

"Sir, your campaign manager is here."

"Great. Send him in. And bring me a cup of coffee."

With or without rat poison, sir?

Augie opened the large pretentious door to the Mayor's large pretentious office and strode confidently in. Neither his stride nor his confidence lasted very long. At that particular moment, the carpeting decided to bunch up and present an obstacle to striding confidently. The campaign manager obliged by tripping and performing an exquisite belly flop on the floor.

"Well, *honk!*" he muttered and struggled to pick himself up.

He took two more steps. At that particular moment, one of the large pretentious chairs decided to shift its position to a point in his path. Augie obliged by barking his shin and staggering backwards.

"Well, *honk!*" he muttered and limped toward another large pretentious chair.

He lowered himself to a sitting position. At this particular moment, the large pretentious chair decided it had important business elsewhere and moved backwards six inches. Augie obliged by sitting on thin air and performing an exquisite one-point landing on the floor.

"Well, *honk!*" he muttered and struggled to pick himself up.

He made it to his hands and knees. At this particular moment, the large pretentious chair which had decided that it had important business elsewhere changed its mind, returned to its original position, and struck the campaign manager squarely on the buttocks. Augie obliged by pitching forward and banging his head on the Mayor's large pretentious desk.

"Well, *honk!*" he muttered and decided to stay right where he was.

"Honethtly, Augie," Triple-A admonished, "mutht you carry on tho?"

"Are you quite through?" His Honor admonished. "We have a speech to write."

"Well, *honk!*" Augie muttered. "I thought Triple-A had already written the honking thing."

"I don't like it. I want to make some changes. Take a look at it and see what you think."

Reluctantly, Triple-A handed his masterpiece to the campaign manager. The latter began reading; and the more he read, the more wide-eyed he became. When he had finished reading, he began to roll across the floor. He rolled and rolled and rolled and rolled all over the floor. And all the while, he laughed and laughed and laughed and laughed until he ran out of breath at which time he stopped rolling and laughing. When he had taken a new breath, he waved the speech at its writer.

"By damn, Triple-A! You've outdone yourself this time!"

"You mean, you like that poo, Augie?" His Honor queried.

"Oh, hell, no! I wouldn't give this speech even at a DAR meeting. Those old ladies would die from hyperglycemia."

"We were making changes to it when you arrived. Care to help?"

"If it'll do any good, yeah. What we really need here is less philosophy and more image-building. We need to make you dynamic."

"I hate dynamic. People expect great things from dynamic. I'd rather be just a man-in-the-street type."

Augie now pulled a pen out of his coat pocket and began crossing out word after word, phrase after phrase, sentence after sentence, and once a whole paragraph. Tears came to Triple-A's eyes. Smiles came to His Honor's eyes. Ideas came to Augie's brain and, in half an hour, he had written the Perfect Campaign Speech (more or less).

"Okay," he crowed triumphantly, "let's get this thing typed up. We'll be right back, Delbert."

Augie stood up and strode toward the large pretentious door, speech firmly in hand and Triple-A dejectedly in tow. Neither his stride nor his triumphalism lasted very long; for, at that moment, the carpet took umbrage at his attitude and decided to bunch up and present an obstacle to the striding and triumphant campaign manager. Augie duly tripped and performed an exquisite belly flop on the floor.

"Well, *honk!*" he muttered and struggled to pick himself up.

He took two more steps. One of the large pretentious chairs also took umbrage at his attitude and decided to shift its position into his path. Augie duly barked his shin and staggered backward.

"Well, *honk!*" he muttered and limped his way toward and through the large pretentious door.

Triple-A followed, shaking his head every step of the way. His Honor, Mayor Delbert Orville Richmond Kildare leaned back in his large pretentious chair and stared blankly at the large pretentious window.

VI

08:51:08 am
(except on Tommy's watch which, due to a
manufacturing defect, was one second behind)

Tommy asked for committee reports as was his usual practice as it gave him an opportunity to jump-start his brain, because he was still unused to the idea of waking up early on a Saturday morning and would not have done so if it weren't for the fact that he was running a political campaign and therefore needed to spend extra time in preparing speeches, making appointments with potential donors, holding press conferences, making speeches before potential voters, and getting everything in order lest the whole enterprise fall to pieces, although he would rather have spent the time snuggling up with Amber – except that she insisted on his concentrating on the campaign and assured him that there would be plenty of time after the election for some serious snuggling which promise he was definitely going to hold her to and the election could not come any time too soon, because (1) he wanted to win and (2) he wanted to snuggle, and so he asked for committee reports as was his usual practice.

Amber, Finance Committee: currently, two unpaid bills were outstanding – one from the print shop which printed the campaign flyers and one from a lawyer who was handling a libel suit against the Mayor's own campaign committee for calling one Thomas A. Russell a "thug" and a "hoodlum" because of his past associations (which he once was but was no more) – and the campaign's bank account held insufficient funds to cover both. Which one, Amber asked, should she pay first? The consensus was that they needed the flyers sooner than the lawyer's representation. If Tommy won the election, the lawyer would

176

be willing to wait indefinitely for his money if he knew what was good for him.

Segue to Alice, Donations Committee: (1) the local bankers' association was divided on the question of donating any money to either campaign as a group – two of the group had strong financial ties to the current Mayor – and so had tabled the motion (individuals were, of course, free to contribute up to the legal limit if they so desired); (2) the matriarch of one of the oldest families in Cythera had flatly refused to contribute "one single dime to anyone with an Irish name" (or words to that effect), because of some slight suffered by one of her ancestors at the hands of an immigrant from Dublin, even though he had not been a Russell; (3) the downtown merchants' association had voted to contribute an equal amount to both campaigns – hedging their bets, as it were – and the check was in the mail; and (4) a local judge declared that he would give the Russell campaign whatever amount of money it needed to "throw that self-serving, sniveling, sorry son-of-a-bitch, Mayor Dork, out of office and back on the streets where he belongs" (or words to that effect).

Willy (?), Propaganda Committee (his words): he opened up his briefcase, extracted a handful of flyers and passed them around. They were updated versions of previous publications and featured prominently on one side a color photo of Mr. and Mrs. Russell, one with a garbage-eating grin, the other with a demure smile. On the other side, Tommy's qualifications to be the next Mayor of Cythera, although it was plain to see that the statements were slight exaggerations which every politician learned to cultivate for the sake of wooing the voters. In the present instance, Thomas A. Russell was listed as a "Director of a youth group," a "campus leader at Cythera College," and a "community activist," referring to his stint as a Commissioner on the Cythera City Council. Willy (?) said gleefully that a number of youth groups, including some in the African-American and Hispanic communities, were "handing out flyers left and right, even as we speak" (or words to that effect).

Wally (?), Drone Committee (his words): he opened his briefcase, extracted a handful of posters, and passed them around. A photo of Tommy with the same garbage-eating grin was prominent. Above the photo were the words "VOTE FOR RUSSELL"; below the photo were the words "THE PEOPLE'S CHOICE." The photo was also an updated version of a previous one which had featured a grim-faced Tommy and which sorely need re-touching if he hoped to win over the voters. Not only were the aforementioned flyers "being handed out left and right" but the posters were "being plastered on every utility pole in Cythera and distributed to any merchant or homeowner willing to display them on their property, even as we speak" (or words to that effect).

Donny, Security Committee: a specially trained team of volunteers will roam through the crowd at the rally, keeping a sharp eye out for *agents provocateur* and reporting the presence of any such to the Head of Security. Also, said specially trained volunteers will take note of any illegal activities – ingesting controlled substances, soliciting for sex, disorderly conduct, excessive farting and belching in order to cause a public disturbance, etc., etc. – and exhort the perpetrators to cease and desist.

"What happens if you catch any perps?" Tommy asked guilelessly.

"Best you don't know, fearless leader," came the equally guileful reply. "Plausible deniability, and all that, don't you know?"

"Right. Anybody have anything to add?"

"I'd like to make an announcement," Amber piped up. "I was going to wait until after the rally. But, if there's going to be trouble, I might not get the chance."

"And what's that, sweet thing?"

Amber paused dramatically. Then:

"I'm pregnant."

The entire group gasped dramatically. Alice reached over and patted Amber's hand. The Bookends pursed their lips and nodded their heads in unison. Donny imitated a well-known Cheshire cat. Tommy imitated a well-known painting by Edvard Grieg.

"You're going to have my child?" Tommy asked witlessly.

"No, I'm going to have *Brooke's* child, honey," Amber answered artlessly. "Of course, I'm having your child. Who else have I been with?" She waggled a finger at him. "Don't answer that!"

"This is stupendous news, fearless leader!"

"You're telling me?"

"We can use this in the campaign."

"How so?" Amber asked suspiciously.

"As a married man, Tommy has a certain respectability attached to him. Now that he's going to be a *family* man, he's sure to get the female vote."

"Brooke, leave my child out of this! I don't want it involved in some vote-getting scheme."

"Me neither, Donny."

Donny threw up his hands in surrender.

"OK, suit yourself. I think you're missing a good bet."

"I'd like to have a baby," Alice said to Donny in a husky, lust-filled voice, designed to send him provocative signals and to raise certain hopes.

"Marvelous," Donny responded in a steady, neutral voice, designed to send her non-provocative signals and to dash certain hopes.

"If there's nothing else to discuss," Tommy declared, "we'll adjourn for now and reconvene at Weldon Park at a quarter after ten. Move out, troops!"

"Can we drop you –"

"—off someplace, Alice?"

Yes, at Donny's place. I'll prepare a surprise for him, one he'll never forget.

"Yes, at my place. I want to change into something more suitable for the rally." *Like sack-cloth and ashes.*

"What a man-eater!" Donny murmured as soon as Alice and the Bookends had departed. "I swear she'd've smothered me if we had been alone."

"She's got the hots for you all right, old buddy."

"You should go for it, Brooke. You need a girlfriend." Amber eyed him slyly. "Keep you out of trouble."

"I *was* going to fix him up with Solongo after we got together, sweet thing. Except – Solongo disappeared." Tommy stared off into the distance. "I wonder whatever happened to her."

"If you two are through planning my life for me, I'll be off. I want to check on a few things before the rally starts. *Au revoir, mes amis.*"

"Well, Mrs. Russell, shall we go over my speech once more?"

"We shall" – she smiled sweetly – "*Daddy.*"

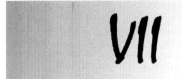 

VII

09:00 am
(unless the clock downtown
is badly in need of repairs)

As municipal parks went, McKleckney Park on Cythera's near-east side was not all that spectacular. It was a small park, covering only one city block; and it was sandwiched between two busy thoroughfares which carried the bulk of east-west traffic through the City. Unless one were on foot – and one would not want to be on foot in that part of the City of Cythera if one were in one's right mind – one tended not to notice the otherwise scenic view as one whizzed by on one's way to other, more pleasant neighborhoods.

This sad state of affairs had not always been so, of course. In the early days of Cythera, when the traffic consisted of horses and carriages and one whizzed by only if one whipped one's horse unmercifully, the good folk of the City visited McKleckney Park on a regular basis on foot to enjoy the view and to be entertained. Even when the horse-and-carriage had given way to the horseless carriage, the good folk of the City came to the park (either by foot or by horseless carriage) to enjoy the view and to be entertained. The park, like many other municipal parks of the nineteenth century, had one thing that most modern parks unfortunately did not have; it had a bandstand in the exact center of the park and held concerts every Saturday night during late spring through early autumn, featuring mostly local bands plus a few traveling bands from out-of-state.

On these occasions, the park was quite crowded. Whole families gathered to listen to uplifting, wholesome, patriotic music while sipping lemonade and eating popcorn and ice cream. And they dressed up for the occasion – Dad in his three-piece suit and bowler hat, Mom in her lacey pinafore and bonnet, Junior and Little Miss in their child-sized, matching attire. Everyone brought a blanket to spread out on the lawn and sit on while listening to uplifting, wholesome, patriotic music and sipping lemonade and eating popcorn and ice cream. It was a grand time to be alive, as anyone could have told you, and only a few complained about the mosquitos.

It has been said by those who have nothing better to do with their time than invent witty aphorisms (at least, in their own minds, they were witty) that all good things come to an end. And so the good times passed into the present-day times (at least, that was what the inventors of witty aphorisms were now saying), more or less. As life in the City of Cythera became more complex and hectic and the good folk became more self-absorbed and busy, old-fashioned entertainment like band concerts in the park on Saturday nights gave way to the Electronic Age.

McKleckney Park thus fell into disuse, and only "old-timers" could be seen there, sitting on the park benches, napping, feeding the squirrels or pigeons, swilling beer and/or spirits, or talking to each other or to themselves about the "good old days." If a concert was ever held there, the bands tended to be Mother's Little Darlings or their clones – loud, discordant, and vulgar, not at all uplifting, wholesome, or patriotic.

The City of Cythera still maintained the park (or tried to, given the current sort of "patronage"). The grass was moved, the walkways were swept/shoveled, the flowers were watered, the trees and shrubbery were trimmed, and the bandstand was repaired. More often than not, however, the City's employees spent most of their time picking up the trash, mountains of trash left behind by the aforementioned "patronage," the lost souls who had no other haven.

The park had one other "attraction" which no other municipality had or wanted to have. This "attraction" had even bothered the lost souls who had no other haven; and, since it was a mobile, rather than a fixed, attraction, no one could determine when it might make its appearance. One had to take one's chances on enjoying the park unannoyed. This "attraction" was none other than the Untouchables.

[Author's note: the Reader has already been introduced to this group in a previous narrative, and so there is no need for redundancy. Suffice it

to say that these stalwarts for the right to be as offensive as they can were sunning themselves in McKleckney Park, as was their usual custom. The Reader might ask him/herself, "Self, why are these stalwarts for the right to be as offensive as they can lounging in a public place in plain sight when their reputation – which precedes them in no uncertain terms and lingers long after they are gone – poses a risk of their being arrested first and asked questions of later by the Keystone – uh, the Cythera Police Department?"

[The answer is quite simple, as the Reader should know. If one wishes to arrest first and ask questions of later the scum, vermin, riff-raff, and animals which infect the streets of the City of Cythera, one must be able to get near the said scum, vermin, riff-raff, and animals which infest the streets of the City of Cythera in order to arrest first and ask questions of later. And no one had been able to come within twelve feet of these stalwarts for the right to be as offensive as they can and stay healthy.]

And so, the Untouchables sunned themselves in McKleckney Park, as was their custom, for as long as they pleased, and no one bothered them in the least.

Except one.

This one was, of course, one Donald A. Brooke III, who knew the The Secret of getting within twelve feet of these stalwarts for the right to be as offensive as they can and staying healthy. [Author's note: The Secret remains a secret, even to the Author, due to the (mistaken) perception that he is a blabbermouth and will cause these stalwarts for the right to be as offensive as they can to be less offensive – and thus less stalwart – and to be liable to be arrested first and asked questions of later by the Key – uh, the Cythera Police Department.] As soon as one Donald A. Brooke III came within twelve feet of the Untouchables, he invoked The Secret. He stopped breathing.

For as long as he was in the presence of these stalwarts for the right to be as offensive as they can, he employed a yoga technique – taught to him by his father – to cease respiration and to exist on oxygen stored up in his body. He had not learned this technique overnight, of course; he required many long years – and many thumps on the head by his father – before he learned this technique. But, once he had learned this technique – and avoided additional thumps on the head by his father – invoking it became second-nature to him, as easy as, well, breathing.

With the exception of Poohead, who had gotten civilized for some unfathomable reason and therefore had gotten himself removed from the list of the scum, vermin, riff-raff, and animals which infected the streets of the City of Cythera, the whole gang was there sunning themselves, as was their usual custom. Meathead was picking bits of food out of his yellowing teeth, Knucklehead was picking lint off his shabby clothing, Airhead was picking lice out his disheveled hair, and Dopehead was picking wax out his hairy ears. As soon as one of them (it matters not which one) spotted Donny, he broke out in a grin, whooped, and yelled, "Yo! Gung Ho is here!"

Two of the Untouchables then also broke out in a grin, whooped, and yelled, "Yo! Gung Ho is here!" The one exception was Dopehead, who preferred to speak in shorthand; he broke out into a grin, whooped, and yelled," YGHIH!" Donny slapped each of them on the right hand, which was the proper greeting between members of different and non-belligerent organizations.

When Donny reported in his Committee Report that he had engaged a "specially trained team of volunteers" to provide security for the rally, he had not identified the said "specially trained team of volunteers" for good reason. The team he had in mind was the same team he and Tommy had employed once before, i.e. the Untouchables. This time, he had kept Tommy out of the loop so as to provide him with additional plausible deniability and respectability. It would not have done Tommy any good to be linked to a leading collection of scum, vermin, riff-raff, and animals which infected the streets of the City of Cythera; more than likely, such an association would have cost him the election. Therefore, Donny had hastened to "check out a few things," i.e. hire the Untouchables discreetly to provide the security for the rally.

"What it is, Gung Ho?" Meathead completed the ritual.

"It be fine. Who's in charge here, now that Poohead is off the streets?"

"I am, on account of no one else wanted the honking job. I didn't either, but these honkers needed guidance – if you know what I mean – and, out the goodness of my heart, I honking volunteered."

"Stout fellow."

"So, what's the haps?"

"I have an assignment for you – same thing you did at the college. This time, it's at Tommy's political rally."

"I heard a rumor he was running for mayor. Izzat really true?"

"Really. You interested?"

"Same rate of pay as before?"

"Uh-huh."

"OK. It's a deal. Having Tommy as 'Hizzoner' will be a honking blast. Maybe life in this honking town will be a lot easier."

"It couldn't be any worse than with Mayor Dork in office. The rally will be in Weldon Park at 10:30. Be there fifteen minutes before."

"Right on, Gung Ho."

"OK. See you later."

"Hey, Gung Ho!" Knucklehead called out. "We get to knock some heads?"

"Maybe."

"I'd really like to knock some heads, man."

"We'll see."

Donny and Meathead slapped each other's right hand again. Meathead then returned to his bench and resumed picking bits of food out of his yellowing teeth. Knucklehead resumed picking lint off his shabby clothing. Airhead resumed picking lice out of his disheveled hair. Dopehead resumed picking wax out of his hairy ears.

When he was twelve feet away from the Untouchables, Donny resumed breathing.

VIII

15:15 GMT
(if anybody cares)

Having successfully escaped once again the miasma of the Untouchables, Donny decided to check on the progress of the setting up of the "grandstand" in Weldon Park for Tommy's rally, both in his capacity as the #2 person in the campaign and in his position as head of the Security Committee (which consisted of one person – himself). The Construction Committee had been instructed to begin their task at 8 am, and he wanted to make sure that they were on schedule. Some of the work crew he could count on, because they had worked in a similar capacity at the aforementioned college event; the rest were recent volunteers who had offered their services, because (1) they didn't like Mayor Dor – uh, Delbert Orville Richmond Kildare, either personally or professionally, (2) they saw in Tommy a breath of fresh air, (3) they liked the idea of putting an ex-gang-banger into the Mayor's office, (4) they hoped the new Mayor would turn Cythera upside-down, inside-out, and every which way but loose, and (5) most importantly, they didn't have anything better to do.

Donny quick-marched from McKleckney Park to Weldon Park in fifteen minutes. He had learned to quick-march from his ex-Marine father who had insisted that he not waste his time in needless activity (that, and a few thumps on the head to instill a proper attitude). As soon as he arrived at the park, he breathed a sigh of relief. The crew were scurrying about like squirrels on steroids, hard at work at putting the finishing touches on the "grandstand." All they needed was a few encouraging words; and he had all the right encouraging words, plus a hard stare for good measure.

The "grandstand" was little more than a pair of risers set end-to-end. Upon them would be placed a podium, a microphone, and a dozen folding chairs for the Central Committee and any volunteer speakers who wanted to vent their spleen on Tommy's behalf. At each end of the stage, monster loudspeakers had been set up which were guaranteed to rattle the windows of buildings two blocks away. The City Fathers had originally objected to the use of loudspeakers on the grounds that they did not want to invite lawsuits from the park's neighbors. But, since the park was public property and Tommy had a valid permit to hold the rally at Weldon Park and threatened to call the American Civil Liberties Union to pursue a free-speech grievance, the City Fathers had reluctantly relented.

Other volunteers from the Propaganda and Drone Committees scurried back and forth like squirrels on steroids, putting up posters and banners and arranging stacks of flyers and boxes of buttons to be distributed to anyone who cared to take one (and anyone who didn't care to take one). Once the "grandstand" had been completed, they would set up the podium and microphone and position the folding chairs.

At times, the scurrying back and forth like squirrels on steroids resulted in a few collisions. These collisions produced embarrassed smiles, conciliating hand gestures, and mumbled apologies. No one wanted to antagonize anyone else if (s)he could possibly help it. Tommy needed a solid front with which to confront the entrenched administration of Mayor Dor – uh, Delbert Orville Richmond Kildare – and turn it out of office.

Just as Donny entered Weldon Park, he was hailed by a plump blonde – made plumper by the fact that she was seven months pregnant – dressed in sweatshirt and sweatpants bearing Cythera College's logo of a cougar with fangs bared. The sweat clothes were much too small, due to the added "baby bump," and threatened to fall down, thereby exposing several body parts, some of which were better off *not* being exposed. The woman steamed toward him like a Mack truck on high octane, smiling toothily, red-faced from her exertions, thanks to the added load.

"Maxine!" Donny greeted her cheerfully (more or less). "What's the haps?"

Maxine pulled up in front of him and took a deep breath. She had a hawk-like nose to go with a round face and large ears; otherwise, she was not altogether unpleasant to look at if one did not look too closely. Curiously, her left eyelid tended to tic, giving her the appearance of someone ready to fall asleep on the spot.

"I got good news, Donny. The Zombies Against Corruption will be showing up for the rally."

"No poo?" He suppressed a desire to roll his eyes heavenward. The "Z's" – as the club was known far and wide – could count its membership on one hand, and the members were reputed not to possess all of their faculties. "That *is* good news."

"Say," she said suspiciously, fixing him with a steely glare, "you don't sound too honking enthusiastic."

"Who, *me*? I'm very enthusiastic."

"I'm glad to hear it. You know, my husband is now the Chapter President."

"So I've heard." He eyed the "baby bump." "I see you're expecting again. Number three?"

"Number four, but who's counting?"

"Not me. Look, I got to check on the others here. See you later."

May you live in interesting times, Maxine.

Halfway to the "grandstand," Donny was hailed again, this time by a slender red-head – made plump by the fact that she was seven months pregnant – dressed in a sweat shirt and sweatpants, the former of which bore the slogan "Dressed to Kill." The sweat clothes were much too large, despite the added "baby bump," and threatened to fall down, thereby exposing several body parts, some of which were better off *not* being exposed. The woman steamed toward him like a Mack truck on high octane, smiling toothily, red-faced from her exertions, thanks to the added load.

"Christine!" Donny greeted her cheerfully (more or less). "What's the haps?"

Christine pulled up in front of him and took a deep breath. She had bushy eyebrows and a tremendous overbite which distracted from an otherwise pleasant-looking face if one did not look too closely.

"I got good news, Donny. I finally convinced the Darth Vader Fan Club (Cythera Chapter) to join the rally."

"No poo?" Donny suppressed a desire to roll his eyes heavenward. The Vaderites – as they were derogatorily called by those who misunderstood their mission – could count their membership on one hand, and the members were reputed not to possess any sense of humor. "That *is* good news."

"Say," Christine said suspiciously, fixing him with a steely glare, "you don't sound too enthusiastic."

"Who, *me*? I'm very enthusiastic."

"I'm glad to hear it. You know, my fiancé is still the Regional Director of the Club."

"So I've heard." He eyed her "baby bump." "I see you're expecting again. Second one?"

"Third, but who's counting?"

"Not me. Look, I got to check on the others. See you later."

May you live in interesting times, Christine.

Donny resumed his straight-line path to the "grandstand." No one else – pregnant or otherwise – flagged him down, though many called out to him in support of the upcoming event. He flashed his winning smile and made the peace sign to one and all.

As he approached the "grandstand," an extremely battered blue van pulled up to the curb of the adjacent street on the north side of the park. It coughed and wheezed and shuddered hugely, and it was self-evident that the muffler was either deficient or missing altogether. The van died a slow, agonizing death and became deathly still, prompting much idle and raucous speculation over whether it could be resurrected.

Out of this wretched piece of machinery emerged four bare-chested, jeans-clad skinheads which alarmed not a few of the crew who had never seen or heard of them before. This unruly quartet was, in point of fact, the band which called themselves "Mother's Little Darlings," although "Mother" would have had to swallow her pride (and a lot of other things) in order to claim them as her own. They had earned a reputation for being discordant, off-key, and very loud, endearing qualities which attracted no one to them. Tommy had hoped they would volunteer their talents for The Cause, but they had insisted upon getting some "expense money" upfront without specifying what sort of expenses they intended to incur (although one could hazard a shrewd guess). After much haggling, Tommy had rejected their little extortion scheme and dismissed them.

Donny was astonished that Mother's Little Darlings had arrived anyway. It was quite uncharacteristic of them. The problem with this was that, since the "grandstand" was not yet complete, they had no place to put all of their equipment – all of the standard pieces in various degrees of usefulness – rumored to have been stolen. Which meant that they would simply hang around, making nuisances of themselves and annoying the workers. As soon as he had concluded his primary business here, he would have to lay down some rules of conduct for them (not that he expected them to comply, but one could hope, couldn't one?)

The closer he neared the "grandstand," the more he had to dodge the construction crew, scurrying about like squirrels on steroids. And one of the squirrels actually collided with him, because he was carrying a large plywood panel which partially blocked his vision. Donny fell to the ground; the squirrel fell to the ground; and the plywood panel fell to the ground – all at the same time. Donny got to his feet, and the squirrel got to his feet – at nearly the same time. The plywood panel did not get to its feet but just laid on the ground like a stupid lump, thinking stupid thoughts.

"Sorry, buddy," the squirrel apologized. "Didn't see ya comin' there."

"No harm done," Donny lied. "Carry on."

Donny limped away, rubbing his sore buttocks. In his younger days, when he had been a member of the Commandos, he might have been tempted to wrap that plywood panel around that squirrel. But, he was older and wiser now, and he had to behave like a proper young gentleman, whether he liked it or not.

He finally found the crew chief, a tall, lanky, horse-faced individual by the name of Horace Shoemaker. Said crew chief was, at that moment, busy staring off into the distance and seeing what no one else could see. Donny tapped him on the shoulder. Horace turned around slowly, looked at and through Donny, and saw what no one else could see.

"Hiya, Mr. Brooke," he said vacantly.

"Hi, Horace. How's it going?"

"Goin' good. Right on schedule."

"Great. Do you have enough material to work with?"

"Yup. Could use some earplugs, though, just in case those so-called 'musicians' start to play."

"OK. I'll get you some. Carry on."

"Thanks."

Horace turned around slowly, looked off into the distance, and saw what no one else could see. Donny limped away, rubbing his sore buttocks, and headed toward downtown and the nearest drugstore. On the way, he collided with the same squirrel who was still carrying the same plywood panel which partially blocked his vision. Donny fell to the ground; the squirrel fell to the ground; and the plywood panel fell to the ground – all at the same time. Donny got to his feet, and the squirrel got to his feet – at nearly the same time. The plywood panel did not get to its feet but just laid on the ground like a stupid lump, thinking stupid thoughts.

"Oops," the squirrel said awkwardly. "Did it again. Sorry."

"No harm done," Donny lied again. "Carry on."

I'll have to tell Horace to fire that honker. He's a menace to society.

He limped off, rubbing his *really* sore buttocks. He *really* needed to get to the drugstore.

ten seconds before 09:30

Chief Ozzie stormed into the Office of the Mayor of the City of Cythera, wearing the fiercest scowl he could manage (and he could manage quite a few when he put his mind to it) and startling Ms. Tix, the Dream Woman of many a wretched male, out of ten year's growth (which would have been unfortunate as she was only twenty-two years of age and could not have afforded such a large loss). The office lights glinted off the Chief's bald pate as he quick-marched past her desk, temporarily blinding her (which was unfortunate as she had been about to sit down and now could not find her chair). The Chief yanked open the large pretentious door to the Mayor's large pretentious office and steamed through it. Before he slammed it shut, Ms. Tix regained her eyesight and shook a fist at the Chief's backside. *[Author's note: ordinarily, the term "backside" is a euphemism for one's buttocks, used in polite company where the term "ass" would not be appropriate. In the present circumstance, however, Ms. Tix did not shake her fist at Chief Ozzie's a – uh, backside, but at the Chief's entire back side of his body. The Reader can breathe a sigh of relief at not being offended by a misinterpretation.]*

The steaming into his large pretentious office by the Chief, who was wearing the fiercest scowl he could manage (and he could manage quite a few when he put his mind to it) also startled His Honor because (1) the Chief had not been announced as protocol in this Administration dictated, and (2) His Honor was in the act of improving his golf putt and was concentrating very, very hard at an attempt to putt the golf ball into a small plastic cup. *[Author's note: the golf ball scooted across the carpet and disappeared under a nearby large pretentious credenza, in case the Reader cares about such things.]*

The Mayor turned around in shock and was instantly blinded by the glinting of the large pretentious office's lights off of Chief Ozzie's bald pate -- which was unfortunate because it caused him to drop his putter, to trip over the said putter when he attempted to return to his large pretentious desk, to crash to the floor, and to bang his head against the said large pretentious desk. When he finally recovered his wits, his equilibrium, and his putter (not necessarily in that order), he stared at Chief Ozzie in bewilderment.

"Chief Ozzie!" he exclaimed in bewilderment. "What's the meaning of this storming into my office unannounced? And why are you wearing that fierce scowl?"

In response, Chief Ozzie switched to a different scowl and regarded the Mayor with undisguised contempt. His Honor quailed.

"I've just been informed," the Chief growled, "that the permit that Russell the Rat has to hold a rally in Weldon Park has been upheld by the municipal court."

"Do tell, do tell," His Honor murmured.

"How did he ever get a permit in the first place?" the Chief growled some more. "He's got a criminal record and shouldn't have been issued one."

[Author's note: this was an exaggeration on the Chief's part. Tommy Russell had been arrested many times when he had led the Commandos but had been released each time for lack of sufficient evidence of criminal activities.]

"Do tell, do tell," His Honor murmured.

"What are you going to do about it?" the Chief growled even more.

"My hands are tied, Chief. I don't oversee the permits, and the Court has spoken."

"Damnation!" the Chief growled intensely. "That's no excuse. Well, I'll tell you what *I'm* going to do about it. I'm going to throw a monkey wrench into Mr. Russell the Rat's little party."

"Do tell, do tell," His Honor murmured.

"I won't tell you exactly what I'm going to do, however, because you'll need some plausible deniability."

Whereupon Chief Ozzie pivoted, steamed toward the large pretentious door, yanked it open, and slammed it shut behind him. He quick-marched past the desk of Ms. Tix – who was now comfortably seated – and stormed out of the Office of the Mayor of the City of Cythera, but not before the office lights glinted off his bald pate and blinded her again. Ms. Tix shook another fist at his, um, backside.

"Ms. Tix," His Honor called over the intercom, "I've just developed a terrific headache. Get me some aspirin, will you?"

How about a hammer instead, sir?

"I'll get right on it, Mr. Mayor."

The Dream Woman of many a wretched male heaved a huge sigh, rose to her feet, and departed the Office of the Mayor of the City of Cythera. She was bound for the nearest drug store. What she really wanted was a stiff drink.

X

five minutes later

Hallman's Drug Store on the corner of River and Fox Streets was the oldest of its kind in Cythera, having been established right after the American Civil War. Prior to that establishment and that War, the Hallmans were patent-medicine salespersons who always managed to remain one step ahead of disgruntled customers, the sheriff, and the competition in every state east of the Appalachian Mountains and north of the Potomac River. The War in particular gave them a brief respite and time to re-evaluate their position in society and their prospects for the future.

In short, they decided to go west and become legitimate purveyors (more or less) of prescription medicines, medical devices, and other sundry items related to the health and well-being of the average human.

The establishment on the corner of River and Fox Streets was, at the time of this narrative, in its fourth generation, which generation was desperately attempting to persuade Generation #5 to continue the family business. Said Generation #5 was not convinced, once it had learned of the unsavory characters perched in the family tree. Said Generation #5 was seriously eyeing the hardware business, because (1) there had been no shenanigans involved in purveying hammers, saws, wrenches, and other sundry items related to construction and repair and (2) one of the brothers in said Generation #5 was engaged to be married to the daughter of the proprietor of the local outlet of the A-One chain of hardware stores, and his future father-in-law wanted to continue *his* family's dynasty. *[Author's note: use of the word "shenanigans" wasn't what the Author would have used. He was merely quoting one of the brothers (it matters not which one) who had used that expression repeatedly in an interview made to obtain the preceding background material.] [Author's further note: if the Reader detects a similarity to a Romeo and Juliet scenario, that can't be helped. Poo happens.]*

Family squabbles aside, Hallman's Drug Store was a thriving business because it stocked everything everybody was looking for in the way of prescription medicines, medical devices, and sundry items relating to the health and well-being of the average human. If the average human did not find a desired item at Hallman's, it probably hadn't been invented yet; but, once it had been invented, one would surely find it on the shelves of Hallman's Drug Store – *guaranteed.*

In the present instance, it carried two brands of earplugs and half a dozen brands of aspirin – all waiting for customers to buy them as the need arose.

In the present instance, Need #1 was evinced by one Donald A. Brooke III, former member of the Commandos street gang and currently chief of security for the Thomas A. Russell political campaign. He entered Hallman's Drug Store, still limping and rubbing his sore buttocks (discreetly, of course), and began his search for earplugs. Never having been in this establishment for many long years, he had lost his familiarity with it – not that having familiarity with it would have done him any good, as the proprietor insisted on re-arranging the merchandise every month or so just to keep his customers and would-be customers on their toes and to make sure that they looked at *everything* in stock before finding what they really needed – and so he began to walk up and down the aisles, looking this way and that way very carefully lest he miss what he was really looking for. So intent was he in walking up and down the aisles and looking very carefully lest he miss what he was really looking for that he was not watching where he was going until it was too late.

In the present instance, Need #2 was evinced by one Apollonia Tix, the Dream Woman of many a wretched male and executive secretary of the Mayor of the City of Cythera. She entered Hallman's Drug Store, busily composing new and colorful pejoratives for the Administration of Mayor Delbert Orville Richmond Kildare in general and for Mayor Delbert Orville Richmond Kildare in particular and wishing she could find more suitable employment for her considerable talents, and began her search for aspirin. Never having been in this establishment at all during her short existence and therefore not having any familiarity with it at all, she walked up and down the aisles, looking this way and that way very carefully lest she miss what she was really looking for. So intent was she in walking up and down the aisles looking very carefully lest she miss what she was really looking for that she was not watching where she was going until it was too late.

That which neither Donald A. Brooke III nor Apollonia Tix wanted to happen happened. It was like a train wreck in slow motion: two trains running on the same track, colliding with each other, and de-railing. One train spun around and crashed into a display of suppositories; the other train spun around and crashed into a display of condoms (it matters not who spun into what – the outcome was the same).

Donny, upon recovering his equipoise, his wits, and his balance (not necessarily in that order), turned toward what he had crashed into and prepared to address it with several colorful expressions he had cultivated while a member of the Commandos. The first colorful expression he had cultivated while a member of the Commandos died aborning as he caught sight of the other train. The other train was the most gorgeous creature he had ever laid eyes on, and he was instantly smitten. He then put aside all of the colorful expressions he had cultivated while a member of the Commandos and consulted his mental French dictionary for something more appropriate.

Apollonia Tix, upon recovering her equipoise, her wits, and her balance (not necessarily in that order), turned toward what she had crashed into and prepared to address it with several colorful expressions she had cultivated while a student at a Catholic high school. The first colorful expression she had cultivated while a student at a Catholic high school died aborning as she caught sight of the other train. The other train was the most gorgeous creature she had ever laid eyes on, and she was instantly smitten. She then put aside all of the colorful expressions she had cultivated while a student at a Catholic high school and consulted her mental German dictionary for something more appropriate.

"*Pardonnez moi, mademoiselle* [pardon me, miss]," Donny said in a gentle tone. "*Je suis tres maladroit* [I am very clumsy]."

"*Entschultigen Sie mir, mein Herr* [pardon me, sir]," Apollonia said in a gentle tone. "*Ich bin sehr ungeschickt* [I am very clumsy]."

"*Merci* [thank you]."

"*Danke* [thank you]."

"Allow me to introduce myself. I'm Donald Brooke. My friends call me 'Donny.'"

"Can I be your friend?" *And a lot more?*

"Yes, you can." *And a lot more!*

"I'm Apollonia Tix. *My* friends call me 'Polly.'"

"Can I be your friend?" *And a lot more?*

"Yes, you can." *And a lot more!*

"What is your function in society, Polly?" *Other than being the Woman of My Dreams.*

"I'm Mayor Kildare's executive secretary."

"*No poo?*"

"No poo. And what is *your* function in society, Donny?" *Other than being the Man of My Dreams.*

"Currently, I'm the chief of security for the Russell mayoral campaign.

"*No poo?*"

"No poo."

"We shouldn't be talking to each other."

"No, we shouldn't."

"But, I don't care. I don't like 'His Honor' either. I'd like to see him run out of town."

"Then we've got one thing in common."

Ask me out, so we can find out what else we have in common.

"There's a rally at 10:30. How about we get together at McGillicuddy's afterwards? *And find out what else we have in common.*

"I thought you'd never ask. I'll see you later."

"Wonderful. So long."

Both Donny and Apollonia departed Hallman's Drug Store after obtaining what they both came there for. One of them walked back to Weldon Park with earplugs in his hand and stars in his eyes. The other one walked back to the Mayor's Office with aspirin in her hand and stars in her eyes. Neither of them was concerned about his/her function in society.

 # XI

ten minutes and ten seconds later

No sooner had he departed Hallman's Drug Store than Donny realized he should have bought earplugs for himself. The cacophony issuing from Weldon Park was enough to raise the dead and kill them all over again. Mother's Little Darlings were in fine form, and they were playing what they were pleased to call "music" with reckless abandon (with the emphasis on "reckless"). All the way back, he heard babies crying, dogs howling, cats meowing, horns beeping, and drunks cursing; and he saw people passing out, people dashing headlong down the streets, people vomiting, people writhing in agony, and people flagellating themselves. The closer he came to the epicenter, the more bodies he had to step over.

No sooner had he entered the park than a dead silence abruptly fell over it. He looked at the "grandstand" (miraculously still standing) and spied Horace Shoemaker threatening Mother's Little Darlings with a hammer. This behavior would not do, he thought, as it would tend to give the Russell campaign a black mark if the good citizens of Cythera equated violence with it. He started toward the melee but soon collided with the same squirrel carrying the same plywood panel which blocked his vision. Donny fell to the ground; the squirrel fell to the ground; and the plywood panel fell to the ground – all at the same time. Donny got to his feet, and the squirrel got to his feet – at nearly the same time. The plywood panel did not get to its feet but just laid on the ground like a stupid lump, thinking stupid thoughts.

"Oops," the squirrel said awkwardly. "Did it again. Sorry."

"No harm done," Donny lied again. "Carry on."

He limped off, rubbing his *really, really* sore buttocks. He *really, really* needed to have Horace fire that honker.

He arrived at the "grandstand" just as Horace was chasing Mother's Little Darlings back to their van. The latter were cursing, shaking their fists, making obscene gestures, threatening to sue the Russell campaign for defamation of character, and accusing Horace of being a Communist opposed to free enterprise, free speech, and free love. Horace, for his part, was cursing, shaking his fist, making obscene gestures, threatening to have them arrested for disturbing the peace, vandalism, and indecent behavior, and accusing Mother's Little Darlings of being terrorists opposing the American way of life, democracy, and civil liberties. Donny took in this exchange of viewpoints with much aplomb and its consequences with much satisfaction.

"Good show, Horace," he observed as soon as the crew chief had vented his spleen and returned to the "grandstand."

"Maybe I won't need those earplugs after all."

"Well, here they are anyway." He handed over the earplugs in his hand but not the stars in his eyes. "Just in case."

"Oakie-doakie. Thanks, Mister Brooke."

"You're welcome. By the way, who's that…*person* over there, the one with the large plywood panel?"

He pointed to the squirrel in question. Horace followed the pointing finger (it matters not which one), squinted, and focused on the squirrel. He shook his head.

"Dunno. I never saw him before in my life. What's he up to?"

"That's what I'd like to know. He doesn't seem to be contributing anything to The Cause."

"You want me to run him off?"

"If you don't mind. But, be careful" – Donny rubbed his very sore buttocks again – "he's dangerous."

"Oakie-doakie."

As Horace walked away in the direction of the squirrel, Donny gazed around at the rally site and noted that everything was nearly ready for the rally. The campaign volunteers who were scurrying around like squirrels on steroids were just now putting the finishing touches on the "grandstand," affixing the last of the posters and banners to every available surface, and arranging stacks of flyers and boxes of buttons. Already a number of potential voters were wandering into the park, drawn mostly by curiosity; they were immediately deluged with flyers and admonitions to "Vote for Russell." Donny nodded with satisfaction.

It was going to be a BITCH *of a rally, as Tommy would say.*

And then he spotted something which instantly soured his mood.

Off to the southern regions of Weldon Park, four suspicious-looking individuals stood behind a tree, surveying the rally unabashedly. They were dressed like hippies, right down to the bandanas on their heads and sandals on their feet. But their body postures told him – an expert in such things – that they were *not* hippies at all.

Some of Chief Ozzie's goons, I'll wager, he deduced decidedly. *They're here to disrupt the rally. I'd better warn Tommy ASAP.*

He limped off, rubbing his very sore buttocks again.

the exact same time

Ms. Apollonia Tix, the Dream Woman of many a wretched male, ambled into the Office of the Mayor of the City of Cythera with aspirin in her hand and stars in her eyes, clicked on the intercom, and announced that she had the desired aspirin.

"Great, Ms. Tix, and not a moment too soon. I'm in a brain session, and my brain is hurting."

I'll get a drill, sir, and relieve some of the pressure.

She ambled into the large pretentious office and noted that Mayor Kildare was not alone. His "brain trust" – which, in her humble opinion, lacked one-and-a-half brains -- one Anthony Algernon Armstrong, a.k.a. "Triple-A," the Mayor's speech writer, and one Spencer K. Augustus, a.k.a. "Augie," the Mayor's campaign manager, had returned during her absence and managed to find their way to the Mayor's large pretentious office without anyone's assistance. All three gazed at her lecherously, and she gazed at them contemptuously. She handed His Honor the aspirin in her hand but not the stars in her eyes, pivoted, and ambled back to her own domain.

The three wretched males followed her every step of the way with their eyes and wished they could follow her every step of the way with their feet. *[Author's note: the Reader may surmise that this action takes a heavy toll on one's eyes. It has not been recommended by any credible ophthalmologist.]*

"Where were we?" the Mayor asked artlessly.

"You were rehearsing the speech for your own rally, Bertie," Augie reminded him artlessly.

"Ah, yes. And don't call me 'Bertie.'"

"We wanted you to emphathithe Ruthell'th criminal background, Delbert," Triple-A reminded him artlessly.

[Author's note: the Reader should be aware that Delbert Orville Richmond Kildare was extremely touchy concerning his name. His parents had bestowed upon him a collection of odd names in honor of their ancestors – a noble gesture, to be sure – but, when placed in juxtaposition with each other, the collection was difficult to say, and speakers ended up tripping over their own tongues (which was painful at best and embarrassing at worst). Therefore, Delbert Orville Richmond Kildare was called, to his eternal chagrin, "Bertie," "Del," "Orv," "Rich," or "Dork," to name a few of the more frequent ones. What he preferred to be called had never quite been decided; something suitable to his self-image had seemed to have eluded him, and he spent all of his spare time pondering the question. But the Author digresses and begs the Reader's indulgence.]

"You should quote extensively from the police reports. I've got them right here." Augie tapped his briefcase. "Chief Ozzie edited them himself."

"And make thure the thitithenry underthandth that thith criminal mathtermind hath never been brought to juthithe."

"I certainly will. Augie, how are the preparations for my own rally going?"

"Quite well, B – uh, Delbert. I've got a number of people from the Cythera Chamber of Commerce, the Downtown Business Association, and the Industrial League lined up to speak prior to your own speech. I tried to get a few of those Ivy Leaguers from Cythera College, but they refused to speak against one of their alumni, no matter what his background was. And the rumor is that a couple of them will show up to support him."

"Who needth them, Delbert? They're nothing but a hotbed of radicalithm."

[Author's note: the Reader should be aware that, had the current Administration of Cythera College heard the above comments, it would have laughed its collective backside off. (Author's additional note: use of the word "backside" here actually does refer to the human posterior in the common, vulgar way.) Furthermore, the said current Administration

of Cythera College would have reminded the current Administration of the City of Cythera that most of the staff and faculty had voted for him in the previous election. Furthermore, the said current Administration of Cythera College would have cautioned the said current Administration of the City of Cythera not to vilify the school in such reckless terms lest the said current Administration of Cythera College be forced to re-evaluate its political stance. But the Author digresses again and begs the Reader's indulgence.]

"How about the social organizations, Augie?"

"*Humph!*" Augie *humph*ed vigorously. "They're a mixed bag. I'm still working on that angle."

"*Humph!*" Triple-A *humph*ed vigorously. "A bunch of bleeding hearth, every thingle one of them."

[Author's note: the Author will forego commentary here as he does not wish to beg the Reader's indulgence anymore.]

Before either Augie or Triple-A could offer more advice, Chief Ozzie stormed into the large pretentious office (having bypassed Ms. Tix once again). The "brain trust" looked at him in shock. Chief Ozzie was smiling!

"Chief!" the Mayor shouted. "What's going on here? And why are you smiling?"

Chief Ozzie marched across the large pretentious office in a military fashion, came to a military halt, executed a military right-face, and finished off with a military parade-rest, all the while murmuring the execution commands to himself in a military manner. He still did not salute His Honor, however.

"I'm making my report – sir. And it's a goodie. I've got some of my people in Weldon Park even as we speak, ready at a pre-programmed moment to disrupt Russell the Rat's rally and put his backside in a sling. Also, I've got a little surprise for him."

"What thort of thurprithe?" Triple-A asked boldly.

"Well, now, if I told you what it was, it wouldn't be a surprise, would it, you dunderhead? Besides, His Honor needs all of the plausible deniability he can get, doesn't he? You'll find out soon enough."

"Thanks for the update, Chief. Anything else?"

"No, sir, not at the moment."

Chief Ozzie came to a military attention, executed a military right-face, and marched out of the large pretentious office in a military manner, all the while murmuring the execution commands to himself in a military manner. The "brain trust" looked alternately relieved and worried.

"I don't like 'surprises,'" Augie growled. "It means having to issue special press releases."

"Leave that to me, Augie. I'll whip up thome preth releatheth to end all preth releatheth."

"I'll bet you will." His Honor grumbled as he reached for the bottle of aspirin Ms. Tix, the Dream Woman of many a wretched male, had thoughtfully obtained for him. "I don't like surprises either."

XIII

09:59:59 am
(plus 59 nanoseconds)

The construction of the "grandstand" has been completed, and the volunteers congratulate each other for a job well done. They then join the other campaign workers in distributing flyers, posters, banners, and buttons to the accumulating curiosity-seekers in Weldon Park. The construction-crew chief, Horace Shoemaker, takes one last look at the construction, congratulates himself for a job well done, and departs the park for a well-deserved bottle of beer (or three) at McGillicuddy's.

Seeing that the coast is clear, Mother's Little Darlings sneak back into the park and quickly set up their instruments on the "grandstand." Soon, Weldon Park is rocking and rolling (literally!) as the band belts out tunes of its own devising.

* * *

"Where'd this band come from?"

"WHAT?"

"I SAID, WHERE'D THIS BAND COME FROM?"

"DUNNO. AWFUL, AIN'T IT?"

"OH, I WOULDN'T SAY THAT. I THINK IT'S GOT A CERTAIN *JOIE DE VIVRE*."

"IT'S GOT *WHAT*?"

"*JOIE DE VIVRE*. YOU KNOW, AMBIENCE."

"ARE YOU FOR REAL?"

* * *

Now the curiosity-seekers gathered in earnest. Some were interested in seeing what all the fuss was about. Some, who had heard that the notorious Russell the Rat was running for public office, wanted to know if he was serious and, if he was, then what his campaign was all about. And some just liked to be part of a crowd (not necessarily for legitimate reasons) and enjoy the ambience. Whyever they came, they were immediately inundated with flyers, posters, banners, and buttons by the campaign volunteers who were working the crowd for all they were worth.

Alice Monomoy was definitely not working the crowd for all she was worth. In fact, she was not working the crowd at all. She had no interest in politics in general and in this particular campaign in particular; she was here to bask in the presence of one Donald A. Brooke III and to persuade him to impregnate her. Surreptitiously, she had walked into Weldon Park and was keeping a low profile; she hoped no one – especially friends and business associates of her parents – would recognize her, although, in the back of her mind, she was positive that none of them would be caught dead or alive at this event. Still, one could not be too careful, could one?

Even though Alice wandered about in a low profile while keeping an eye out for Donny, several of the volunteers who were working the crowd for all they were worth recognized her and flashed toothy smiles and the peace sign. Alice supposed she had to reciprocate on the off-chance that one or more of the volunteers might report her "disloyal attitude" to the Executive Committee, i.e. Tommy and Amber Russell. And so, she flashed a big toothy smile (which looked more like a grimace) and the peace sign (surreptitiously, in case some of her parents' friends and business associates actually were at this event) and kept on moving in a low profile.

Invariably, while she wandered about in a low profile, she spotted someone else who was wandering about in a low profile. Immediately, Alice experienced (1) recognition, (2) surprise, (3) chagrin, (4) surprise again, and finally, (5) embarrassment. The other party was an old classmate of hers at the University of Illinois (Chicago), one who she had had no use for then and one who she had no use for now.

The other party to this chance encounter was none other than Harriet Methune Beiderbeck, star reporter (in her humble estimation) for the Cythera *Clarion-News*, who had won several awards for her reporting which (in her humble estimation) she deserved. Her reputation for sniffing out a story and pursuing it until (1) it became old news or (2) some other story needed to be sniffed out and pursued was legion, inside and outside of Cythera. It was rumored -- sometimes true, sometimes not –that she could sniff out a story before it ever became a story and that any number of unsuspecting individuals found themselves confronted by her without a clear reason why they had been blessed by her attentions. Thanks to her reputation for sniffing out a story and pursuing it until (1) it became old news or (2) some other story needed to be sniffed out and pursued, Harriet Methune Beiderbeck, star reporter (in her humble estimation) for the Cythera *Clarion-News*, had earned the colorful sobriquet of "Harry the Hatchet." It was not an epithet she particularly cared for (as one might imagine), and hearing it provoked rockets' red glare and bombs bursting in air (so to speak). Needless to say, only the extremely foolhardy spoke the epithet in her presence, and they spoke it only once. Then they died. Not a literal death, of course, but a death of the spirit and of the mind, leaving the victim to wish (s) he had suffered a literal death.

Harry – uh, Harriet was in Weldon Park on assignment. It was the first assignment since the birth of her baby, and her beloved publisher, the redoubtable Michael John McNamara, the great-great-great-great-grandson of the founder of the *Clarion-News*, believed she was ready to "get back into harness – heh-heh-heh" (or words to that effect). Needless to say, she did not view this assignment very enthusiastically; political rallies were (in her humble estimation) the most boring events in the world, and she'd rather pull her fingernails out than cover one.

Invariably, while she wandered about in a low profile, she spotted someone else who was also wandering about in a low profile. Immediately, she experienced (1) recognition, (2) surprise, (3) chagrin, (4) surprise again, and finally, (5) embarrassment. The other party was an old classmate of hers at the University of Illinois (Chicago), one who she had had no use for then and one who she had no use for now.

"Alice!"

"Harry!"

"What a pleasant surprise!"

"Likewise!"

"It's good to see you after all these years."

"Yes, it is."

"How've you been?"

"Just great. You?"

"Just great. Still operating a book store?"

"Uh-huh. Still reporting?"

"Uh-huh. I'm on assignment here."

"What an incredible co-incidence. So am I. I'm on the campaign committee."

"You're kidding?"

"Uh-uh. I'm in charge of donations."

"You married?"

"Uh-uh. Still shopping around. Heh-heh-heh. You?"

"Uh-huh. Got a kid too."

"You're kidding?"

"Uh-uh. Met a great guy. Swept me off my feet."

"I'm happy for you."

"Thanks. Good luck in your shopping."

"Thanks. Well, I've got to move along here."

"Me too."

"We should do lunch some time."

"Love to. Bye."

"Bye."

Stupid bitch!

Stupid bitch!

[Author's note: the preceding exchange was not a verbatim one but was the gist of one. It was relayed to the Author by a third party who had overheard it in passing and relayed it to him as best she could remember it.]

Once she had recovered her bearings, Alice headed straight for the "grandstand" where she would duly wait for the arrival of her "fearless leader" and "show the colors." She sighed heavily. If only Donny would pay more attention to her, all of this going through the motions would be worth the agony (but no ecstasy). If someone like "Harry the Hatchet" could snag some guy, then she could too – hands down.

Once she had recovered her bearings, Harriet headed straight for the western edge of Weldon Park where she would duly wait for the arrival of the mayoral candidate and seek an interview. She sighed heavily. If only McNamara would give her better assignments, all of this going through the motions would be worth the agony (but not the ecstasy). If someone like Alice Monomoy could go about as she pleased, then she could too – hands down.

XIV

(not too much later)

The Bookends – Willy and Wally (or Wally and Willy in some circles) – were definitely working the crowd for all they were worth in their own inimitable fashion. That is to say, they were sowing confusion in everyone they encountered, either by word of mouth or by mirror-image pantomiming, both of which they excelled at.

A typical example:

"Hi, I'm Willy!"

"Hi, I'm Wally!"

"We're here to ask you to…"

"…vote for Tommy Russell because…"

"…he will clean up the corruption…"

"…at City Hall and return Cythera…"

"…to its democratic past and to…"

"…a more vibrant and prosperous economy."

"Thank you, and have a nice day."

"Thank you, and have a nice day."

At the next encounter, they would switch positions:

"Hi, I'm Wally!"

"Hi, I'm Willy!"

"We're here to ask you to…"

"…vote for Tommy Russell because…"

"…he will rid the streets of the…"

"…criminal element which the…"

"…current corrupt Administration…"

"…has failed to do, making the…"

"…streets unsafe for decent people…"

"…to walk along them for fear of…"

"…being assaulted and/or murdered."

"Thank you, and have a nice day."

"Thank you, and have a nice day."

They would continue to switch positions, thusly:

"Hi, I'm Willy!"

"Hi, I'm Wally!"

"We're here to ask you to…"

"…vote for Tommy Russell because…"

"…he will reform the political…"

"…process so that every citizen…"

"…of Cythera has an equal say in…"

"…the affairs of the City which the…"

"…current corrupt Administration…"

"…has co-opted for its own…"

"…selfish purposes and sold the…"

"…City to the highest bidder."

"Thank you, and have a nice day."

"Thank you, and have a nice day."

These and other examples repeated over and over again whenever a curiosity-seeker chanced to cross their paths (which was increasingly the case) had the said curiosity-seeker coming and going, going and coming, and never sure where (s)he was. Thereafter, the said curiosity-seeker would walk around in a daze and often collide with other curiosity-seekers.

10:10:10 am
(unless your watch was fast)

The supporters of Thomas A. Russell, the non-supporters of Thomas A. Russell, and the undecided of Thomas A. Russell were now gathering in earnest and were fully caught up in the spirit of the event. They clapped, cheered, booed, whistled, waved banners and posters, threw away banners and posters, chanted anti-incumbent slogans, chanted pro-incumbent slogans, shook heads in wonderment of it all, danced (where space was available), sang (though one had to get close to the singing in order to hear what was being sung, due to the output of Mother's Little Darlings), and generally enjoyed/hated the spectacle of a political campaign.

While the crowd was gathered for one purpose (more or less), each individual or group served that purpose (or not) in unique ways. In point of fact, there were nearly as many mini-dramas as there were people, and no two mini-dramas (like people) were similar.

XVI

10.11:11 am
(mini-drama #1)

Fifty-four feet and forty inches southwest of the "grandstand," four couples – two heterosexual, two homosexual – form a "square" and begin to dance. None of the dancers fits the description of traditional square dancers. That is to say, none of them, especially the homosexual couples, are dressed in traditional rural costumes. That is to say further, none of the "gentlemen" wear plaid shirts, bibbed overalls, and boots; and none of the "ladies" wear fluffy blouses, crinoline skirts, and slippers. Rather, all of them, especially the homosexual couples, wear T-shirts and short shorts. All of the "ladies," however, wear a yellow ribbon in their hair, presumably to distinguish themselves from the "gentlemen."

One of the "gentlemen" (it matters not which one) also acts as the "caller," and "his" expertise leaves something to be desired. "He" seems to be making up the calls, more or less, as "he" goes whether or not they make any sense. Nevertheless, what "he" lacks in expertise, "he" makes up for in enthusiasm – and so do all of the dancers. The surrounding onlookers get into the spirit of the occasion by clapping rhythmically and offering suggestions for further calls. For some unfathomable reason, Alice Monomoy, who is wandering across the park in a low profile, declines to clap rhythmically and offer suggestions for further calls.

The calls themselves are an admixture of traditional square-dance language and political messaging. For example:

"Swing your partner, do-si-do!
Tell the Mayor he's got to go!"
And:

"Ladies, now aleman left.
Gentlemen, aleman right!
Mayor Dork is not too bright!"
And:
"Everyone promenade around!
Make Russell City Hall bound!"
And so it goes, one after another.

10:11:13 am
(mini-drama #2)

The horns are tooting!

The flags are flying!

Look there! Coming from the parking lot east of the "grandstand," it's the Universal Union of Unicycles (Cythera Chapter) – all five of them!

Gaily festooned with red-white-and-blue bunting, these intrepid cyclists skillfully maneuver their magnificent machines through the crowd and accept accolades from one and all. Their magnificent machines, painted a fire-engine red (more or less), are also festooned with red-white-and-blue bunting and wheel noiselessly across Weldon Park.

In the lead is the Chapter President, a muscular fellow with a resplendent handle-bar moustache. Abruptly, he blows a whistle hung around his neck, and the "U's" form a circle. They pedal in the circle for one lap. Then, the President blows his whistle again and pushes himself upward; his cycle rises to a height of three feet. The other cyclists follow suit. When they return to the ground, they all toot their horns and circle another lap. They repeat this maneuver four more times.

The President blows his whistle again. Now, the "U's" pedal *backwards* for one lap and leap into the air. This maneuver is performed as many times as before. They then wheel through the crowd, tooting, to wild applause, cheers, whistles, and lewd suggestions. Alice Monomoy, who is still wandering across the park in a low profile, has to jump out of the way to avoid being run over.

Since this is a political rally, the "U's" have come prepared to lend their support to Tommy Russell's campaign. Each of the cyclists wears a placard on his back.

The first placard reads: "On the highway of Life, the powers-that-be"

The second placard reads: "Attempt to control our destiny."

The third placard reads: "But We the People will go our own way,"

The fourth placard reads: "And to the Mayor we have this to say:"

The fifth placard reads: "*[expletive deleted]*!"

[Author's note: the expletive wasn't deleted on the placard, of course, but it has been in this narrative in order to avoid offending the Reader's sensibilities.]

XVIII

10:11:15 am
(mini-drama #3)

Look out!

They are among us, lurching and staggering and creeping, ominously seeking fresh victims to eat.

They are the Zombies Against Corruption. They are here to frighten everyone into being non-corrupt, and they are here to frighten everyone into voting against a corrupt government.

There are six of them. Five of them wear ragged, torn, and filthy clothing and garish make-up, and they growl and scream ominously. The sixth wears a freshly-pressed suit and matching tie and speaks passable English, but he still wears garish make-up. He is the Chapter President and the husband of the aforementioned pregnant Maxine. The five do the frightening, while the sixth utters slogans appropriate to the occasion.

With one exception, no one in the crowd is the least frightened by the "Z's" as zombies have been around since Time immemorial and are so commonplace that few think anything of their presence. In point of fact, with one exception, the crowd thinks that the "Z's" are a comical bunch, and they laugh and laugh and laugh at the alleged frightening behavior. (The one exception is Alice Monomoy, who immediately ducks behind a lilac bush and hopes the "Z's" do not spot her.) On the other hand, they take the slogans to heart – slogans like "Rip the Mayor's heart out and eat it!" and "Tear the Mayor apart – he makes us all fart!" and "The Mayor is more frightening than we are. Don't vote for him!"

For the slogans then and not the behavior, the crowd applauds, cheers, whistles, and makes lewd suggestions. The Zombies Against

Corruption continue to lurch, stagger, and creep ominously while seeking fresh victims to eat, and they also continue to growl and scream ominously, frightening no one (with one exception).

XIX

10:11:17 am
(mini-drama #4)

Look!

Up in the sky!

It's a bird! It's a plane!

No, it's a kite!

No, it's *four* kites!

It's four magnificent kites decorated to resemble the City Flag of Cythera, a not-so-subtle message that the Russell campaign is in solidarity with a beleaguered social organization which had suffered from the policies of the Kildare Administration, a fount of corruption, cronyism, and conflict-of-interest.

The box kites are being flown by the entire membership of the Klassic Kite Konsortium (Cythera Chapter) (they of a most unfortunate acronym), who, it must be admitted, are last-minute recruits to the Russell campaign. Previously, they had maintained a studious apolitical stance (more or less) on city issues. But, after the Mayor had announced that he favored the banning of kite flying within the city limits on the grounds that they interfered with the operation of his surveillance drones, the KKK had hopped off the fence (so to speak) and onto the offence.

The Regional Director of the KKK, a stocky fellow who has shaved his head to reflect a recent trend skillfully maneuvers his kite in a series of dips and rises. His fellow members follow suit, and soon all four magnificent kites are creating imaginary figure-eights which either conjoin with each other or cross each other's path. At one point, the Regional Director dips his kite low to the ground – and his fellow members follow suit – so that the crowd can read the slogans painted on the sides of the box – slogans like "Mr. Mayor, go fly a kite!" or "Kites for Russell!" or "Kite, yes – Kildare, no!"

As the KKK wend their way across the park, the crowd goes wild, applauding, cheering, whistling, and making lewd suggestions. Alice Monomoy, fresh from her disappearance behind a lilac bush, has to duck in order to avoid being struck in the head by an errant kite.

XX

10:11:19 am
(mini-drama #5)

Fifty-four feet and forty inches due south of the "grandstand," a group of campaign volunteers (having ceased their labors and scurrying about like squirrels on steroids) form a conga line (more or less) and begin snaking their way through the crowd. It is abundantly clear that they lack co-ordination; some of them are kicking left while others are kicking right, and some of them – perhaps out of confusion – are not kicking at all. For this bit of ineptitude, they receive numerous boos and catcalls and lewd suggestions. The conga line ignores the boos and catcalls and lewd suggestions (although one enterprising individual tosses back his own lewd suggestions) and keeps on snaking.

The gist of their message is this:

"Dump Mayor Dork – *now!*

Vote for Russell – *now!*"

At one point, the conga line nearly collides with the "U's," but a major catastrophe is avoided when the Chapter President (he with the resplendent handle-bar moustache) halts and backpedals in order to allow the line to proceed. On a whim, he maneuvers his magnificent machine toward the rear of the line (and his fellow members follow suit); and, when the moment to kick either left or right arrives, the "U's" leap into the air in unison and toot their horns. The crowd goes wild, applauding, cheering, whistling, and making lewd suggestions.

At another point, Alice Monomoy, who has resumed wandering across the park in a low profile, is enticed to join the conga line. But, for some unfathomable reason, she declines.

XXI

10:11:21 am
(mini-drama #6)

No one has invited them – and, if anyone had known they were even in the neighborhood, they surely would have been invited to leave the neighborhood – but the Future Suicide Bombers of America have put in their appearance nevertheless.

The stated goal of the FSBA is to train the youth of America to immolate the rotting infrastructure of the current Cythera city government and root out all of the corruption, cronyism, and conflicts-of-interest. This, on the face of it, is a noble goal. It is the *methodology* of the FSBA which has pushed them, not to the fringes of polite society but beyond the bounds of polite society and into the wilderness. This methodology consists of wearing phony explosives – made from plastic and aluminum, complete with wiring and a "triggering device" – on their bodies, running wildly about, and shouting "Boom! Boom! Boom!" as loud as they can. Needless to say their tactics scare the bejabbers out of many in the crowd. *[Author's note: for the Reader's information, "bejabbers" is a technical psychological term – although some in the profession insist that there is a* biological *element at work – and the Reader is invited to consult the relevant literature.]*

Still, as the City of Cythera is not a police state – yet – the FSBA is tolerated (more or less), and it is free to make whatever statement they care to. And, on this day, they have chosen to make a statement in Weldon Park in support of the Russell campaign on the grounds that the Kildare Administration has overstepped the bounds of decency and morality. A half dozen of them now run wildly through the park and shout "Boom! Boom! Boom!" as loud as they can. In their hands, they carry placards reading:

"To bomb or not to bomb:

There is no question.

Mayor Kildare is our target!"

The crowd parts before them and offers no resistance beyond a few boos, catcalls, and lewd suggestions. Alice Monomoy, who is still wandering across the park in a low profile, has the bejabbers scared out of her, and she hides behind a tree. The FSBA circle the park once, then depart as quickly as they had arrived. They have played their part here, and they are off to play a part elsewhere.

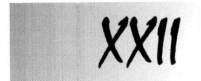 

XXII

10:11:23 am
(mini-drama #7)

Hot on the heels of the Future Suicide Bombers of America, another unwanted group makes its presence known. Although they have been invited, they are still troubling enough to raise some eyebrows, some hackles, and some fists, elicit some "tsk-tsk's," and shake some heads in disgust.

They are the Darth Vader Fan Club (Cythera Chapter), and they are in full regalia. The part of "Darth Vader" is played by the Regional Director of the Club (whose fiancee is the aforementioned pregnant Christine), and the other four members are outfitted as "storm troopers" marching in lock step behind him. He might have been a more imposing and intimidating sight had he been a tad taller; as it happens, he stands only five-feet-six-inches in his stocking feet, half a foot shorter than his "troopers" (who *are* imposing and intimidating). Nevertheless, he and they receive boos, catcalls, and lewd suggestions from the crowd. Upon his signal, the "troopers" wave their "weapons" in a menacing manner. Alice Monomoy, who starts to emerge from behind the tree where she had been hiding, is duly menaced and remains where she is.

The Club circles the park in their imposing, intimidating, and menacing manner. They wear placards on their uniforms, all of which read "The Force is with Tommy Russell." They intend to leave as quickly as they have arrived. They have played their part here, and they intend to go off to play a part elsewhere.

XXIII

10:11:25 am
(mini-drama #8)

Your attention please!

Fifty-four feet and forty inches due north of the "grandstand" – that is to say, on the sidewalk adjacent to Weldon Park – the Tap Dancers Against Dirty Politics are performing for your edification. Each of them carries several placards, the faces of which are temporarily turned away from the crowd. They begin a routine inspired by Billy Bojangles in a Shirley Temple film and segue into one inspired by Gregory Hines in *White Lightning*. This lifts the spirits of those who had been put off by the appearances of the Future Suicide Bombers of America and the Darth Vader Fan Club (which had been just about everyone, more or less) and provokes them into applauding, cheering, whistling, and making lewd suggestions. Even Alice Monomoy is persuaded to emerge from behind the tree where she had been hiding.

It may be fairly said that not everyone is pleased with this impromptu performance, because the impromptu performers tend to draw attention away from their own impromptu performance (erratic though it is). What they can also do, and what they now do is to play discordant "music" – which is everything they play – with the dance routine in the hopes that the dancers will be discouraged from continuing.

No such luck. The Tap Dancers Against Dirty Politics are here to make a statement, and they throw themselves even more vigorously into their performances.

Once the group routines have run their course, each of the individuals perform a routine of his/her own devising, involving many different and complex maneuvers. As each dancer goes through his/her routine, the remaining two stand on the sidelines and flash their placards, the faces of which had been turned away from the crowd but now face toward the said crowd. The placards carry various political slogans, such as:

"Dance and vote for Russell!"

And:

"Tappity-tap-tap, Kildare politics are a trap!"

And:

"Tommy sets my feet to tapping!"

And so it goes, one after another.

XXIV

10:11:27 am
(mini-drama #9)

Last, but not least, they are here for your further edification.

The Cythera College Kazoo and Whistle Marching Band step smartly and precisely across the park, a dozen stalwarts playing eight kazoos and four whistles. They have formed two columns of six individuals each – a whistle in the first and sixth positions and a kazoo in the central positions. Their uniforms – red shirts and blue trousers for the six men and blue blouses and red skirts for the six women – are clean and pressed and are complemented by golden slippers and beanies (minus propellers, of course).

One might think that kazoos and whistles are an incompatible combination, scarcely suited to each other. Those thoughts are thought by those who have played neither kazoo nor whistle and certainly have not played either in concert with the other. Kazoos provide the melody while whistles provide the beat; and, in the hands – or should we say "mouths"? – of experts, the combination creates a rousing music designed to uplift one's spirits.

The Cythera College Kazoo and Whistle Marching Band wends its way smartly and precisely though the crowd, carefully avoiding the "U's," the conga line, and the KKK, and plays a more moving and intelligible rendition of "Blowin' in the Wind" than one would have heard from Mother's Little Darlings. This performance elicits its fair share (more or less) of applause, cheers, whistles, and lewd suggestions. They then play another Dylan classic, "This Land Is Your Land," which provokes a bit of impromptu singing of the lyrics -- not necessarily in key or in harmony, but most assuredly with gusto. It does not, however,

provoke Alice Monomoy into a bit of impromptu singing of the lyrics –
not necessarily in key or in harmony -- and she remains behind her
favorite tree to avoid being trampled to death by the band.

10:15 am
(for the benefit of the clock-watchers)

Tommy Russell made his Grand Entrance by exiting a city bus (which had had the foresight to drive past Weldon Park during its rounds) and thus demonstrating that he was a "man of the people." He was accompanied, as usual, by Amber and Donny (who no longer was rubbing his sore buttocks).

Upon seeing him, the crowd parted like the Red Sea in order to give him passage to the "grandstand." Those who were involved in his campaign or were ardent supporters of his platform broke out in applause, cheering, and whistling (but no lewd suggestions, except from those who were *not* involved in his campaign or were *not* ardent supporters of his platform). Tommy waved to one and all, regardless of where on the political spectrum they happened to be. He especially gave the high sign to the "U's" in the conga line. *[Author's note: "high sign" in this context is the "peace sign" in another context, because that was the only "high sign" Tommy knew, despite efforts by his supporters to persuade him to adopt one which was unique to him.]*

If everyone was having this much fun, he reasoned, then they would be more receptive to his message. He might have been more pleased if more people had shown up if only out of simple curiosity; he might have been more pleased if all of them had been only passive supporters of his platform. But, this bunch had turned the rally into a carnival, and they were whooping it up, cavorting about, and throwing themselves into the spirit of the occasion. It was Tommy's best attempt at organizing, and it was beginning to be successful beyond his wildest imaginings. It would not have been an overstatement to say that he was, at that very point in time, in a highly exultant frame of mind and that he believed to the core of his very being that he would be the next Mayor of Cythera.

"Man, oh, man!" he crowed. "This is going to be one BITCH of a rally!"

"It does indeed, fearless leader," Donny said casually, "thanks to your keen organizing skills."

"Say," Amber piped up, "isn't that Alice, hiding behind that tree over there?"

Tommy and Donny followed her pointing finger (it matters not which one) and spotted their chairperson for the campaign's Donations Committee (of which she was the sole member) peering from behind the said tree even as she attempted to become one with the said tree. Tommy frowned. Donny grimaced. Amber smirked.

"So it is," the chairperson for the campaign's Security Committee (of which he was the sole member) observed. "I guess I'd better rescue her."

"She's liable to attach herself to you even more, Brooke," Amber observed. "I'd better get her myself."

Amber sauntered away and instantly a great deal of attraction was diverted toward her. As it has been stated in a previous narrative, she was petite, slender, and exceedingly buxom, the centerpiece of many sexual fantasies by males of all ethnic persuasions and of many jealous fits by females of all ethnic persuasions. She wore her hair in braids, alternately dyed magenta and purple, which contrasted well with the jeans and sweaters she fancied most of the time.

As she sauntered away, the crowd parted like the Red Sea in order to give her passage to the tree behind which Alice was hiding when she was not wandering about in a low profile. When Amber arrived at the said tree, she gave Alice a stern look. Alice returned the stern look because she didn't want one.

"Girl," Amber said surprisingly softly, "stop acting like a ninny and come with me."

"Is it safe?"

"Of course it's safe. I wouldn't be here otherwise, would I?"

"I guess not. All right."

Stupid bitch.

Stupid bitch.

10:16 am
(and ticking)

His Honor, Mayor Delbert Orville Richmond Kildare, was not enjoying the fruits of his labor. True, he now stood at the large pretentious window of his large pretentious office from which he could watch the Wolf River flow gently down the stream and survey his kingdom to his heart's content as befitted his position, but he was not enjoying what he saw. For, in his kingdom which he could survey to his heart's content as befitted his position, there was a menacing dragon on the horizon, and this menacing dragon on the horizon was threatening to put His Honor out of a job – an unthinkable thing to think about inasmuch as he had no other skills than politicking to fall back on. He had to defeat this menacing dragon on the horizon by any and all means available, or else the unthinkable would become the thinkable.

Also present in his large pretentious office were his "brain trust": Anthony Algernon Armstrong, a.k.a. "Triple-A" (for that was what he wished to be called), His Honor's speech writer; and Spencer K. Augustus, a.k.a. "Augie" (for that was he wished to be called), His Honor's campaign manager. Neither of them was standing at the large pretentious window surveying His Honor's kingdom to their heart's content. Instead, they were sitting in large pretentious chairs surveying His Honor to no one's content and waiting for him to give them new marching orders. Said marching orders were not forthcoming because His Honor had none to give – not until, that is, his Chief of Police returned to update him on the latest developments in his war against the menacing dragon on the horizon. In the meanwhile, both men remained quiet, thinking thoughts that only they could think which pleased them immensely.

Curiously, both men were thinking the very same thought at this moment: how to score with Ms. Apollonia Tix, the Dream Woman of many a wretched male. Had both men known in what little regard Ms. Tix held either of them, they might have given up the chase altogether. The one would have believed that his speech impediment had earned him the little regard in which she held him; the other would have believed that his short stature had earned him the little regard in which she held him. Both men, however, would have been entirely incorrect. Ms. Tix held both of them in little regard, not because of any speech impediment or of any short stature but simply because they were both associates of His Honor, one Delbert Orville Richmond Kildare, whom she held in less regard than both of them put together.

And truth to tell, now that Ms. Apollonia Tix, the Dream Woman of many a wretched male, had found her own Dream Man in the person of one Donald A. Brooke III, no other male would do.

The surveying of one's kingdom and the thinking of thoughts about dream women came to an abrupt halt by the forceful opening of the large pretentious door to the large pretentious office and the storming in of Chief Ozzie. His Honor and his "brain trust" were duly startled, first, by the manner of his entrance (although they should have been used to that manner by now) and, second, by the enormous grin on Chief Ozzie's face – especially since Chief Ozzie was seldom given to displaying enormous grins on his face.

Chief Ozzie marched across the floor in a military fashion, came to a military halt in front of His Honor's large pretentious desk, executed a military left-face, and assumed a military parade-rest, all the while murmuring the execution commands to himself in a military manner. He still did not salute His Honor.

"Chief," His Honor sputtered, "what's wrong? Why are you smiling?"

"I have implemented the surprise for Mr. Russell the Rat, Mr. Mayor. The moment he opens his mouth to speak, it'll be shut real quick."

"Are you quite sure that this…surprise can't be traced back to me?"

"Yes, sir. The surprise was designed to fit in with the Russell crowd. No one will recognize it until it's too late."

His Honor responded with an enormous grin of his own, and Triple-A and Augie followed suit. The Mayor returned to his large pretentious desk and flicked on the intercom.

"Ms. Tix, we're going to celebrate my upcoming re-election. I've got some champagne in here. Won't you join us?"

"Thank you, sir. I'll be in as soon as I clear off my desk." *And as soon as I can find that dead skunk I keep for special occasions.*

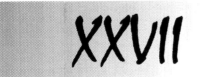 

XXVII

twenty minutes after the hour
(the count-down begins)

Mayoral candidate Thomas A. Russell clambered up the steps of the "grandstand" and nearly put his foot through one board which had not been thoroughly installed by the construction crew who had been scurrying back and forth like squirrels on steroids. He swore briefly under his breath, recovered his equipoise, and continued on. Once safely on the stage, he surveyed all of the mini-dramas taking place and all the people gathering together with great relish. He had not surveyed for very long before he spotted two scenarios which fit the bill as "flies in the ointment."

"Donny," Tommy said quietly and pointed off to the north, "what are the Untouchables doing here?"

"Ah, they're the 'special security team' I promised you."

"And you didn't think to tell me that you were going to hire them whether I wanted you to or not?"

"Plausible denial, fearless leader, plausible denial. As far as anyone knows, they're here because they feel like it."

"How much are they getting for this 'security'?"

"The usual."

"OK. Now, look over there – the tree next to the one Alice is hiding behind. Recognize them?"

Donny squinted off into the distance and spotted the other "fly in the ointment" – four males endeavoring to pass themselves off as "hippies." They were dressed like "hippies," right down to the bandanas on their heads and the sandals on their feet. But their body postures said that they were something else entirely.

"Indeed I do. I saw them earlier. Chief Ozzie has sent his 'elite squad' to disrupt our rally."

"Uh-huh. Well, you know what to do."

"Right on. I'll unleash the Untouchables."

Donny clambered down the steps of the "grandstand" and nearly put his foot through a board which had not been thoroughly installed by the construction crew who had been scurrying back and forth like squirrels on steroids. He swore briefly under his breath, recovered his equipoise, and continued on toward the northern edge of Weldon Park, where the said Untouchables were milling about and being bored stiff by all of the inaction.

All Hell was about to break loose.

XXVIII

twenty-two minutes after the hour
(the count-down continues)

Behind the tree next to the tree Alice Monomoy was hiding behind, the four males who were dressed like "hippies" right down to the bandanas on their heads and the sandals on their feet but who could not disguise the fact that they stood too rigidly to be "laid back" like "hippies" had braced themselves to take action once Tommy Russell showed up at the rally.

That moment had come.

"There he is, men," one of the "hippies" remarked. His name was Monroe; and, as it happened, he was the officer-in-charge of Chief Ozzie's "elite squad" and had specific orders to carry out. "You all know what to do. Russell the Rat is a clear and present danger to the decent folk of Cythera, and it's up to us to stop him before he tears this city apart."

The other three nodded in agreement.

"Michaels, your job is to target Brooke. Make sure you separate him from Russell. You don't have to be polite about it."

"Yes, sir," Michaels responded enthusiastically.

"Mitchell, your job is to target Mrs. Russell. Make sure you separate her from her husband. You don't have to be polite about it."

"Yes, sir," Mitchell responded enthusiastically.

"Mason, your job is to target those twins. Make sure you separate them from the others. You don't have to be polite about it."

"Yes, sir," Mason responded enthusiastically.

"Once all those people are separated from their leader, I'll deal with

Mr. Russell the Rat personally. And I don't intend to be polite about it. Are you prepared to do your duty, gentlemen?"

As with one voice, the "elite team" responded in the affirmative enthusiastically.

"Then go forth!"

The "elite squad" went forth.

All Hell was about to break loose.

XXIX

twenty-four minutes after the hour
(the count-down continues)

Donny approached the Untouchables with his usual precautions. Happily, the breeze was upwind of them, and therefore no odorous emanations could be detected until one was near enough to touch them (although why one would want to be near enough to touch them was a great mystery). Still, he wasn't about to take any chances and stopped breathing.

The Untouchables were shifting their collective weight from one foot to the other, bored stiff by all of the inaction. Simultaneously, for lack of anything else to do, they all picked at something or other – Meathead his teeth, Knucklehead his lint, Airhead his lice, and Dopehead his ears.

Out of the corner of his eye, Donny observed a suspicious movement of bodies on the opposite side of the park. He knew what it meant, and he was determined to stop it in its tracks by any and all means at his disposal. The Untouchables were just the right any and all means to stop it in its tracks.

"Heads up, guys!" he alerted the smelly bunch. He pointed at Chief Ozzie's "elite squad." "You see those four bozos? They're cops, and they want to disrupt the rally."

"So, now we get to earn our pay?" Meathead asked.

"You got it."

"We get to knock some heads, man?" Knucklehead asked.

"Be my guest. Just make sure you knock the right heads."

"LGFI," Dopehead murmured.

"Huh?"

"'Let's go for it,'" Meathead translated.

"All right. Move out!"
The Untouchables moved out.
All Hell was about to break loose.

XXX

twenty-six minutes after the hour
(the count-down continues)

Picture: two runaway trains rushing toward each other on the same track.

Picture: many obstacles upon the said track through which the said runaway trains must pass.

Picture: the said obstacles on the said track oblivious to the said runaway trains approaching them.

Picture: the said runaway trains on the said track making contact with the said oblivious obstacles.

From her vantage point west of the "grandstand," one Harriet Methune Beiderbeck, a.k.a. "Harry the Hatchet," star reporter (in her humble estimation) for the Cythera *Clarion-News*, who had won several awards (which, in her humble estimation, she deserved) for sniffing out a story and pursuing it until either (1) it became old news or (2) some other story needed to be sniffed out and pursued, watched the rally unfold with much detachment and even more disgust. She had probably spent a more boring hour during her illustrious career, but she was hard pressed at the moment to remember when. Her perpetual frown had deepened with each passing minute; and, for the umpteenth time, she reminded herself to confront her publisher, the redoubtable Michael John McNamara, and scratch his eyes out for assigning this event to her.

A political rally was not (in her humble estimation) a decent story. It was not even a half-decent story. For one thing, she had seen political rallies before (too many times before, in her humble estimation), and they all looked alike to her. For another thing, she had heard too much hot air blown out by too many windbags (in her humble estimation)

240

to give them any credibility, much less any column space. And, for a third thing, she had never questioned Mayor Delbert Orville Richmond Kildare's policies – well, maybe a teensy, weensy bit when he refused to hold any press conferences unless he needed some photo-ops to puff up his ego – and she wasn't about to start now. *[Author's note: for the Reader's information, the expression "teensy-weensy" describes an amount of anything between "small" and "infinitesimal." It is often misused when the other two should be used.]* In short, she would rather have been covering the dog show taking place at the Cythera Animal Shelter at this very minute than standing here being bored (in her humble estimation).

While she was standing there being bored, her cameraman Ichabod finally showed up but offered no reason for his tardiness. Harriet had no inclination to ask him for a reason; whatever Ichabod's reasons for doing anything was of no interest to her, and she could have cared less if he had decided not to show up at all. Therefore, Ichabod stood idly by and wondered what he should shoot first. And had Harriet been more enthusiastic about her present assignment and given him some clues about what to shoot first, he might have shot half a cassette in the first two minutes of being on the scene. But she didn't even have the energy to browbeat him for standing around and gawking like a schoolboy at a nudist camp.

To pass the time, she lit up one of her special brand of cigarette (made from camel shit), inhaled deeply, and blew out a large cloud of smoke. Ichabod hacked and wheezed and nearly dropped his camera.

"I don't know how much more of this I can take. I suppose I'll have to *interview* someone – even Russell the Rat, for God's sake!"

"I never saw so many *ca-razy* people in my life!" Ichabod twanged. "All those *ca-razy* things they're doing – it's nothing but *ca-raziness*! I don't know why I'm here. I'm just going *ca-razy* myself, I tell you!"

"Well, it'll soon be over with. And then, I can -- Hello? What's this?"

"This" was the appearance in Weldon Park of two disparate groups of people – the aforementioned runaway trains on the same track – walking quickly and deliberately toward each other. From her vantage point west of the "grandstand," Harriet immediately recognized one of the groups, and she didn't have to *smell* it in order to recognize it. The other group looked vaguely familiar, but she couldn't put her finger on its identity just then. But she did realize that both groups seemed to be on a collision course and that the said collision course was going to be a big surprise to at least one of them.

"Well, well, well," enthused Harriet Methune Beiderbeck, a.k.a. "Harry the Hatchet," star reporter (in her humble estimation) for the Cythera *Clarion-News*, who had won several awards (which, in her humble estimation, she deserved), "it looks like I'm going to get a decent story after all. All Hell is about to break loose!"

XXXI

twenty-six minutes and thirty seconds after the hour
(the count-down reaches zero)

All Hell broke loose!

All Hell broke loose in pieces.

The first piece of Hell which broke loose broke loose immediately in the vicinity of Chief Ozzie's "elite squad" whose assignment was to disrupt Tommy Russell's rally by any and all means available to it and who did not have to be polite about it. The said immediate vicinity, as it happened, was the tree behind which Alice Monomoy had been hiding and from which Amber Russell had just succeeded in prying her. The two women proceeded toward the "grandstand" at a slow, cautious pace (Alice) and a slow, agonizing pace (Amber).

The two women took barely six (slow, cautious/slow, agonizing) paces before they were overtaken by the "elite squad" moving at a brisk pace toward the "grandstand." Chief Ozzie's boys whizzed by Alice and Amber and nearly bowled them over. Alice screeched in mortal fear. Amber cursed in mortal anger. *[Author's note: a debate arose after the event and has continued (more or less) to the present day whether Alice's screeching or Amber's cursing was the louder. Those in favor of the former claimed that the windows for two blocks around were either shattered or rattled. Those in favor of the latter claimed that people for two blocks around either fainted or ran incontinently in all directions. The Reader may judge for him/herself.]* The "elite squad" ignored both the screeching and the cursing by reason of the fact that they had taken the precaution of wearing earplugs in order not to have to listen to the several noisy performances of rally supporters. Alice raced back to her tree, and

Amber trailed. Mitchell, satisfied that his target had been duly separated even without being not polite about it, continued on with his comrades.

The second piece of Hell which broke loose broke loose in the vicinity of the conga line which had been winding its way hither and yon throughout the park and which had had the bad taste to end up in the northern part of the park, not ten yards from the position of the Untouchables moving at a brisk pace toward the "grandstand." The Untouchables ignored the conga dancers, passed through the line at various points, and continued on. Those nearest the smelly bunch wisely chose to pass out on the instant, while the remainder had to be content with gagging and retching interminably. Happily, Donny trailed his "army" and offered whatever assistance he could.

The third piece of Hell which broke loose broke loose in the vicinity where the square dancers had been dancing. They would have continued to dance were it not for the fact that they were alerted to a dangerous situation. The said dangerous situation was, of course, Chief Ozzie's "elite squad" moving at a brisk pace toward the "grandstand," and the alert came in the form of Alice's screeching and Amber's cursing. Immediately, all dancing ceased, and the dancers turned in the direction of the screeching and cursing to learn why there was screeching and cursing, only to discover a group of men charging in their direction like a herd of buffalo. The said dancers wisely panicked and scattered in all directions. The said herd of buffalo ignored them and continued on.

The fourth piece of Hell which broke loose broke loose in the vicinity where the Darth Vader Fan Club (Cythera Chapter) had made their final act of menacing, which was the conga dancers whom they believed were not in the proper spirit of the occasion and whom they believed ought to be put back on the True Path. The members of the Darth Vader Fan Club had not, however, expected to encounter a force greater than theirs, but they were wrong. When some of the conga dancers wisely passed out and the rest were content to gag and retch interminably, the Club sought out the reason why and immediately spied a greater force than theirs charging in their direction like a herd of buffalo. Fortunately for them, they were close to the "grandstand"; they dropped their "weapons," ran toward it, and crawled underneath it for protection against the greater force. The Untouchables ignored them and continued on. At Tommy's command, one of the Bookends (Willy or Wally) was dispatched to lend assistance.

The fifth piece of Hell which broke loose broke loose in the vicinity where the Zombies Against Corruption had made their final act of frightening, which was the square dancers whom they believed were not in the proper spirit of the occasion and whom they believed ought to be put back on the True Path. The "Z's" had not, however, expected to encounter creatures more frightful than they were, but they were wrong. When the said square dancers wisely panicked and scattered in all directions, the "Z's" sought out the reason why and immediately spied the creatures more frightful than they were, charging in their direction like a herd of buffalo. Fortunately for them, they were also close to the "grandstand"; they dropped their pretense of being frightful, ran toward it, and crawled underneath it for protection against the creatures more frightful than they were. Chief Ozzie's "elite squad" ignored them and continued on. At Tommy's command, one of the Bookends (Wally or Willy) was dispatched to lend assistance.

The sixth piece of Hell which broke loose broke loose in the vicinity of the northwest corner of the "grandstand" where the Klassic Kite Konsortium (they of the unfortunate acronym) were regaling the crowd with their kite-flying skills. Their kites dipped and rose with precision and created imaginary figure-eights which either conjoined with each other or crossed each other's path. This demonstration of kite-flying would have continued, but the Regional Director of the KKK (the stocky fellow with the shaved head) noticed something extremely curious, to wit: the Darth Vader Fan Club (Cythera Chapter) running like hell toward the "grandstand" and crawling underneath it. He also noted *why* the Club was running like hell toward the "grandstand" and crawling underneath it, to wit: the Untouchables charging toward the KKK like a herd of buffalo.

Now, as has been observed in a previous narrative, the KKK was made of sterner stuff and resolutely refused to run like hell and crawl underneath something. Instead, they calmly and coolly maneuvered their kites to form a blockade against the charging herd of buffalo (while keeping their distance from the same!). The Untouchables ignored the blockade, detoured around it, felled some unfortunate members of the crowd who could not get out of their way fast enough, and continued on.

The seventh piece of Hell which broke loose broke loose in the vicinity of the southwest corner of the "grandstand" where the Universal Union of Unicyclists (Cythera Chapter) were regaling the crowd with their cycling skills. The "U's" were now performing their special performance whereby the Chapter President (the muscular fellow with the resplendent handlebar moustache) pushed himself upward, causing cycle and cyclist to rise to a height of three feet, at which point he twisted himself and his cycle into an 180-degree turn, lighted on the ground, and pedaled *backwards* in the direction toward which he had been pedaling forwards. In their turn, the Chapter Vice President and the other members executed the same maneuver. As soon as the last of the quintet became earth-bound, all five would have tooted their horns three times in unison.

They did not toot their horns in unison, however, because they observed something extremely curious, to wit: the Zombies Against Corruption running like hell toward the "grandstand" and crawling underneath it. They also noted *why* the "Z's" were running like hell and crawling underneath it, to wit: the "elite squad" charging toward them like a herd of buffalo. Now, as has been told in a previous narrative, the "U's" were made of sterner stuff and resolutely refused to run like hell and crawl underneath something. Instead, they calmly and coolly maneuvered their magnificent machines to form a blockade against the charging herd of buffalo. The "elite squad" ignored the blockade, detoured around it, felled some unfortunate members of the crowd who could not get out of their way fast enough, and continued on.

The eighth piece of Hell which broke loose broke loose in the vicinity of the front of the "grandstand" where the Cythera College Kazoo and Whistle Marching Band had stopped marching and were playing a medley of Sousa marches *in situ*. Therefore, it was their extreme misfortune to be where two herds of buffalo, a.k.a. two runaway trains on the same track, were charging toward them from opposite directions. Upon seeing the said charging herds of buffalo, a.k.a. the runaway trains on the same track, the Band behaved in the only way they knew how, to wit: the women screeched in mortal fear, and the men cursed in mortal anger. *[Author's note: a debate arose after the event and has continued (more or less) to the present day whether the women's screeching or the men's cursing was the louder. The fact of the matter was that nobody ever heard their screeching and cursing because, by that time, everybody in Weldon Park was screeching or cursing, running like hell, and looking for a place to crawl underneath.]* Then they dropped their instruments, did an about-face (not necessarily in a military fashion), and crawled underneath the "grandstrand." At Tommy's command, the Bookends (Willy and Wally/Wally and Willy) were dispatched to lend assistance.

The ninth, and final, piece of Hell which broke loose broke loose when the two charging herds of buffalo, a.k.a. the two runaway trains on the same track, had the field to themselves and came face-to-face with each other (more or less). Interesting enough, neither group had heard of the other, a fact which was to prove disastrous to one of them.

The first individual to make a move was Monroe, the officer-in-charge of the "elite squd." He scowled fiercely at the Untouchables, took one bold step forward, and said in his best authoritative voice:

"You people! You are all under arrest on the charges of disturbing the peace, assault-and-battery, willful destruction of public property, incitement to riot, and loitering."

The second individual to make a move was Meathead, the nominal leader of the Untouchables. He smiled wickedly at the "elite squad," took a bold step forward, and said in his best sneering voice:

"Honk you, pigs! Add resisting arrest to your honking charges!"

"Have it your way, scumbag," Monroe sneered back. "Michaels, Mitchell, Mason, put the cuffs on these clowns."

Michaels, Mitchell, and Mason stepped forward, cuffs in hand, ready to arrest the clowns, a.k.a. the Untouchables. Their demeanor was grim, their body posture was confident, and their attitude was officious. When Michaels, Mitchell, and Mason approached to within twelve feet of the clowns, a.k.a. the Untouchables, they stopped abruptly, for they had reached the optimum range of the Untouchables' effectiveness. Instantly, grimness turned to confusion, confidence turned to anxiety, and officiousness turned to fear.

"The world is spinning around me!" Michaels observed. "I fear I must barf!"

He fell to the ground and squeaked like a mouse.

"The world is all topsy-turvy!" Mitchell observed. "I fear I must puke!"

He fell to the ground and brayed like a mule.

"The world is turning inside out!" Mason observed. "I fear I must upchuck!"

He fell to the ground and cawed like a crow.

"Three down, one to go!" Meathead hooted.

"Knock some heads!" Knucklehead hooted.

"Kick buttocks!" Airhead hooted.

"LTFB!" Dopehead hooted. *[Author's note: it was determined later on that "LTFB" was Dopehead's shorthand for "let the fun begin." The Author has no reason to dispute this interpretation.]*

Monroe evaluated the situation, assessed his chances for resolution of the problem, and arrived at the logical conclusion.

He turned and ran like hell. The Untouchables followed in hot pursuit. The chased and the chasers nearly collided with a young male of medium height with a slight paunch and an owlish expression who had wandered into Weldon Park out of curiosity. A whiff of the Untouchables persuaded the said young male of medium height with a slight paunch and an owlish expression to fall down and writhe in agony. The chased and the chasers continued on.

10:30 am
(the anticlimax)

From his vantage point on the "grandstand," Tommy Russell observed all of Hell breaking loose piece by piece with increasing dismay. He did like the confrontation between Chief Ozzie's "elite squad" and the Untouchables, however. Perhaps there was some justice in this world after all.

If the attendant crowd were having this much terror, he reasoned, then they would not likely vote for him. Worse, they would tell their friends and neighbors not to vote for him. This crowd had turned his rally into a panic, and they were screeching and cursing and running like hell and looking for a place to hide like squirrels on steroids. It would not have been an understatement to say that he was in a deeply blue funk and that he believed to the core of his being that he was finished politically. *[Author's note: a "blue funk" is one step above a severe depression but one step below a neurosis. There are three degrees of blue funks – deep, deeper, and deeply. The Reader is invited to read the relevant literature on this subject.]*

"Man, oh, man!" he moaned. "This is the mother of all disasters."

"On the surface, yes, fearless leader," remarked Donny, who had joined him after rescuing the conga line and who had watched all Hell breaking loose piece by piece himself. "I see a silver lining in all this. After all, it wouldn't have happened if Mayor Dork hadn't been so desperate to win re-election. We can turn this disaster to our advantage."

"That's what I like about you, old buddy. You're so optimistic."

"I get that from my old man. Let's assess the damage and see what we can salvage."

The pair exited the "grandstand" and nearly put a foot apiece through a board which hadn't been thoroughly installed by the construction crew which had been scurrying about like squirrels on steroids. Both swore briefly, recovered their equipoise, and continued on. Once safely on the ground, they were joined by the Bookends, who had come to the assistance of the Darth Vader Fan Club (Willy), the Zombies Against Corruption (Wally), and the Cythera College Kazoo and Whistle Marching Band (Willy and Wally), all of whom had crawled underneath the "grandstand" for protection, and by Amber and Alice coming from the tree behind which they had been hiding. The Bookends had used all of their powers of persuasion to coax everyone out and had succeeded, and they both now wore comedy masks. Amber had used all of her powers of persuasion to coax Alice out, because Alice was about to totally lose it, and succeeded. She did not, however, wear a comedy mask.

"Honey!" she (Amber) wailed. "What a four-star disaster!"

Upon seeing Donny, Alice perked up a fraction, and only a sense of propriety prevented her from rushing headlong into his arms and seeking comfort there.

"You know it, sweet thing." He sighed. "Well, it's time for damage control, if possible. Donny thinks we can blame Mayor Dork for this." He sighed deeply. "Willy, Wally, check out whoever of the volunteers are left and see if they're all right."

"Will do," Willy said cheerfully.

"Will do," Wally said cheerfully.

The Bookends hurried off on their mission of mercy.

"Alice, tell Mother's Little Darlings the show's over."

"Will do," she said dourly. "Are they expecting a fee for 'services' rendered?"

"They may think they are." He reached into his pocket and pulled out a rumpled ten-dollar bill. "Give 'em this and tell them they're damned lucky to get it."

Alice hurried off on her mission of mercantilism.

"What do you want me to do, fearless leader?" Donny asked gratuitously.

"Keep an eye out for those smelly honkers. If they come back, tell 'em anything. Just get 'em out of the park."

"I hear and I obey. I'll -- Uh-oh, this I hadn't counted on."

"This" was the sudden appearance in the park of a tall, statuesque female who might have walked out of a Greek legend, who carried herself in a regal fashion, and who was approaching deliberately toward what was left of the Russell campaign. As it happened, she was Ms. Apollonia Tix, the executive secretary of the Mayor of Cythera and the Dream Woman of many a wretched male. She possessed a headful of long, flowing jet-black hair and stood exactly six-feet-two-and-one-half-inches tall in her stocking feet; and, since she was not in the habit of walking around in public in her stocking feet (or any other kind of feet), the shoes she wore added another half inch to her stature.

"Man, oh, man," Tommy murmured appreciatively. "Now, *there's* a tall drink of water."

"Put your eyes back in your head, Russell," Amber said unappreciatively.

"Yes, dear," Tommy said correctly.

"Just remember who and what you are."

"Yes, dear."

"Think of your unborn child."

"Yes, dear."

"And stop saying that!"

A pause.

"Yes, dear."

Tommy groaned as Amber planted a sharp jab into his ribs.

"Oh-h-h-h! Spousal abuse, for sure. Somebody call the police."

"Chill out, honey, or I'll give you another one."

"Yes, dear." Another pause. "Oh-h-h-h!"

Ms. Apollonia Tix, the Dream Woman of many a wretched male, approached Donny with an expression of concern. Donny approached Ms. Apollonia Tix with an expression of pleasure.

She gazed longingly into his eyes. He gazed longingly into her eyes. They embraced and kissed longingly.

[Author's note: the Author apologizes to the Reader for giving the impression that (s)he has walked into a Barbara Cartland novel. It just seemed appropriate at the moment.]

"Polly," Donny asked when they both came up for air, "what are you doing here?"

"I was worried about you," she answered when they both came up for air. "I overheard the Mayor and the Chief discuss what they were planning to do here. I left the office at the first opportunity to warn you, but it looks like I was too late."

"Yeah. You missed all the fun. I'm glad you're here though."

"Say," Tommy interjected, "are you gonna introduce your...friend, old buddy?"

"Oh, sure. Polly, you know everybody here?"

"Of course. Their reputation precedes them."

"Guys, this is Apollonia Tix, the Mayor's executive secretary – and my fiancée."

Shock. Dismay. Horror. Apprehension. Concern. Fear. (Not necessarily in that order.)

"You have got to be pooing me!" Tommy exclaimed.

"Brooke!" Amber exclaimed. "what's got into you, hobnobbing with the Enemy?"

"I'm *not* the 'Enemy,' Mrs. Russell," Polly said resolutely. "I don't like Mayor Kildare any more than you do. He's a bore, a lecher, and a nincompoop – not necessarily in that order – and I'll do anything I can to put him out of office and sweeping streets (which more suits his talents)."

"Far out!" Tommy exulted

"We'll see," Amber said neutrally.

"We've got a mole in the Mayor's office!" Donny exulted.

"We'll see," Amber said neutrally.

At this point in time, the Bookends (Willy and Wally/Wally and Willy?) re-joined the group. They eyed the newcomer with wonder and wondered if she were available for some stimulating intellectual conversation. Also at this point in time, Alice re-joined the group. She eyed the newcomer with wonder and wondered why she was standing so close to Donny and holding his hand.

At the next point in time, Harriet Methune Beiderbeck, star reporter (in her humble estimation) for the Cythera *Clarion-News*, who had won several awards (which, in her humble estimation, she deserved) for her reporting and who had the reputation for sniffing out a story and pursuing it until (1) it became old news or (2) some other story needed to be sniffed out and pursued, approached the group with a Cheshire-cat grin on her face. Ichabod trailed behind her, looking this way and that way for any more signs of *ca-raziness.*

"Harry the Hatchet!" Tommy boomed. "Long time, no see!"

"Russell the Rat!" Harriet boomed back. "Still up to no good, I see!"

"I'm sure you've got a good story today, Harry."

"Don't I always?" She cocked her head. "Hmmm. I hear sirens in the distance, and I think they're coming this way."

"One of Chief Ozzie's stormtroopers managed to call for back-up," Donny observed. "What's the game plan, fearless leader?"

"All of you – and especially you, Ms. Tix – scatter. No need for you to get involved with the law. Meet back at my place in an hour for lunch and some brainstorming."

"What do we do in the meantime, honey?" Amber inquired with no little concern.

"We stay right here. I'm a candidate for Mayor. That gives me immunity from arrest. Besides, the Keystone Kops aren't going to do anything as long as the *Clarion*'s star reporter is a witness. Now, scram!"

"We're off," said Willy (Wally?).

"To see the Wizard," said Wally (Willy?).

The Bookends scrammed northward.

"Oh, God!" Alice murmured and scrammed westward.

"Where to, darling?" Donny asked Polly.

"To Mcgillicuddy's, to celebrate our engagement," Polly answered Donny.

Donny and Polly scrammed southward.

"How long has the Mayor's secretary been a part of your campaign?" Harriet asked Tommy.

"Oh, all of ten minutes. Donny recruited her, apparently."

"In more ways than one, I should judge."

"So, you want a statement now or later?"

"Let's make it now. That way, we can annoy the Kops even more."

XXXIII

11:12:13 am
(or thereabouts)

Weldon Park is deserted now, except for the clean-up crew who are scurrying back and forth like squirrels on steroids, striking the "grandstand," hauling away equipment, and picking up tons (more or less) of litter. One enterprising individual, a young male of medium height with a slight paunch and an owlish expression, is picking up loose change, a consequence of the crash of bodies to the ground. Soon, they will all be gone.

Weldon Park will then return to normalcy (more or less) until the next brouhaha (which in Cythera is usually just around the corner, so to speak).

POSTSCRIPT

(because the Author does not like loose ends)

Mayor-elect and Mrs. Thomas A. Russell became the proud parents of a bouncing baby boy. Despite numerous pleas, the child was *not* named "Rat, Jr."

Donald A. Brooke III and Apollonia Tix married one month after the election. The couple are expecting the arrival of Donald A. Brooke IV any day now.

Stricken by unrequited love, Alice Monomoy sold her book store and joined a convent. Her parents disowned her.

William and Wallace Nicholson, a.k.a. the "Bookends," bought Alice's bookstore and are doing a thriving business selling adult literature.

Former Mayor Dor – uh, Delbert Orville Richmond Kildare is now selling vacuum cleaners door to door and hating it.

Former Chief of Police Luther Ozymandias Oglesby resides at an old soldier's home and hating it.

Ichabod still works at the Cythera *Clarion-News* despite all of the *ca-raziness* he sees daily, and nothing more can be said.

[Author's note: for the insatiably curious Reader, it should be mentioned – needlessly and pointlessly – that that the squirrel in Weldon Park who carried a large plywood panel which blocked his vision was eventually identified as the mad scribbler who usually hung out at McGillicuddy's. When asked why he had been in Weldon Park carrying a large plywood panel which blocked his vision, he said he was "gathering background material." He refused to elaborate, and Horace Shoemaker subsequently chased him out of the park on the grounds that he was a terrorist opposed to the American way of life, democracy, and civil

liberties. What the scribbler thought the chaser was cannot be printed here.]

THE END
(until the next exciting episode)

Printed in the United States
By Bookmasters